# KC's
# REDEMPTION

## JUDY DOYLE

WESTBOW
P R E S S®
A DIVISION OF THOMAS NELSON
& ZONDERVAN

THE HOLY BIBLE, NEW INTERNATIONAL VERSION®, NIV® Copyright © 1973, 1978, 1984, 2011 by Biblica, Inc.® Used by permission. All rights reserved worldwide.

This is a work of fiction. All of the characters, names, incidents, organizations, and dialogue in this novel are either the products of the author's imagination or are used fictitiously.

WestBow Press books may be ordered through booksellers or by contacting:

WestBow Press
A Division of Thomas Nelson & Zondervan
1663 Liberty Drive
Bloomington, IN 47403
www.westbowpress.com
1 (866) 928-1240

Because of the dynamic nature of the Internet, any web addresses or links contained in this book may have changed since publication and may no longer be valid. The views expressed in this work are solely those of the author and do not necessarily reflect the views of the publisher, and the publisher hereby disclaims any responsibility for them.

Any people depicted in stock imagery provided by Thinkstock are models, and such images are being used for illustrative purposes only. Certain stock imagery © Thinkstock.

ISBN: 978-1-5127-7741-3 (sc)
ISBN: 978-1-5127-7740-6 (hc)
ISBN: 978-1-5127-7742-0 (e)

Library of Congress Control Number: 2017903348

Print information available on the last page.

WestBow Press rev. date: 03/09/2017

# Dedication

This book is dedicated to the memory of three females who have impacted my life. First is my mother, Clara Welch. She was a quiet, Christian lady who apparently enjoyed writing. I wasn't aware of her writing ability until the birth of my nephew. Mom penned a beautiful letter to her first grandchild. It was then I realized she had an ability to put her love not only into action but onto a blank piece of paper.

Second, I wish to acknowledge the one who is unseen but ever present throughout this book, Kimberly Christine. Kim, our daughter, was born with multiple birth defects and lived six weeks. Rarely a day passes that I don't think of her. The main character has our Kim's initials, and her prisoner number (03011980) is actually Kim's birthdate. Although this little baby never left the hospital, she made a huge difference in our world. She made me a more sensitive individual. As a pastor, I have officiated at funerals for infants, and because of Kim's death, I can and do empathize with the heartbroken parents and family.

Third, I dedicate this book to the memory of a lady who became my best friend but was also like a big sister, second mom, and mentor, Shirley Berg. Although her first thought of me as the associate pastor was, *Oh, no, not another female pastor,* Shirley became my friend and confidant. She was my encourager. She'd read my stories and was very affirming. I regret that this project was not completed before her death in November 2014. I always said her critiques was prejudiced as she was such a good friend. It wasn't until another friend, Heather Robertson, read part of this book that I began to realize that Shirley was being honest with me.

Fourth, I wish to thank my God, who for whatever reason called me into ministry. Through that ministry I was introduced to Shirley and Heather.

# Contents

# Acknowledgments

I really don't know where to begin. I had a very tolerant fifth-grade teacher who encouraged his students. For whatever reason, I wrote skits, and Mr. Tom Franks allowed classmates to perform them. Although he has no idea, he was instrumental in encouraging me.

Thanks to a sudden period of unemployment, I was able to attend college, where Professor Craig Shurtleff was my creative writing instructor. He read a piece I had written that I considered a short story and said, "This is a novel idea." He also made suggestions that I wasn't ready to incorporate, and the manuscript was put on a shelf, where it sat for several years. Due to my vocation as a full-time minister, working on the book was a hit-and-miss venture.

I wish to thank my husband, Ron, for tolerating all the times I was so into writing that I forgot to prepare his meals. He's been my constant, my rock, and my confidant.

Our son, Tim, in my opinion, has the ability to write as well. If you could read some of his Facebook posts, especially to Mother Nature, you would see his sense of humor. Where he got that, I've no idea.

Upon hearing that I was writing a novel, I had the encouragement and support of Louise Spalding. Louise was one of many people who kept prodding me to complete this project.

But I must also acknowledge the help and encouragement I received from Jim and Jan Donahue. Jim was the Tazewell County Sheriff for many years and served on the State of Illinois Parole Board. Jan, his late wife, was his chief clerk. Both read drafts of the book and gave me insight into the operation of the parole board.

Deputy Chief Jim Kaminski of the Pekin Police Department would answer questions as well. During my ministry, I had the opportunity to meet Rob Conover, a private investigator. He, too, offered his expertise. Mr. Dale Thomas also shared his expert advice as a criminal attorney.

Last, I want to thank Patti Lacy. Patti was an instructor at the Green Lake Writers Conference in Green Lake, Wisconsin. She and I connected. She has become a good friend and a prayer warrior, and I appreciate her expertise.

Without a doubt, I have forgotten someone, and I beg your forgiveness. Please know, for everything you said or did to help get this story on paper, I thank you.

I pray that this book will be a source of encouragement and inspiration. Although it is a work of fiction, I believe God can and will use it to aid the reader to see that God can make something good out of something bad (Rom. 8:28).

God bless you.

CHAPTER 1

*H* *ope it isn't the old battle-ax. What a bitter old woman!* Handcuffed, shackled about the waist, and wearing leg irons, KC stumbled. *Handcuffs are one thing, but do they really think I'm a hardened criminal?* It struck her as funny. *Of course they do. I'm in prison.*

"Watch your step, clumsy!" barked the guard. He grabbed her belt. She glared at him. *You try walking with leg irons, buddy!* Her eyes burned with anger.

He pushed her toward the administrative office. Not a word was uttered. Static from his radio broke the silence.

"Open gate 101," he said as he leaned his head toward the radio. With a loud buzz, the electronic door slid open. The two stepped inside, and the metal gate banged shut.

"That way." The guard shoved KC toward the left. She heard his keys rattle as he reached to unlock the gray metal door. "Prisoner Elliott, 03011980," he announced in a monotone.

"Elliott, sit down," a raspy voice demanded.

*Oh, great! It* is *the battle-ax. God, what did I do to get her? I thought she retired. It had to be a rumor.* KC sat on a hard, metal chair. *She hasn't changed much since the last time. Hair has gotten grayer, and it isn't even a distinguished gray. Must still be smoking—fingers nicotine-stained yellow and a deep smoker's voice. Others have said she has a three-pack-a-day voice too.* Protocol required her to remain silent until addressed.

*Well, she's sure takin' her sweet time.* Her stomach growled, breaking the stillness in the room. "Oh, excuse me." It was out of her mouth before she realized she'd uttered it.

"Quiet!" Geraldine Grossman demanded as she glowered at KC. *Disposition hasn't improved either. Demanding, arrogant, and insensitive.*

"Well, Elliott, I see you've applied for parole, again," Grossman spoke. "What makes you think the state should grant it this time?"

*She's baiting me.* Her stomach churned. The shackles kept her from squirming. With her hands clasped together, she kneaded her forefingers with her thumbs.

"I completed college and received a degree in computer programming and web design. Richard Goen, the owner of Advanced Web Designs, offered me a job after he heard I had completed college, and as soon as I'm—"

"Oh, yes, I've heard of Richard Goen," Grossman interrupted. "He's such a sucker. Thinks he can rehabilitate every con. I've lost track of the number he's tried to help. Few made it. What makes you think you can? He's demanding. Think you can work for him?"

"I've been freelancing for him. Money hasn't been great. Most of it applied toward restitution. I intend to repay what I stole," KC replied with pride.

"You do, do you?" Contempt spewed from Grossman's voice. She paused. "I see you were written up for possession of cannabis. As I recall, parole was denied because of that violation." She peered over her reading glasses at KC. "You denied the pot was yours. Still sticking to your story?" Her left eyebrow rose.

KC knew she was being taunted. *The truth? Would Grossman even accept the truth? No.* KC squirmed. It was a lose-lose situation. She needed a godsend—hard when one's faith was gone. Yet she sent a quick prayer to her unknown and uncaring god. Sitting on the edge of the chair with her back straight, she addressed her nemesis. "Mrs. Grossman, I stated the drugs weren't mine then, and I assure you today they weren't mine. I have no idea how they got in my cell. I'll take a polygraph to prove it." She settled back into the chair and offered no other explanation—none was needed.

Skeptical, Grossman lowered her head, peered over her glasses, and clipped, "Thank you, Ms. Elliott. You'll hear from the parole board. You're excused." She pressed a button, and a guard returned.

KC looked intently at Mrs. Grossman for a few seconds, trying to read her face.

The tautness in her stomach eased. Content she'd provided all the necessary answers, she stood. Back straight and head held high, she walked from the room.

The walk back to her cell seemed as if it were miles long, but it was only three or four city blocks in length. She was silent as she walked. Her eyes narrowed as she remembered a scripture. *What was that verse? "Then you will know the truth, and the truth will set you free." If that's true, I should be free.* She tried to imagine what life would be like outside the walls. It was a hot and humid summer day. Despite the high humidity, KC longed for her freedom. A swim in the lake sounded so good.

Mrs. Grossman sat at the metal table in the interview room writing her report. "Inmate 03011980, Kimberly Christine Elliott. Crime: embezzlement. Sentence: ten years. Parole eligibility: two and half years. Elliott applied. Denied. Cannabis found in her cell. Prisoner denied it was hers. This year Elliott reapplied for parole. She's completed college, degree in computer programming, employment is in place, continues to deny contraband was hers." Grossman's eyes narrowed. Her mouth filled with the taste of vomit. *I hate to admit it, but I'm inclined to believe her. She says she'd take a lie detector test to prove it.* "Recommendation: release inmate with a two-year parole period. Further recommendation: weekly random drug tests, employment must continue, and restitution must be made within five years." Annoyed, Grossman slapped shut KC's file. She hated recommending parole. *It makes me sick to admit it, but Elliott is ready to be released,* she thought

*I need a cigarette right now. Who in their right mind wrote a law prohibiting smoking in state buildings? I gotta get out of here for a while.* She banged on the door in frustration. *Tick-tick-tick.* The clock's second hand broke the stillness. She heard the guard's keys jangling in the lock.

"Took you long enough," she said as she glared at the guard. "I need a cigarette. Where can I smoke?" she asked, pulling a pack of Camels from her purse.

"Not in he—"

"I know, fool! Where?"

"Outside the front entrance where everyone else goes." He nodded his head toward the front.

The *click, click* of her high heels echoed as she scurried down the hall. She needed a hit to feed her nicotine addiction. Pulling a cigarette from the pack, her hands trembled as she tried to light it. A long, satisfying draw eased her body's desire for the drug. She exhaled, appreciating the temporary fix. Glancing at her watch, she knew it was time to return. *One more drag before I go in to see the next imbecile.* She dropped the butt in the receptacle by the door.

After her last interview, she flicked her wrist toward her to check the time. *Ugh, it's been a long day. Finally, I can go home.* She jammed the files into her briefcase. *Why have I stayed with the job so long?* She shoved a note into the warden's mailbox: "Be back tomorrow, 9:00 a.m." She turned sharply on her high-heeled shoes and left. *What an exhausting day. Home for the night.* She pined for a night at home, alone to do whatever she wanted.

Once in her car, Geraldine Grossman took a deep, cleansing breath. Stuck at a stoplight, she tapped her long acrylic nails on the steering wheel. The light changed to green. Not five seconds passed. Ever the impatient one, she blared her horn at the car ahead of her. "Move it!" she shouted. "There's only one shade of green."

Pressing the gas pedal, her BMW lunged toward the car ahead of her. Her head jerked forward and back as she stomped on the brake. Within an inch of colliding with the Ford Escort, Geraldine released the breath she'd stored in her lungs. *That was close,* she complained with a mixture of relief and anger. *I thought I left all the idiots in prison today.* No collision, no injuries. Grossman continued on her way.

Chewing on her lower lip, Grossman pondered her interview with KC Elliott. *Why do I hate that woman? I mean, other than because she's a prisoner.* With her eyes narrowed, brow knitted together, and index finger bent and resting on her chin, she tried to ascertain who Elliott reminded her of. Slamming her hand against the steering wheel, she sputtered, "Now I know! She looks like Logan's ex-wife. I hate her for leaving him." She felt as if someone was staring at her. Glancing toward the man in the car stopped next to her, she realized she was right. She gave a sheepish smile and raised her palms, gesturing her surprise that she was talking to no one in particular. *He thinks I'm an idiot now.* Embarrassed, she focused her eyes forward. She returned to her thoughts. *I know Logan could be an uncaring jerk, but that shrew left him with nothing. Nothing. She destroyed him.*

Arriving home, she reached up and pressed the garage door remote. Pulling into the garage, she shuddered and shook her head. *I will not cry.* She wiped a tear from her eye and sniffled. *She ruined our family. I hate Elliott because she reminds me of that spiteful wench. I think psychologists would call that transference. Better get myself together or I'll be forced to see a shrink myself,* she sneered. *Never mind, I don't have to see that woman again unless ...*

KC returned to her cell. "Didn't go well, huh?" Cali, her cellmate, remarked.

KC stared in disbelief.

"Your eyes tell it all." She put her hand on KC's shoulder and squeezed.

"No," KC answered, flopping down on the hard, plastic mattress.

"It was Grossman, Ms. No-parole. Of all people." Disappointment hung on every word, and she struggled to keep her tears dammed in her eyes.

"Oh, tough luck," Cali offered. She knew exactly what KC was talking about. Only three months ago, she'd had her parole hearing, and Grossman had interviewed her. Cali was in prison for child abuse. She knew she belonged there. But KC was guilty of a white-collar crime. "I wish she'd just retire," Cali declared.

KC didn't answer. She lay on her bed for minutes with her hands behind her head, staring at the ceiling. She should call her mother, but she didn't want her to know how discouraged she was. When she left the cell, she did what that old song from the musical *Bye Bye Birdie*" said to do: she put on a happy face. It was either that or commit suicide.

KC knew it would be several weeks before she'd hear from the parole board. Time was not going to be her best friend. She spent hours working on projects for her boss, Richard Goen, but Grossman's disparaging comment intimidated her. With renewed determination, KC designed and redesigned websites for Goen, often resulting in blurry eyesight for her diligence. Resting in her cell wasn't an option. "Gotta keep busy," was her mantra.

She held the envelope in a vise-like grip. The return address read "Department of Corrections." KC wanted to tear it open, but fear paralyzed her. Sitting on her bunk, she turned it over and over in her hands.

Finally, Cali snapped at her, "Will ya just open it!"

"I'm afraid to." KC laughed and cried at the same time. Seconds clicked off the clock. Finally, she tore open the envelope. Her eyes widened and filled with tears as she read, "Inmate 03011980, Kimberly Christine, has been granted parole effective October eighteen of this year. Conditions of parole: two-year probation, weekly random drug tests, $30,000 restitution to be repaid within five years." Taken aback, KC fell back on the bunk and covered her face with her pillow. For the first time in years, she wept unabated. *There is a light at the end of the tunnel.*

"KC, I'm so sorry." Cali touched her empty hand. Melancholy permeated the nine-by-twelve-foot cell. "I thought for sure ya would get parole this time." A hush filled the cell despite the cacophony around them. "In my opinion, you've been a model prisoner. Whoever snuck that pot into your cell really screwed things up for ya. I'm so sorry." She sat on her bunk with her head down and her hands in her lap, shaking her head.

Eventually, KC composed herself. She stood, pumped her fist in celebration, and muffled a shout of jubilation. "I got it, Cali. I got it! I can't believe it. The old battle-ax granted me parole. My last day here is October 18."

Cali, smiling, jumped from her bunk and gave KC a quick hug. Although both were prisoners, they'd become friends. *Oh my, what's my next cell mate going to be like?* Cali tried to imagine that. *No time for imagining.*

"KC, the next six weeks are going to be more difficult than you can imagine. Once the other inmates learn of your parole, you're gonna be the target for all kindsa trouble." She shook her head and locked her jaws together. Her lips formed a small thin line. "Be careful who you tell," she whispered "Don't ever let the guards know. You've gotta keep your nose clean. Watch ya back."

Cali's warnings disturbed KC. Although she'd given up on believing in God, she breathed a quick prayer for help. Her stomach gnarled in knots, and she felt as if she was going to vomit. *I'll never tell another person of the parole board's decision.* She pressed her eyes together as if to shut out all her troubles.

Unfortunately, the word had already spread throughout the prison. In the dining hall, a prisoner "accidentally" spilled coffee on KC. In the television room, KC was shoved off a chair. Still, she maintained self-control. Cali had warned her, but she didn't expect it to begin so quickly. KC sought refuge in the library. She tried to lose herself in a good mystery. She browsed the mystery books and found one written by Agatha Christie. As she checked out the book, *Endless Night*, the librarian, an inmate, whispered, "Watch your back, girl! Trouble's comin'."

Life wasn't easy for KC. The showers were an especially dangerous area. Once, her head was slammed against the wall, and her nose bled from the impact. She didn't report it. Another time, someone slashed her forearm, but she and Cali were able to bandage it, avoiding a trip to the infirmary and many questions. The warnings not only impacted KC but Cali as well. Both women were in a dangerous situation. For Cali, it was only because of her proximity to KC. They took turns sleeping as the risks seemed to increase at night. It was a fact that prison guards often escorted women to a secluded location and repeatedly raped them. Once the inmate reported the rape, she was sent to solitary confinement.

October seventeenth arrived, and KC's anticipation could barely be contained. She selected the things she really wanted to take with her and told the guards what she didn't want.

"This is my journal," she declared. "I'm taking this." She turned to Cali. With a mischievous grin, she added, "Smile—I didn't write much about you." KC pointed to a stack of books and announced, "These books stay." The reality that she would soon enjoy freedom was exhilarating. Finally, KC had everything packed. Early the next morning she was to be released from prison. For the first time in five years, she'd walk free and breathe fresh air. She'd get to decide what time to eat and when to go to bed. The thought of freedom filled every fiber of her being. Yet, KC was nervous. She lay back on the prison bunk for the last time. She rolled up the flat pillow, snuggled under the rough woolen blanket, and tried to sleep. She was surprised by the tears rolling down her cheeks. Years ago, she had learned that an inmate shouldn't cry; it was a sign of weakness, and weakness was not a characteristic a prisoner wanted others to know about. It was common knowledge that a weak prisoner was a target for other prisoners. KC stifled her sobs with a pillow.

Sleep came quickly that night, but the same dream that had been her companion for years also came quickly. In it, KC was a little girl. "Oh, Daddy, thank you. I love my doll. I think I'll call her Suzy." She held Suzy close and kissed her new little companion. Suzy was dressed in cute little pink pajamas. When KC laid Suzy down, she cried, "Mama, Mama." KC picked her up, held her tightly in her arms, and rocked her.

That part of the dream was pleasant, but it soon took on an ominous tone. KC, her drunken daddy, and her dolly were enjoying a tea party. KC spilled the water, and her father began yelling at her, "You're so stupid and clumsy!" He grabbed the doll and threw it across the room.

"I'm sorry, Daddy. Please don't hurt Suzy. She didn't spill; I did." Tears spilling down her face, KC ran to comfort Suzy.

Mr. Elliott continued his diatribe. "You are so stupid! You can't even take care of that stupid doll. Give her to me." He reached for Suzy, but KC held her tightly in her arms.

Mr. Elliott was furious, so he struck KC across the cheek with the back of his hand. The force of the slap was so strong that it knocked KC off the chair. She lay on the floor sobbing,

"I'm sorry, Suzy. I'll take better care of you. I'm sorry." She held the little doll tightly as she wept and held her smarting cheek. Her father staggered off to the kitchen. He opened the refrigerator and swore loudly when he found no beer. He slammed the door and swore again. He dropped into a chair and lit a cigarette.

The enormity of his actions began to overwhelm him. He wanted to apologize to his little girl. Walking into the family room, he saw that KC had fallen asleep on the floor with her plump arm wrapped tightly around Suzy. Picking her up in his strong, tattooed arms, he carried her to her bedroom, which was decorated with princesses and painted light pink. He pulled back the covers and laid her on the bed. He opened the dresser drawer and pulled out a pair of pink pajamas. He stumbled. Although soused, he removed KC's T-shirt and slacks. He began caressing her forehead. He cried as he did, pleading for KC's forgiveness. "I didn't mean to hit you. You're daddy's little girl." But daddy's little girl or not, he began doing things to KC that no daddy should ever do to his children.

KC woke in a cold sweat. The smell of a thousand imprisoned women reminded her of the acrid smell of stale beer, tobacco, and perspiration that she remembered as a small child. She asked herself, *Will I ever get over what Dad did to me?* She renewed the vow she made every day: *If I ever get married and have children, I will* never *allow my husband to touch my children the way my dad touched me. Never!* Screams from one of the new inmates startled KC. She knew what was happening. Assaults on new inmates were common. KC remembered fighting off the women who had attacked her. She covered her ears, hoping to block out the cries of the inmate being attacked by another.

Morning dawned, and KC was met by a guard.

"Inmate 03011980, get your gear together."

*Such efficiency.* KC glanced at the guard. *If she smiled, her face would break.*

"I don't ever want to see your face in this place again. Understood?" Compassion wasn't acceptable. Guards must remain indifferent.

"Yes, ma'am. Understood. I have no intention of being seen here again." She looked back at Cali, and tears welled in her eyes. Afraid to say anything, she mouthed, "Good luck, my friend." KC grabbed her belongings and followed the guard down the long corridors. As they passed through each cell block, the electronic doors clanged opened and then closed behind them. From time to time, another inmate would shout words of encouragement, while others hurled threats and curses. KC kept her face forward, fearful that one false move would negate her parole. She walked to the check-out point without incident.

"You are to go to your residence and remain there for forty-eight hours or until your parole officer arrives. If you go anywhere but home, your parole can and will be revoked. Understand?" The corrections officer clipped off the requirements in a monotone. It was obvious to KC that he had repeated the statements so often that it was as normal as breathing. "The parole officer will tell you what you can and cannot do."

KC signed the necessary papers, releasing her from prison. It was a chapter in her life she wanted to forget but knew she never would. "I understand, sir," she replied. "I will be like the American Express credit card. I won't leave home without it—that is, authorization from my parole officer."

The corrections officer glared at her attempt of humor. He signed the release and handed KC her copy. "Elliott, keep your nose clean." He glanced about the room and then cautiously added, "You have so much to offer society. I really don't want to see you back here." The CO turned curtly and walked away. KC stood looking at his back. *Did he really say that? I can't believe someone here has a heart.* She shook her head as if clearing it. With her arms full of her belongings and her stomach knotted with apprehension, she walked out. She was free—free from prison. But was she really free?

Twisting a small white handkerchief, Rose Phillips waited. This was the day she'd been praying about for years. She took a step toward the thin, blonde girl and stopped. She took a couple more steps. Eyeing each other, a smile broke on the face of the older woman. Her arms opened, bidding the younger woman to allow her to embrace her. "I love you, KC."

KC dropped her belongings and ran with abandon to greet her mother. She hugged her for the first time in five years. Both wept openly and without reserve. Rose broke off the hug, held her daughter at arm's length, and smiled. "I love you so much." The tears flowed again.

A laugh mixed with tears broke the silence. "It's so good to actually hug you, Mom. It's been so long. I'm never coming back here." They'd had their differences, they'd argued about her crime, but their love for each other was strong.

Rose had been brought up in a strict, religious home. Her parents had passed those strict values down to her, and Rose had expected KC to abide by the same values. When KC was arrested for embezzlement, Rose's heart was broken. She wept for days on end; her eyes became red and swollen. She was so disappointed in KC. Her daughter had brought dishonor to the family, and it was more than Rose could bear. She lost weight, and her eyes darkened from lack of sleep. The smile that had brightened a room had faded. KC was painfully aware that she was the cause of the change in her mother's appearance. Almost on a weekly basis, they argued. Words, shouted in bitterness but never meant, would haunt both women. In the end, though, their loved remained.

"Oh, Mom," KC finally managed to whimper. "It is so good to hug you. I've missed that. Our visits were always so short. We've got a lot of catching up to do. Let's go home."

"Let's go. I don't ever want to see this place again," Rose responded quickly. "But first, I want to introduce you to Charles. I know you know we've been married for a year. Charles never wanted to interfere with our time together, so he made the decision to remain home when I visited. Now you get to meet the man who has been my rock."

Standing aside was her stepfather, Charles, who had been Rose's high school friend. After Rose divorced KC's father, she refused to remarry until he died. However, Charles was the one person to whom Rose turned when she needed help. She and Charles were married while KC was in prison.

"Nice to meet you, Charles. Thank you for taking care of my mother." KC responded, but the tone in her voice was reserved. She offered her right hand to Charles, who grasped it gently in his rough, calloused hand. She smiled, but there was no warmth in the smile.

"It's good to meet you too, KC. I hope we can become friends," he said with a smile.

It was the smile that made KC wary of him. It reminded her of her father. Yet, in those brief moments, she could see that he truly loved her mother.

"Well, young lady, let's get your bag into the car. We've got a long ride ahead of us." He quickly and effortlessly tossed her bag into the trunk. KC started to open the car door, but Charles stopped her. "Listen, young lady, I want to help. Please allow me to be a gentleman." He smiled but suddenly knew he'd spoken too quickly and sternly. His smile faded quickly as he said, "I'm sorry. I didn't mean to offend you. Chalk it up to my age. My parents taught me to treat the ladies with respect. I'll try to remember that you need your independence."

"No problem," KC responded.

He opened the door for KC's mom. He then climbed into the car, revved the engine, and drove them off. KC never looked back.

CHAPTER 2

Logan Parsons, the parole officer assigned to KC Elliott, hated his job almost as much as he hated his mother. He'd always wanted to get a degree in theater arts and move to California. Like thousands of other young people, he believed he'd be discovered by an agent who would declare him to be the next Brad Pitt or Matt Damon. However, his hopes and dreams didn't come to fruition. He had spent all of his savings hoping to be discovered. With no money and no signed contract, Logan returned home, where his bitter mother constantly berated his abilities. As Logan drove to 919 Pleasant to meet his new parolee, KC Elliott, he thought of his mother. *Oh, how I hate that woman. I can't recall a single time when she encouraged me. Her mantra was, "You're just like your father. You'll never amount to anything." I didn't even know my father. How in the world could I be just like him? One of these days, I'm going to search for him and see if I'm just like him. Until then, I am going to live my life the way I want, and Mother can just go to—* A car horn jarred Logan from his daydreaming.

Arriving at the assigned address, Logan was shocked. It wasn't the stereotypical convict's home. Most of his parolees lived in run-down government housing. Occasionally, he'd be assigned to a parolee who lived in a middle-class neighborhood. However, this house looked like it belonged in an issue of *Better Homes and Gardens.* Located on a small lake, it was a log cabin with a wraparound

15

porch. The lawn was well landscaped and manicured. If he was in the market for purchasing a house, this would be the one he wanted. *I can't believe an ex-con lives here,* he thought, blinking his eyes. Reaching across the car, he opened the Elliott file to double-check the address. Incredulously, he declared aloud, "Nope, this is the right address." He slammed his hand against the steering wheel as the green monster of jealousy consumed him. *Can't believe it,* he thought. *My parolee lives in a better house than I grew up in and better than what I live in now. Life's not fair!*

Logan gathered the necessary paperwork and untangled his six-foot, six-inch frame from his Ford Focus. Slamming the door, he thought, *One of these days I'll be able to afford that Ford Expedition I really want—and a home like this.* He walked determinedly toward the house with his head held high, walking with long, decisive strides and an air of authority. He hated to use the doorbell. He knocked loudly as if announcing his power.

Within seconds, an elderly, white-haired lady greeted Logan. "May I help you?" she inquired.

"Yes, I'm Logan Parsons from the Department of Corrections," he retorted as he flashed his identification badge. "I'm here to see Kimberly Christine Elliott."

"Oh, yes. She's expecting you. Please come in." She opened the door to Logan. "I'm KC's mother, Rose Phillips." She showed Logan to the great room. "I'll let her know you're here." Standing in the middle of the room, Logan gazed around. The beautiful stone fireplace provided warmth, but he was drawn to the glass wall and the gorgeous view of the small lake. The water was so calm. It was almost like a mirror, and the trees reflected in the stillness.

"Mr. Parsons?" a soft voice inquired.

"Yes," Parsons turned toward the voice. "You must be Kimberly Christine Elliott, my newly assigned parolee," Logan replied, unsmiling and with arrogance. He always reminded his parolees that he was superior to them.

"Correct. I am your new parolee. I prefer to be called KC. Now, could I get you something to drink? Coffee, ice tea, or a soda?" KC might have spent years in prison, but she had never lost her gift of hospitality. It was only on hold.

"Ice tea would be fine."

He watched as she retreated to the kitchen. *Hmm,* he thought. *Very attractive, long blonde hair, and hospitable. What a body!*

"Here you are, Mr. Parsons," KC said as she placed his tea on the table. KC noticed that he'd barely taken his eyes off of her and asked, "You like the view?"

"Of course." He blushed slightly. "This glass wall offers a panoramic view of the lake and woods in the distance. An artist or photographer would love this place."

*He's smooth,* KC thought. *He hadn't been looking out the windows. I know exactly what caught his attention.* The realization both pleased and frightened her.

She sat across the table from Mr. Smooth, as she had dubbed him.

"Ms. Elliott, you understand that there are certain conditions to your parole, correct?" he was very businesslike.

"Yes, sir. I do," she replied with reserve. For the next thirty minutes, Parsons and KC reviewed the sixteen rules of parole.

"Any questions?" he asked as he prepared the paperwork for KC's signature.

"Yes, just one," she replied hesitantly. "Mr. Goen, my employer at Advanced Web Designs, hires former convicts. How am I to avoid associating with convicts when I work with them?"

"I'm aware of Mr. Goen. While I appreciate his efforts to hire ex-cons, I think he is misguided. Yes, you will have to work with them, but you are not to associate with them after work." He glared at KC as if to threaten her. "Keep your nose to the grindstone, as they say, and you'll be free from parole in two years. If not, well, there will be a room for you at the state's expense."

He shoved the papers toward KC, and walking behind her, he reached into his suit coat pocket to retrieve a black pen. Carefully, he pointed to each line she needed to sign and date. He could smell her freshly shampooed hair and was sure she used almond-scented shampoo. But he was keenly aware of KC's beauty.

"Thank you for your time this morning, Ms. Elliott. I will be seeing you." He closed the door tightly behind him. He thought, *Oh, yes, I will be seeing you.*

"That didn't take long," KC's mother remarked. "Mr. Parsons seems like a nice guy." Rose was always so optimistic. She almost always saw the good in people.

"Glad you think so, Mom. You aren't the one who has to deal with him. There's something sinister about that man. I don't like him." KC's voice sounded dubious. "He's got a dark side. You mark my word."

"Well, you've got no one to blame …" The words were out before she realized it. Although Rose could see the good in others, since her daughter's conviction she saw mostly the bad in KC.

"Fine!" KC shouted at her mother. "I'm a bad person. But, Mom, whatever happened to that grace you're always talking about? Does it exist for everyone but your daughter?" KC turned on her heels and stomped out of the room.

Rose walked toward the windows and shook her head. A tear cascaded down her cheek. She was painfully aware that she'd both angered and hurt her daughter. She didn't mean to do it, but there was truth in what she had begun to say. Rose slipped out the door and sat in a chair on the deck. She prayed, "Oh, God, the psalmist said, 'Set a guard over my mouth, O LORD; keep watch over the door of my lips'" (Ps. 141:3). I really need your help to guard my words. I didn't mean to hurt KC. Forgive me. I need to ask KC's forgiveness too. I have missed her so much. I can't believe I said that. I'm so ashamed of myself. Please forgive me." She sat quietly for several minutes before going back inside. Like toothpaste squeezed from the tube, the words that had hurt KC could not be taken back. She had only one option—she needed to apologize. Unfortunately, Rose wasn't sure her daughter would even talk to her now.

CHAPTER 3

R ose tapped lightly at KC's door but got no answer. She tried again—still no response. "KC," she called.

Rose spoke gently and with hesitation. "KC, I'm so sorry. I know you are humiliated. I was careless. It was mean-spirited. I hope we can talk about it sometime." She briefly waited outside KC's bedroom but heard no response and no noise. With contrition, Rose quietly walked down the hallway.

Sitting pensively before the massive fireplace was her husband. Charles didn't say a thing. When the exchange of words occurred, Charles had just walked into the house. He'd vowed to never interfere and never to contradict his wife in front of anyone else, especially her daughter. Although they had been married only a year, he knew Rose would eventually talk about it.

Rose stopped in the kitchen and poured herself a glass of iced tea. Sighing heavily, she walked into the great room and sat opposite her husband. Silence hung in the air. Charles sat quietly, and Rose replayed the terrible scene in her mind. There was no question about it; she was wrong. She'd acted vindictively. "Umph," she cleared her throat. "Charles, I really messed up."

He reached for his iced tea and took a sip. "So you say," he responded.

"Did you hear me?" she inquired. "I really messed up." Resignation of defeat hung in the air.

"Want to talk about it?" Charles asked.

"I s'pose." But she didn't make a sound. The silence seemed to linger for an hour, but it was only five minutes. When she finally spoke, her voice quivered. Tears fell like a waterfall. She choked out the words. "Charles ... Charles ... I'm afraid our relationship is over."

The quiet, reserved man resolutely stood and walked to his wife. He knelt before Rose and gently covered her trembling hands with his. His hands were strong, calloused from years of hard work, but tender.

"Oh, Charles," Rose sobbed. "I love her so much. How could I have hurt her so?" She sniffed as she reached for a tissue. "I don't think she'll ever forgive me."

"Rose, you were wrong. You know it, I know it, and KC knows it." Rose started to respond, but Charles placed his index finger over her mouth. "Hear me out." He firmly and calmly continued. "You are a strong woman. You have high values, and you're a wonderful Christian lady. You're patient with all people except your daughter. KC was right when she questioned your ability to extend grace to everyone but her. But truthfully, I think it more of a pride problem." He reached over and wiped tears from her eyes. "KC will come around. But you need to give her time." With his strong, compassionate hands, he cupped her chin, covered her lips with his, and kissed her tenderly. Then he looked intently at his wife and asked, "Can we pray about this?"

As Rose nodded her assent, the tears began to flow again. Charles began praying, "Oh God, we are in a pickle here, and we need your help. KC has been through so much. We confess much of it was her own fault, but we are people of faith. We are going to trust you to begin working in her life. Harsh words have been uttered tonight by the lady I love. I ask, on her behalf, to forgive her. I love Rose with all my heart, but sometimes her pride gets in the way. Please, loving God, forgive her for the stinging words she said to KC. Help Rose to humble herself before you and with KC. Loving and forgiving God, help me to be the man you want me to be. We all have a lot of adjusting to do, and we need your help." He squeezed Rose's hand and asked, "Would you like to pray too?"

She hesitated but finally agreed. "Dear Jesus, I'm reminded that you gave up everything to come to this sinful earth. Paul said you humbled yourself. He said you told him, 'My grace is sufficient for you, for my power is made perfect in weakness.' Lord, I am weak. I need your grace, and I need to extend grace to my daughter. Please God, help me. Amen."

It was lonely in her room. However, KC was not prepared to confront her mother. As she looked at her reflection in the mirror, she realized that she looked like a pouting teenager. Her arms were crossed, and a scowl made her usually pleasant face look angry. Red blotches marred her creamy-hued skin. Her head was pounding from the headache she'd acquired from crying and fuming. *Okay, okay,* she thought, *I behaved badly. But Mom's words were cutting and unnecessary. I know I did wrong. I don't need Mom reminding me. Daily I'm reminded of the branding I will endure for the rest of my life. It's as if an ugly red C has been burned into my forehead.* KC uncrossed her arms, shook her hands, and stretched out her arms. *I didn't realize I was so tense,* she thought. She lay across the bed and eventually fell asleep, but restful sleep eluded her.

"No!" KC screamed as she drew her legs to her chest. "Don't! Please don't!"

CHAPTER 4

Startled by the screams, Charles tore up the stairway. The glass that Rose had been drying dropped and shattered on the floor as Rose shouted, "What in the world?" She threw her towel on the counter and hurried in the direction of the screaming.

Charles didn't even knock at KC's door. Bursting through the door, he noted that, physically, KC was all right. Something prevented him from approaching her. "KC, you're okay! You're okay." He spoke softly but firmly. However, nothing he said calmed her. KC was weeping convulsively. Although he wasn't her father, he wanted to clutch her in his arms to assure her that she was safe, but he didn't. It was a good decision since she was flailing her arms about and could have hurt him.

"No! No, please don't!" she shouted over and over again. She splayed her hands through her thick, blonde hair and swayed violently as she wept.

Rose pushed past Charles to see what was happening. Her hands flew to her mouth to restrain the scream. Despite the curt words exchanged earlier, Rose wanted—no, she needed—to tightly hold her daughter and comfort her. As she started toward KC, Charles stepped between them. He tenderly held his wife and carefully escorted her from the room.

"Not now, Rose," he whispered as he combed his hands through her hair. "Whatever KC experienced, she needs time to work through this." Rose started to respond, but Charles put his index finger over her lips. "Rose, trust me," he said as he led her from the room. In the hallway, he continued, "KC experienced things in prison she needs to forget. But I'm afraid she'll be haunted by them for the rest of her life if she doesn't get help. When she settles down, we can broach the subject of counseling." Tears slipped silently down Rose's cheeks as she sought comfort in the arms of her husband.

"Honey, we need to pray for KC. We need to ask God to direct us to the right counselor." He paused. Emphasizing the next words, he continued, "And we need to pray that KC will be open to counseling." Rose quietly nodded her agreement. "Honey, you may need to go to counseling too."

Her head jerked up, and she looked defiantly at Charles. "What do you mean? You think I need counseling?"

He hesitated, choosing his words carefully. "Honey, you have a lot of anger toward KC." She started to answer, but Charles continued unyieldingly. "Your pride was injured when KC was convicted and imprisoned. Until you deal with that anger, there will always be a rift in your relationship with your daughter." He looked away briefly and then continued. "And it could also cause problems between us. I don't want our relationship to be damaged, do you?"

"No," she whispered, clearly feeling rebuked by her husband.

Rose quietly walked to her sewing room. She hated to be reprimanded by her husband, but she knew he was usually right. She loved him so much. The sewing room was a place of tranquility. It faced the lake, and her old rocking chair was there. She often secluded herself in the sewing room when she needed to think and pray. She sat quietly with her hands folded in her lap. The tears began again, and she let them flow unhindered. Rose tried to pray, but she couldn't form the sentences. *Okay, God,* she thought, *I'm going to rely upon the scripture that says the Holy Spirit intercedes for us when we don't know what we ought to pray for.* She reached for her Bible and read, "In the same way, the Spirit comes to help our weakness. We don't know what we should pray, but the Spirit himself pleads our case with unexpressed groans. The one who searches hearts knows how the Spirit thinks, because he pleads for the saints, consistent with God's will. We know that God works all things together for good for the ones who love God, for those who are called according to his purpose" (Rom. 8:26–28 Common English Bible, or CEB). She slowly reread the verses, closed the book, and placed it on the end table near her rocker. Still feeling defeated and like a failure, Rose stood looking over the lake for several minutes. She pursed her lips together, shook her head, and knelt in front of her rocker. "Lord Jesus, I've been a fool and a proud one at that. Please forgive me. I've been more concerned about what people think of me than about KC's relationship with me and with you. I tried to be supportive of her while she was in prison, but it broke my heart to see her there. Oh, yes, God, I know she needed to be there. She broke the law." She paused and then continued, "Just saying the words 'she broke the law' is hard for me. I'm afraid the way I said it is judgmental, but it is true. She broke the law." Silence filled the room as she examined her own life. The tears began to fall again. As she sobbed, she rocked forward and backward. When the tears subsided, she continued praying. "And I broke the law too. I broke your law. Jesus said, 'Do not judge, or you too will be judged. For in the same you judge others, you will be judged, and with the measure you use, it will be measured to you'" (Matt. 7:1–2 New International Version, or NIV). "Charles was right in chastising me for the way I've treated KC. But his words stung …" Rose quickly lifted her head. "Oh my, now I understand how KC must have felt." The tears began again. "Oh, God, I'm so sorry. Please forgive me. King David prayed, 'Create in me a clean heart and renew a right spirit in me.' That's what I want, dear Jesus. Please give me a clean heart and right spirit. Help me to love KC unconditionally." She remained in prayer and tried to listen to God for several minutes. Then Rose tried to stand, but her arthritic knees were uncooperative. She reached for the end table.

*Crash!* Glass shattered, and the book tumbled to the floor.

CHAPTER 5

"I 'm okay! I'm okay!" Rose assured anyone who could hear her. As it turned out, no one heard. When no one hurried to her rescue, Rose's ego was bruised. "Fine!" she announced empathically. "Now I know where I stand with this family." A quick personal assessment indicated no apparent broken bones. Unfortunately, the same couldn't be said about the clock or the lamp. She collected the larger pieces of shattered glass and vacuumed up the remaining shards. As she descended the stairs, she heard the door open. She called out, "Hello? Hello? Who's there?"

"For goodness' sake, Rose! It's your husband. Who else could it be?" Charles loved to tease his wife. "Are you okay?"

"You're a little late in asking," she answered jokingly. She kissed him lightly on the cheek.

"You mean you made up with KC?" He was startled that Rose had already talked with her.

"No." Her brow furled questioningly. "I thought we were going to discuss it as a family."

"Yes, I thought we were going to pray about it and then discuss it." He crossed his arms, his head cocked to the left, and he knew they weren't on the same wavelength. "Let's back up. I asked, 'Are you okay?' right?" Rose nodded in agreement. "You responded, 'You're a little late in asking.' What are you talking about?" When

Rose was amused, a sparkle appeared in her eyes, but Charles was confused and getting a little agitated. "Well?"

"After you left, I went upstairs to the sewing room. You know I go there not only to sew but to read, meditate, and pray, right?" He nodded. "Well, I knelt in prayer, and when I was done praying, my knees didn't want to help me up. I leaned on the end table for support, and it tipped over. The lamp and clock are broken, but I'm okay."

Instantly, Charles was concerned about his wife. He hurried to her side and embraced her. "Are you sure you're okay? Do you need to go to the hospital?"

Rose chuckled and gently pushed him. "Oh, for goodness' sake, Charles. I'm fine. I don't have any broken bones." She hesitated and, blushing, added, "The only thing broken is my pride—and of course, the lamp and clock. I'll probably be a little sore for a couple of days, but I'm fine."

"How are you feeling about things now?" he asked. "I mean about our earlier conversation?"

"There is much truth in what you said, Charles. I hate to admit it, but you are right. I don't know how KC will feel about your suggestion, but I like it. I think she should go for counseling."

"Rose?" His voice inflection told her he had a question about her last comment. "Is that all?"

She hung her head with chagrin and continued, "I guess I do have a bit of a pride issue. I probably need to talk with someone too."

He kissed the top of her head, her forehead, and then her lips. "I love you, Rosie." *Rosie* was his term of endearment for the lady he'd loved for years. Yes, he had loved her for years. She had refused to marry him until after her ex-husband died. Reluctantly, he respected her decision, and his love for her continued to grow. The day they married was truly a day of celebration. KC's incarceration had been the only thing dimming the day.

Even before they were married, she had identified Charles as a man of discernment. She had noticed the men from their church consulting Charles. Although she was never privy to their conversations, she could tell that Charles was held in high esteem. Over and over, most of the men who consulted with Charles walked away with their heads held high. Her love for him grew every time someone sought his advice. Now it was she who benefited from his wisdom.

Charles was sitting by the fireplace reading the paper. She looked intently at her husband. Despite the sting of his suggestion that she seek counseling, her love for him continued to grow. She sighed and thought, *I am so fortunate to have married such a godly man. Thank you, God, for bringing Charles into my life.* She cunningly slipped behind him and started to place her hands tenderly on his shoulders.

"Rose, I know you're behind me. What do you want?" He smiled knowing that he'd caught her in the act of trying to surprise him.

"Well," she sputtered. "How did you know I was behind you?"

He reached for her hand and pulled her around in front of him. Smiling, he pulled her to his lap and seductively answered, "I can smell you before I see you. I love the scent." He kissed her tenderly. "By the way, like your perfume, you've become an obsession to me. I love you so much." He kissed her again. It was a long and passionate kiss.

"Oh, please!" they heard KC comment from the kitchen. "Can't you two wait 'til after supper?"

CHAPTER 6

Logan Parsons enjoyed the power he held over his parolees. After working as a parole officer for nearly five years, he could almost always predict who would break parole. Drug offenders rarely were successful. The rate of repeat offenders was over 53 percent. Sex offenders' recidivism was over 55 percent. He and the other parole officers always paid close attention to them. For years, there have been debates on the treatment of and cure for sexual offenders. Can sexual offenders be rehabilitated? In Logan's opinion, the answer was an unequivocal no. He personally had reported men who had violated parole and returned to prison. Logan was a stickler for following the rules. He strictly enforced the law for all parolees on his caseload, and he rarely gave a parolee a second chance.

Logan returned to his office after his initial visit with KC Elliott. He placed his briefcase on his desk with a loud thud, startling the other officers. His eyes were narrowed, his brows furled in disgust, and his teeth clenched tightly together.

"Hey, Parsons, what's the problem? Another successful parolee cleared?" his coworker Dan asked sarcastically.

"Aw, shut up!" He shot a glare as he snapped open his case. "So far, it's a one-for-one day. One was sent back and another released." Logan clamped his teeth together and sighed. "Remember that college girl sent up for embezzlement a few years ago?" He didn't even wait for an answer. "She got paroled. Would ya believe it? She's my newest parolee." Logan plopped down in his black leather executive chair and propped his feet on his desk. "You should see the place she's livin' in!" He was quiet for a few seconds and added, "Ya would think someone livin' in the lap of luxury coulda kept her nose clean. But no," he emphasized the negative by drawing it out. "I expected her to be livin' in a flophouse. Man, she's livin' better'n me."

"You mean that Elliott girl? I remember her. I think I might have gone to school with her." Dan sat quietly thinking. "Yeah, she was a year behind me. I never knew her folks were wealthy. I think they were divorced. Her dad was an alcoholic, as I recall."

"Maybe her *wealth*," Logan said, stressing the word disparagingly, "was supplemented by the money she stole." When Logan was a child, his mother had struggled daily to put a nutritious meal on the table. After he began school, his mom was on the road a lot and usually came home in a foul mood. Rarely did a day pass when she didn't tell him he couldn't make a living as an actor. Although she hated working for the state, she kept telling him she could always get him a job with the Department of Corrections. She resented people who were well-heeled. Logan finally spit out, "If that Elliott woman thinks I'm going to go easy on her because she lives in a fancy house on the lake, she's got another think comin'." He reached for her file. "Ya know that stupid guy who hires ex-cons? That Goen guy? He's given her a job. She's supposed to begin Monday. I think I'll show up on Tuesday. Gonna make her life as miserable as I possibly can."

With that said, he filed the information and slammed the drawer shut. He sat at his desk, his eyes filled with hatred and fire. If looks could kill, everyone in the office—and KC—would be dead. Logan Parsons was so bitter that not even his coworkers wanted to be near him. After muttering for several minutes, he stood and announced, "I think I'll go check out another client, and then I'm gonna go home. Later, Dan." He lifted his hand, gesturing his good-byes.

Dan didn't bother to answer. He'd heard Logan's complaints about people who were better off than he so many times that he could almost repeat the diatribe verbatim. He often thought, *If Logan hates this job so much, why doesn't he quit? He should be able to find a job he likes. He's so negative; he makes all of us miserable. Why doesn't he go to California? He's always talkin' about acting. He'd probably be happier, and the office atmosphere would be much calmer.*

CHAPTER 7

D espite their earlier argument, KC joined her mother and Charles for dinner. Charles seemed to have a calming effect on the two women.

"Charles, Mom has been remiss in telling me how the two of you met," she said with a smile as she drank her milk. "And while you're at it, tell me about yourself. You know, I know nothing about you."

"KC! I don't mind if he tells you about how we met." Her mother was appalled by KC's request. "He has been an outstanding citizen. He's not a—"

"It's okay, Rose." Charles reached over and placed his hand over Rose's. "She has a right to know about us and about me." He smiled and winked at KC. "She needs to know I'm not a serial killer."

"Oh, for Pete's sake, Charles. She doesn't think that." Her face had reddened.

KC laughed, enjoying her mother's embarrassment. "What's the problem, Mom? Did you do something embarrassing to hook this man?"

"Oh, no, nothing like that." She reached for Charles's hand and added, "Go ahead,"

"Mine is not an exciting life, KC. But you do have the right to know about the man who married your mother and loves her beyond measure." He glanced at Rose and breathed a kiss her direction.

"Your mother is my first wife, and if she'll have me for the rest of her life, it will be my only marriage," he said to begin the story of his life. "My father died of a massive heart attack when I was in grade school, and my three sisters doted on me. I've always said they never spoiled me, but they did. Mom never wanted to raise a 'mother's boy.' She was a strong-willed woman." Charles gazed out the windows. Lost in thought, he struggled with ambivalent feelings.

"Charles," Rose spoke with caution. "Are you okay?"

He cleared his throat. "Oh, I'm sorry." He wiped his mouth with the napkins. "Mom could be stern. She insisted we children find jobs for spending money. She never tolerated slothfulness or brashness with any of her children.

"When I was a freshman, I landed a part-time job with the local lumberyard, Black's Lumber, for the summer. I loaded wood for contractors and carried roofing shingles and bags of cement, and by the end of the summer, I'd bulked up and sported a tan. The girls at school were fawning over me." The memory caused him to blush. He looked at KC and laughed, "Can you imagine—girls wanting to go out with me? I was a shy boy. Since I was so backward, I buried myself in my studies. I was a good student, not a jock, so the rumor was that I was gay. As you can imagine, I was an outcast."

KC rose to refill his coffee cup. She touched his shoulder and said, "I'm sorry, Charles. Kids can be so mean."

Rose sniffled and dabbed her eyes.

"Okay, enough of the melodramatics!" he declared. "No more tears." Looking at Rose, he asked, "Can I have some ice cream? Or do I have to go to the dairy barn?"

"Sit still," Rose offered. "I'll get us all a dish of ice cream." She slipped out of the dining room.

"Charles, you don't have to talk if you don't want," KC said. Compassion flooded her voice.

He shook his head slightly to the right, his mouth puckered. He continued his narrative. "Mom was disappointed that I didn't go to college, but I continued working at the lumberyard. Within five years, I was promoted to assistant manager."

KC saw his pride swell. "I saved my money, took a few investment classes, made some good investments. Five years later, Mitchell Black, the owner, announced that he was retiring. I asked if I could buy the business." He paused, savoring the black cherry ice cream. "You should have seen his eyes bulge." Charles laughed at the recollection. "'Son, he said, 'if you can come up with the money and good sound business plan, I'd be delighted to sell you the company.' As they say, the rest is history. It's been thirty-three years since that conversation. I think I did okay for not being a college graduate. I graduated from the school of hard knocks."

"Charles, you have every right to be proud," KC agreed. "I understand why Mom is so protective. But how did you meet Mom?"

"Your mother probably told you I'm a bit of tightwad." He smirked at Rose. "I've always planned ahead." He looked down and then lifted his head. "Our family never had very much and lived very frugally. Even after I bought the company, I rented a small apartment and rode my bike to work, weather permitting. I never had a subscription to a paper—didn't need it. I was at the library every day. I'd decided I wanted to retire comfortably. I bought this land." He glanced toward the lake and added, "I always wanted a house on the lake."

"Shortly before I retired, work began on this house. I was on site every day." He hesitated, a bit chagrined at the memory. "The contractor finally asked me not to come during the day." A smile broke across his face, and he laughed. "Imagine that—the contractor asked me not to come during the day."

Both Rose and KC tried to hide their grins.

"Go ahead. Laugh." He paused, giving them time to laugh. "But I wanted it done right." He stood and looked toward the lake. "I think I did a good job." He swiveled around. "I know, I didn't do the work. But I assure you—I inspected everything. Let's move to the great room where it is more comfortable."

The ladies refreshed their coffee and joined Charles in the great room, where the story of Rose and Charles's initial meeting continued.

"When decisions needed to be made about the appliances, bathroom facilities, and lighting fixtures, I didn't have a clue as to what to do. The contractor kept pushing me for decisions. I finally admitted that I didn't know the first thing about decorating a house. His answer was a woman by the name of Rose Elliott. He gave me the phone number, and I promised I'd call that night." Charles rose, went to his wife's side, bent over, and with a tenderness KC hadn't seen for years, kissed her. "I've never regretted my decision. And every decision she made regarding this house was perfect."

"Why, thank you very much, Mr. Phillips." Rose reached up and touched his hand, which was resting on her shoulder.

"Mom, I still need to be sure Charles is the right man for you," KC said, taking delight in teasing her mother. "Where'd Charles take you for your first date?"

"I don't know if we would call it our first date, but our first working meal was at Kenyon's Palace."

Charles coughed as if gagging.

"What she said was, 'I don't want to go to some greasy spoon to discuss business.' She suggested Kenyon's. Her reasoning? 'They have good salads.'"

Laughing freely, KC declared, "Sounds like Mom. Did you have to eat a salad too?"

"No," he said with a smile. "She promised me they had excellent steaks, fish, and chicken," Charles added.

"Yeah, but be honest," Rose cajoled. "After we ate, you announced, 'Hey, this place is better'n all the greasy spoons I've ever been in. The steak was exactly the way I like it. We've got to come back here sometime.' Remember? That's exactly what you said."

"It's true. It is our favorite place to eat too. Now that I've talked on and on and on, KC, do you have any other questions?"

"No. It is clear to me that you love my Mom. I appreciate all you've done to care for her this past year." She stole a look at her watch and proclaimed, "I think it is time for me to go to bed."

"Will you go to church with us tomorrow?" Charles asked cautiously.

She stopped with her foot on the bottom riser. "I don't know if I'm ready for church. For that matter, I don't know if the church is ready for me, a convicted felon." She didn't wait for a reply. KC continued climbing the stairway.

Charles and Rose sat on the love seat enjoying the sunset. With his arm resting on Rose's shoulders, Charles's chest rose and fell deeply as he sighed. "Guess it was a little too soon to ask the question, huh?"

"Probably," Rose responded. "But it gives her something to think about."

CHAPTER 8

*Well, she certainly hasn't changed,* KC thought, clenching her teeth. *I do not want to go to church tomorrow or anytime in the future. I'm sure she had Charles ask because she knew I'd say no.* She hurried upstairs and closed her bedroom door. *I hope working for Mr. and Mrs. Goen is better than living at home with Mom. Charles seems okay, but Mom is still overbearing.* KC reached for a nightgown in the walk-in closet. It looked like her mother had brought all her clothing to the new house. Some of her bedroom furniture made the move, but her mother must have sold some. Looking around the room, she could definitely see her mother's touch. *Since Charles designed the house, I should tell him I like the design,* she thought with a smile.

Curled up in her bed with a book on web design, KC wanted to refresh her memory on the various types of computer languages. Although the Goens had given her an internship while she was in prison, she wanted—no, needed—to impress them with her computer abilities. She suspected the job was offered to her because they knew her mother from church and felt sorry for KC. *Oh, how I hate the idea that I've become someone's "project,"* she thought. She slammed the book shut with disgust. *I'll do such a good job that they'll never again think of me as a project.* She reached to her left and turned off the light. Snuggling down in her bed, she realized that her mother had bought

41

silk sheets for her. *Memo to self: thank Mom for the sheets.* For the first time in five years, KC's sleep was uninterrupted.

Sunday morning arrived with a beautiful sunrise. It was an autumn dawn, and the foliage was gorgeous. *Freedom,* KC thought as she awoke. She stretched and yawned lazily. The thought of spending this beautiful morning in a stuffy church service didn't appeal to her. Yet she knew her mother wanted her to go to church with her, so she decided to appease her. She threw the covers off and reluctantly got out of bed. The best part of the morning was the long, hot shower she enjoyed. She allowed the hot water to course over her tired body for several minutes. KC leaned her head backward, soaking her long, blonde hair. *Oh, it feels so good to take my time in the shower,* she thought. She massaged a generous amount of almond-fragranced shampoo into her hair. After rinsing her hair, she wrapped a towel around it and toweled off. She slipped into her microfiber body wrap robe. *This is so comfortable.* She relished her freedom. She padded down the hall to her bedroom. Although she'd been out of society for five years, she found an appropriate outfit for church and applied her makeup with precision. It was a treat she hadn't enjoyed since her incarceration. She dressed in a dark blue outfit. The jacket had a single-button closure and faux side pockets, and the pants were wide-legged. The light blue-patterned blouse brought the outfit to life. Looking in the mirror, KC was pleased with her appearance. Her lips pulled to the right in disgust. *It's a shame to waste such a nice outfit on Sunday morning church.* KC's stomach knotted.

Sitting at the dining room table were Rose and Charles. Both were sipping coffee. Charles was reading the sports section of the Sunday newspaper, and Rose was reading the religious section.

"Well, good morning, sunshine," Rose pleasantly greeted her daughter. She noted KC's dress and was pleased. "Oh, KC, I'm so glad you are going to worship with us this morning. I think you'll like the new pastor. Reverend Thomas has been here for about two years. He's done a remarkable job with our young people. Last year, he and fifteen teens went to Kentucky on a work mission. The teens came home changed people. It was wonderful! And—"

Charles broke in. "Rose, give the girl a chance to get a cup of coffee and something to eat. You don't have to bring her up to date on everything this morning." Although he was joking with Rose, he was also being serious. "KC, can I get you a cup of coffee? Cream? Sugar?" Already he was on his feet and pouring her a cup.

"Thanks, Charles, but I really don't care that much for coffee. However, a cup of tea sounds great. I think I should have been English. Cream would be great, and yes, I think I'll keep my pinkie finger up too." She smiled mischievously as she tried to sound British.

After a light breakfast, the three rode to Community Church for worship. Many of the worshipers greeted KC as if nothing had happened. Yet many more were reserved in their acceptance of her. Some couldn't or wouldn't look her in the eyes. She felt the tension and wondered if they really believed in the grace they said their God offers to sinners.

When the service was over, KC immediately walked to the car to wait for her mom and Charles. It seemed as if it were forever before they came to the car.

"Honey, where were you? We have coffee and rolls in the fellowship hall. We've looked all over for you." Rose was almost perturbed.

"Mom, for heaven's sake, I'm not a child. I'm not a prisoner. I can do whatever I want now. I didn't want coffee or rolls. I just wanted out of that place. I needed fresh air. And ..." Her voice trailed off. The words unsaid would have been hurtful, so she left them unsaid.

It was a quiet ride home. Rose was afraid to say something that would anger KC. And fearing what her mother might say, KC remained silent.

That all changed when the three arrived home. The aroma of roast beef, carrots, potatoes, and onions filled the house. *Oh, this is one of the things I've missed the most,* a reluctant and peeved KC thought. "Mom, the house smells so good. I always loved your Sunday dinners. I bet you fixed a coconut cream pie too. Right?"

Rose smiled. "No, honey. I made an apple pie for Charles."

"Rose!" Charles was quick to reprimand her. "Don't lie to her. We just came from church. You know you fixed her favorite."

It was as if the harsh words, both said and unsaid, had never happened. KC gave her mother a quick hug and raced off to change clothes. While it was nice to be dressed up, even if it was for church, she was more comfortable in her blue jeans, sweatshirt, and tennis shoes. She'd made a decision to begin an exercise program that afternoon.

KC joined her mother and Charles at the dining room table. Following the blessing, which Charles offered, she helped herself to the meal she loved. She savored each bite, but she saved room for her mother's famous coconut cream pie.

"Mom, this is the best meal I've had in years," she laughingly quipped. "Best meal in *five* years. I've dreamed of this day. Thank you for making it."

Rose couldn't stop herself. The words were out before she'd given it any thought. "Well, KC if you hadn't stolen …"

That was all KC needed to hear. In what seemed like one motion, she pushed the chair back, scraping it on the ceramic flooring, and stood. "I know I messed up. But are you ever going to forgive me?" With that, she walked out of the house.

Silence! It was so silent that the tick-tick of the second hand on the clock could be heard. Neither Rose nor Charles said a word for several minutes. It was the usually calm Charles who broke the silence.

"Rose," Charles quietly began. "You had that coming. I know her crime bruised your ego, but she's served her time and she deserves a new start. Are you ready to give it to her? Or are you going to hold it over her forever? If you don't forgive her, you'll lose her." He sat at the table drinking his coffee. Rose didn't answer him.

She couldn't. She was too busy damming up the tears in her eyes. If she spoke, she knew the tears would flow. Instead, she stood, looking out the window but not seeing a thing. She knew Charles was right, but she also knew KC had known better. *Whatever possessed me to say that?* she thought for the umpteenth time.

KC was gone all afternoon. She walked to the park. Despite the ugly situation, she managed to enjoy the beauty of the fall leaves. She breathed in the acrid aroma of burning leaves and watched children playing on the swings, slides, monkey bars, and seesaws. All this she'd missed the last five years. KC knew she'd done wrong. She knew she deserved prison. She'd served her time. *Don't I deserve a second chance? Even Mom should cut me some slack!* she thought wistfully.

KC walked from one end of town to the other. She saw a little lost brown puppy and stopped to pet it. She held that puppy so close that she could feel its little heart thumping. Stroking its muzzle, KC decided she'd get a puppy when she had her own place. The little thing licked her hand and occasionally bit her arm. "You little scamp. That hurts," she lovingly scolded.

Eventually, a boy rode up on a bicycle.

"Hey, lady, that's my puppy!" he said accusingly.

"I'm sorry. I saw him walking in the street and was afraid he'd get hit. Here you go. Enjoy your dog," she answered. As soon as the dog was gone, KC felt all alone again.

Dusk was beginning to fall, and there was only one place to enjoy the sunset. KC walked toward the lake. She arrived in time to watch as the sun slipped below the horizon. The brilliance of the sunset was better than she remembered. The bright ball of fire displayed a variety of hues as it left the horizon. There was bright red, pink, purple, and finally darkness. The street lights flickered on, and it was past time for KC to be home. She knew her mother would be worried. KC really didn't care Yet when she arrived home she announced, "Mom, I'm home. I should have called, but I didn't have a phone and didn't have a dime," she remarked.

Laughter rang out from the living room.

"What's so funny?" she asked incredulously.

"A dime? A dime to call home?" Charles was guffawing. "KC, you need at least a quarter to make a phone call. Did you forget? We're glad you're home safe and sound."

"You're too funny. Of course, I knew a phone call costs a quarter. I just forgot." She was laughing too. "It's been a long day and an emotional one too. I think I'll go to bed. Gotta get up early to report to work. Night, Mom. Night, Charles," KC cried out as she walked down the hallway. She removed her makeup, brushed her teeth, slipped into her nightgown, and crawled into bed. Sleep arrived quickly, and so did the nightmares.

CHAPTER 9

*C*hirp, chirp, chirp, chirp—it was early the next morning. KC couldn't figure out what the noise was since it didn't really sound like a bird. Suddenly it dawned on her: *Oh, it's the alarm. Where's the alarm?* She thought. Jumping from the warmth of the bed, KC found the alarm and hit the snooze button. For another ten minutes, she lay in bed enjoying the comfortable blanket and softness of the mattress. *Chirp, chirp,* reminded the alarm.

"Yes, yes, I know. I've got to get up," answered KC sleepily. This time she shut off the alarm. Gathering her clothes for the day, she shuffled down the hallway to the bathroom, where she enjoyed another leisurely shower. Toweling off, she noticed some sore muscles, a reminder of her long walk yesterday. *Better take it easy, not so much in one day,* she reprimanded herself. She dressed in an appropriate business outfit. She wanted to make a good impression on Richard and Joyce Goen. With her makeup applied, she walked to the kitchen for a piece of toast and a cup of tea. She was somewhat relieved that her mother wasn't there, yet she was also a bit peeved. *My first day of work—you'd think she be here to wish me luck,* she thought longingly. Then from the living room she heard, "KC, dear. I didn't hear you. Let me fix you some breakfast."

"Mom, it's okay. I'm having a cup of tea and slice of toast. That's all I need," she answered confidently. "I'll see you at the end of the day. Wish me luck," she said as she went out the door. She couldn't use the family car because she still needed to get her driver's license renewed. She had her walking shoes on and was carrying her business shoes in a bag. Although the air was a bit nippy, it was a great day to walk to work.

Finally, she arrived at Advance Web Designs. Taking a deep breath and summoning all the courage she could, she pushed open the door and walked into the reception area. The woman at the front desk looked up, startled.

"Good morning. How may I help you?" the woman asked.

KC quickly plastered a smile on her face and answered, "Good morning to you too. I'm KC Elliott and—"

"Why, KC, it is good to see you so early this morning. I'm Joyce Goen. Richard and I own this joint." The woman smiled as she reached her hand toward KC's to greet her. There was something about Joyce that KC liked instantly.

"Well, Mr. Goen told me to be here by 8:30 sharp. I think I have about three minutes to spare. Shall I go out and wait three minutes?" KC knew instinctively that she could joke with Joyce.

"No, I think we'd better let Richard know you're here," Joyce replied.

"Okay, let's do it." There was a lilt in her voice but butterflies in her stomach.

The two walked back to Richard's office. Even Joyce knocked on the door and waited for Richard to respond.

"Come in," a gruff voice announced. Immediately KC was on guard. His voice sounded too much like that of many of the guards at the prison.

"Richard, KC is here. And she's early. Now be nice!" Joyce instructed. She glanced at KC and winked.

"KC, sit down," Richard instructed. "I want to talk with you." He was pleased that KC had been paroled but also knew that she needed time to acclimate herself to her freedom. "My wife and I have been helping ex-cons for as long as I can remember." Involuntarily, KC raised her eyebrows. Richard continued, "My father was a convict, and if someone hadn't give him a second chance, I'm convinced our family would have starved. As I've watched new parolees report to work, I've noticed a need to reacclimate to society. I want you to take the month off. Take some time to get to know your mom again—and Charles. He's a good man, KC."

"But, Mr. Goen, I need to work. I have to report to the probation office, and I'll be asked if I'm working," she protested. *What will that creep Parsons do if I don't have a job?* she thought. "And I have restitution money I need to repay. I need this job, and I need the money."

"I know that. But I also know that you need time to enjoy the fresh air and get to know your family again. You take the month off, and I'll send a letter to your parole officer."

Prison had taught KC to be wary of everyone.

"No offense, Mr. Goen, but could you give me that letter now? I haven't been able to trust another person for five years. I'd like to have that letter in my hands before I take time off."

Richard smiled warmly. "I understand. Give me five minutes, and I'll have it ready for you. You also have some paperwork to complete and W-4 forms for taxes. Eventually, after a probationary period—my probationary time, not the state's—you will have the opportunity to have health insurance through our plan. Sound good to you?"

KC took the papers she needed to complete and replied, "Health insurance sounds good. I don't have any right now."

KC sat down at her computer workstation, completed the paperwork, and then ran her fingers over the keyboard. Suddenly the screensaver filled the monitor. Tears filled her eyes as she read the screensaver's marquee: "Welcome to Advanced Web Designs." To the left of her keyboard, she noticed a nameplate. It read, "KC Elliott, Administrative Web Page Designer." The tears that had filled her eyes began gently and quietly streaming down her cheeks.

"KC," said Mr. Goen quietly. "Here's your letter."

She wiped the tears from her face, spun her chair around, and stood respectfully. Richard ignored the tears and continued, "I'm really glad you're here. I'll do everything I can to help you make the transition. My wife and I are the only people who know your background. You are at liberty to tell whomever you wish, whenever you wish. If someone learns of your background, it will never come from us."

"But I thought you hired only ex-cons," she asked. She was surprised by his confidentiality.

"The employees know that, but most of our clients don't. Even if they did, it wouldn't make any difference. Advanced Web Designs has a wonderful reputation. Rarely have I had a parolee reoffend. I know I can trust you."

KC was genuinely moved by the compassion and concern of this couple she'd never met personally until now. However, she suspected the other employees could piece together her background given the Goens' reputation among the parolees and parole officers.

"Thank you, Mr. Goen." She started to leave, but he stopped her.

"KC, sit down. Read the letter. I want to be sure this is what you want."

KC sat down and carefully opened the envelope. She unfolded the letter and read,

To Whom It May Concern:

KC Elliott has recently been employed by Advanced Web Designs. She is the Administrative Web Page Designer. Although she has recently been paroled, she is on paid special assignment for this firm. Ms. Elliott will be developing her portfolio of photos, which she will be using in her position. She is expected to be on special assignment for four weeks and will be reporting to me once a week. If you have questions, please contact me.

Sincerely,

Mr. Richard Goen
President and CEO, Advanced Web Designs

Included in the letter, to KC's astonishment, was a check in the amount of her first month's salary. She was stunned.

"But Mr. Goen, I haven't even—"

"I know," he interrupted. "You haven't even worked a day here. It's okay. You've been helpful while you were living at state expense, and we couldn't pay you what we know you're worth. This is something Mrs. Goen and I want to do. Your assignment is to spend time with your family. No argument, understand?" He said it as sternly as possible but with a broad grin. "And, by the way, in addition to spending time with your family, I want you to take as many digital photos as possible. Take pictures of sunsets, sunrises, rainbows, whatever. This is the beginning of your portfolio, and you'll need them for your position here. Here's a camera for you to use."

"Thank you very much, Mr. Goen. I promise you'll—"

"No promises. KC. I trust you, and I believe in you." He started to walk away but turned and added, "Now, go home." He pointed toward the door.

So KC picked up her camera bag and the letter for her PO and returned home.

It was almost ten o'clock when she reached her mother's house. When she walked in, her mother was shocked.

"What are you doing home? Oh, KC, what happened?" Rose was visibly shaken.

"Oh, Mom." The tears flowed. When she finally stopped crying, she said, "Read this letter. But sit down first!

Rose sat down and read the letter. She was stunned. "You mean, we have almost an entire month together? To do anything we want? When we want?"

A warm smile spread across KC's face. "Looks that way, doesn't it?"

Rose hugged her daughter so tightly that KC had to beg her mother to give her a chance to breathe.

"Well, when Charles and I were dating, he took me to the park at the edge of town and showed me the most wonderful sunsets. We often go there to watch the sunset and admire God's handiwork."

There! It finally happened. "Mom, do we have to talk about God all the time?" KC walked out of the room.

Rose was taken aback. She stood alone in the kitchen and thought about their brief conversations since KC had been released from prison. She couldn't remember mentioning God during any of them. She resisted the urge to clear herself. Rose decided that KC just needed time to adjust. She didn't see KC the rest of the day.

CHAPTER 10

A ngrily, KC grabbed the camera bag and the letter for her parole officer and stormed out of the house. Since she didn't have her driver's license, she walked briskly toward town. *If I'm ever going to be on my own, I'm going to need a driver's license.* Mentally, she began a list of things she needed to do. *First, stop at the Department of Motor Vehicles to get the "Rules of the Road" manual to study. Next stop, parole office.* She frowned as she visualized Logan Parsons. *I don't trust that man. Guess I'll make the best of a bad situation.*

It was a beautiful fall day. The leaves were a gorgeous array of orange and red. With the sun shining brightly, KC instinctively knew she was missing a wonderful photo opportunity. Stepping up her pace, she made it to the DMV office by 10:45. Fortunately, the parole office was only a couple more blocks down the road.

KC arrived at the county courthouse. She shivered as she started up the stairs. It wasn't from the cold. She remembered the day five years ago when she had stood trial and been sentenced to prison. KC's body was reacting in a variety of ways. First she shivered, and next she perspired. Walking across the marble floors, each step echoed. She was approaching the parole office but glanced over her shoulder. Seeing no one she knew, she quickly opened the door and walked in. She instantly bumped into Logan Parsons.

"Oh, excuse me," she said before realizing who it was.

"Well, I should think you should apologize," Logan arrogantly retorted as he looked KC squarely in the eyes. "You really ought to watch where you are going." He looked intently at her. His eyes narrowed. "Why, Miss Elliott, aren't you at work?" he thoroughly enjoyed brandishing his power. "You do know it's a violation of your parole. I could send you back to prison like that," he snapped his fingers.

Although she'd made up her mind not to allow this cocksure, self-important jerk frighten her, she fumbled around in her purse.

"Oh, I have a letter for you, Mr. Parsons," she nervously answered. She dropped the manual she'd gotten at the DMV, and almost everything fell out of her purse. Lipstick, wallet, and pens scattered across the floor. KC knelt down to collect her belongings.

"Elliott, there is no excuse for being away from the job." Logan stood ramrod straight with his arms crossed over his broad chest.

Putting her belongings in her purse, KC groped around inside the camera bag. The more she tried to find the letter, the more flustered she became. "Oh, here it is, Mr. Parsons." She quickly handed the letter to Parsons.

He stood reading the letter from Richard Goen, scowling. "Special assignment, huh?" He glared at KC.

"Yes, sir. I'm to begin working on my portfolio—"

"I can read, Elliott," he snapped. Clearly, Parsons was irritated. *I can't believe I've got a parolee who actually knows the importance of covering her tail. And she does have firm, well-rounded buns*, he thought as he turned to file her report. "Well, Elliott, how does it feel to be free? Any problems?"

She hated the way he addressed her. She wanted to remind him that she preferred to be called KC but didn't want to rock the boat. Although she'd met him only once, she sensed he wasn't a man who liked to be corrected. "Generally speaking, things are going well." She opted to give short, precise answers. *What would he say or do if he knew she and her mother often had harsh words?* she wondered. She wasn't willing to find out, so she said nothing.

Logan slammed the filing drawer closed with a bang. *He's trying to frighten me, but I'm not going to let him,* she thought with a smirk.

"Something funny?" he asked sharply.

"No, sir. Is there a problem with Mr. Goen's letter and assignment?" she inquired.

"No, but you better not miss meeting with him weekly. I'll be checking with him. Miss one meeting and—"

She was surprised to hear herself interrupt. "I know—you'll send me back to prison like that," and she snapped her fingers.

"Don't forget it, either. Now get out of here." As she turned to leave the office, Logan let his eyes linger over her body. "Don't forget, I can stop to check up on you any time I want."

KC raised her hand to acknowledge his comment. She opened the door and left. In the foyer, she sat on one of the old wooden benches to compose herself and straighten her purse. The parole office door opened, and Logan walked out. He glared at KC but kept walking. She grabbed her purse and camera and walked out the opposite door.

CHAPTER 11

KC was filled with mixed feelings. She was incredibly thankful for the gift Joyce and Richard Goen had given her. For a whole month she could sleep in, get to know her mother and Charles, and take photographs. She was determined to never break any law that would land her in prison. KC had studied computer programming, web design, and photography while behind bars. In fact, studying was the easiest thing to do in prison. She'd been given chores to do every day. When she was busy working, she heard the other prisoners joking around and sometimes arguing, usually about the most ridiculous things. In the dining hall, they argued about the portion size of food one of them got. Also, the state had declared the prisons smoke-free environments, but contraband was often smuggled inside. Occasionally, someone got a cigarette, and arguments resulted for a whiff of smoke. Evenings seemed to be the best time to study. KC stayed in the library as long as she was permitted, practicing computer skills. When the library closed, she'd go to her cell and continue study. It wasn't easy, but she was determined. She made many vows, and one was to never go back to prison. Others included getting her degree, getting out of prison, getting a job, and living on her own. KC still couldn't believe her luck. The Goens had given her a job. As a bonus, she had a month to begin adjusting to life in the real world.

*Okay, I got that legal stuff taken care of. What's next?* She hesitated and shifted the weight of the camera to the other shoulder. *Well, it is almost time for lunch.* She furrowed her brow as she thought. *I know. I'll surprise Lisa with lunch.* There was a bounce in her step as she walked toward the children's museum.

The museum had been built while she was in prison. Her mother often talked about how the community had come together to build it. Red bricks were sold to pave the walkway through the gardens separating two buildings. The gardens were well maintained. In good weather, weddings were regular events there. Of course, the museum board of directors sent letters to the more well-to-do and wrote grants to help with the expenses. The children saved coins to help purchase beanbags and cots. The children's museum was a huge success.

KC walked ten minutes before catching her first glimpse of the museum. *Wow,* she thought, *it's everything Mom said it was.* She entered the foyer and discovered that it was well lit, with bright colors greeting the children and their parents. From the moment she stepped inside, she knew it was a place for children. She stood in the middle of the building. It was a hands-on experience for children and grown-ups. The Lego display was phenomenal. In the corner of the room was a long table about two and a half feet tall. Legos were strewn all over the table. Children had connected Legos for their own displays. She saw a science room and sauntered in that direction.

"KC? a familiar voice broke into KC's consciousness. She turned and saw her high school friend approaching.

"Oh, Lisa! It's been so long." The two ladies hugged briefly. "It is so good to see you. I came to surprise you, and I'm the one surprised. Is it too late for lunch?"

Lisa looked around the building. "Oh, no. Not at all. Let's go to the snack bar and get something. We'll take it back to my office."

Half-teasing and half-serious, KC asked, "Are you embarrassed to be seen with me?"

"Heavens, no," her lifelong friend shot back. "There's an

employee I'm trying to avoid. I had to write him up last week, and he's still grumbling."

Lisa ordered a tuna salad sandwich with a side salad and raspberry vinaigrette dressing. KC checked her purse and then made her selection. "I'll have a side salad, and I'll try the honey mustard." Both ordered bottles of water.

"Let's go upstairs," Lisa announced. She turned quickly but not quickly enough.

"Oh, no, he saw me, KC." They quickened their step. However, Lisa had been spotted. Soon, a middle-aged man approached her.

"Hey, I need to talk to you about that letter you gave me," he began.

"Stewart, we'll talk about that later. I'm having lunch with my friend. Please, excuse us," she said, clipping off her response.

"Let's do that, Ms. Know-it-all," he loudly responded.

Lisa turned and glared at him. "Yes, we will!" she firmly retorted.

The two ladies continued walking toward the elevator. "Lisa, are you okay? You are so pale. Are you frightened of him? You aren't going to talk with him alone, are you?" The questions came out of KC's mouth like bullets from an automatic revolver.

The elevator door opened, and the two entered. When the doors closed, Lisa leaned against the stainless steel cage, shaking. "Yes, I'm okay. No, I will not talk with him alone." Personnel issues were confidential, but she added, "It's his second reprimand. He'll be put on probation ..." She looked at her dear friend as she threw out the word. She was horrified that she had used that word. "Oh, KC, I'm so sorry. I shouldn't have said that."

KC laughed at Lisa. "Good gracious, Lisa. If you have to weigh every word around me, we'll never see each other."

The doors opened onto the executive floor. The hallways there were also painted with bright colors. They walked toward Lisa's office, and Lisa nodded briefly at her administrative assistant. "I'm having lunch with my friend. Please don't disturb, okay," she said. The secretary nodded.

Lisa opened the office door. KC was greeted with a smart, well-furnished executive suite. The desk had a well-polished mahogany finish. Behind the desk was a matching credenza with lateral filing drawers. Lisa's desk was clean, without a folder or pen on it.

KC's eyes were wide and her mouth agape. "Wow! Lisa, you've done well for yourself. But you know what they say about a desk as clean as yours, don't you?"

Lisa smiled and asked, "No, what do they say?" Her eyes sparkled. She knew KC had a quick answer.

"A clean desk is a sign of a sick mind," she laughed.

"Then I must have one sick mind." She showed KC to the sofa with the coffee table in front. "Let's eat before our food gets warm," she smiled at her attempt to be funny.

Scanning the room, KC saw a photo of Lisa's parents and a small photo of herself. Tears filled her eyes. "Lisa, I can't believe you kept that picture. I've been such an embarrassment to my family and friends." The tears filled her eyes.

"Oh, cut it out. For goodness' sake, KC, you're going to ruin your salad." Lisa always had a way of breaking the ice.

They laughed together for the entire lunch hour.

"I better go so you can get back to work." KC picked up her purse and stood. "Oh, by the way, I'm working at Advanced Web Designs. I already got paid. Mr. and Mrs. Goen paid me for the time I worked for them while in the joint. He told me to take a month and reacclimate myself to life on the outside. He gave me a digital camera. During the month, I'm to take lots of pictures that will be used for my work. I'm so lucky."

"KC," Lisa stood, put her hand on her friend's shoulder, and said, "that's not luck. That's God."

KC started to snap back an answer but decided to let it go. *God this, God that. Will they ever stop preaching at me?* she thought. "See you later!"

"KC, before you leave, could you or would you explain why your sentence was so long? I've heard of others who embezzled money, and they got probation. Why did you end up with a ten-year sentence? It seems unfair."

KC dropped into the chair again. "Lisa, you're the only person who has asked me. It seems as if everyone else avoids talking to me about my conviction. I'll do the best I can to explain it. Because I stole from an elderly person and did it several times, the district attorney decided to make an example of me and charged me with ten counts of embezzlement. Well, I assure you, I've learned my lesson." Silence filled the room. "I think one of these days, after my parole is over and restitution has been paid, I'll contact an agency working with the elderly and volunteer. I want to help the elderly and families and caregivers with the hazards of elderly financial abuse." She pursed her lips together tightly and added, "Yep, I've learned my lesson, and it was a harsh lesson." Lisa stood, walked over to her friend, and hugged her.

"KC, I'm proud of you. Let me know if I can help, okay?"

KC wiped a tear from her eye and nodded. "Thanks, friend. Right now, I don't want to drag you into my mess. But I'll remember your offer." Once again KC stood, turned, and left.

CHAPTER 12

T he weather had decidedly cooled. When she was first released from prison, KC was greeted with an early Indian summer. She'd walked out of the gates of the prison into a sunny, warm October morning. Almost a month had passed, and the mornings were chilled and darkness fell earlier each day. Her thirty-day paid assignment was almost over. She'd enjoyed getting to know her family and friends again, at least those friends who wanted to be seen with her. Every day, she had worked on the photo portfolio for her web designs. KC had shot photos of sunsets and sunrises, children playing, and dogs and cats; and she'd tried some abstract photography. Each week she met with Richard Goen, her boss, to review the week. She'd shown him her photos, and her self-esteem grew with the praise he lavished on her.

*Today, November 19, is my first official day at work*, she mused. *I've been spoiled this month.* Peering in the mirror, KC checked her makeup for the second time. Running the comb through her blonde hair, she thought she saw a gray hair. She stepped closer to the mirror and parted her hair to search again. *Must have been the way the light hit my hair. I'm too young to have gray hair.* She reached for her purse, camera, and bag. As she walked out the door, she bumped into Charles.

"Oh, excuse me," he said, red-faced. He was still in his pajamas. He'd forgotten to slip on his robe. He scurried back to his room.

KC laughed to herself. "It's not a problem, Charles." She zipped down the stairs to eat a quick breakfast.

"Mom, I don't know what time I'll be home tonight. I want to try to get my driver's license, but I have to see my parole officer too." She grew quiet. Something about that man bothered her. She couldn't quite name it, but she knew two things: one, she didn't like him, and two, she didn't trust him. "Oh, and I have to pee in a bottle again." She lightly clenched together her teeth and added, "Don't know why I have to; that pot wasn't mine. I told them that when they found it. They didn't find any indication in my blood or urine specimen test to suggest differently, but I still have to prove that I'm drug-free. Doesn't seem fair."

"No, honey, life isn't fair," her mom responded. Rose almost added words that were hurtful, but this time she was able to stop them from tumbling out. "Shall I hold supper for you?"

KC patted her stomach. "No, I think you've fattened me up for the kill. If I continue eating like I have, I'll be the turkey for Thanksgiving," she said with a laugh. "Speaking of Thanksgiving, what—"

Her mother interrupted her. "We'll talk about that later. You get out of here. I don't want you to be late for your first official day of work. Good luck. I'll see you tonight."

KC smoothed her black slacks and blazer as she headed out the door.

Walking had been good exercise for KC, but it was getting colder. She was beginning to think about buying a car. She walked swiftly down the lane to the street and turned at the next block. The leaves that had fallen overnight crunched as she stepped on them. She paused briefly and inhaled through her nose. *Yep,* she thought, *someone is burning leaves.* It was both a pleasant aroma and an acrid, pungent odor. It brought memories of her childhood. Raking leaves with her dad was fun, but she also recalled his abusiveness. She checked her watch. *Better snap to it. Don't want to be late.*

*Late* was a word that had never really described KC. She was never late. She would arrive ten or fifteen minutes early but never late. Punctuality was something her mother had emphasized. *Mom said, 'Punctuality is next to godliness' so many times that I really thought it was in the Bible,* she recalled.

It was twenty minutes after eight when KC clocked in. "Well, good morning, young lady," she heard someone cheerily announce.

"Thank you, and good morning to you too, Joyce."

Joyce was the office manager for Advanced Web Designs, as well as the publicist, accountant, and receptionist. Richard was the brains behind the business. Painfully shy, he preferred to remain in the background. Joyce was more social, and she was the one who handled the public.

"Did you have a good weekend?" she inquired. Before waiting for an answer, she continued. "Richard and I drove to the orchard. They have much more than apples and apple cider. Have you been there before?" Not waiting for an answer, she plowed on. "That place once sold only apples, but now? They sell, pies—all flavors— jellies, and a variety of butters."

"I thought butter was butter," KC rejoined.

"Oh, no, they have apple butter, pumpkin butter, peach butter, and honey whipped butter. KC, they have the most delicious apple fritters and apple cider donuts. You really must go there before they close for the season," she raved on.

"Joyce," a gruff voice bellowed from a room down the hall. "Give that girl time to hang her coat and talk with me. You've hardly taken a breath."

"Sorry," she answered. Smiling smugly, she said to KC, "He's all bark. He's really enjoyed the photos you've taken. Says you have an eye for things." She touched KC gently on the forearm and proceeded, "We are so glad you accepted the job." She used her thumb to point over her shoulder and suggest that she go talk with Richard. "Better call him *Mr. Goen.* He's funny about that."

"Thanks, Joyce. I'll be sure I do that." She hung up her coat and slipped her purse in the bottom desk drawer.

KC was so light on her feet that she didn't make a noise as she walked down the hallway. She tapped softly on Richard's door. No response. She tapped a little louder. Still no answer. The third time she was more forceful.

"Come in," he answered with authority.

"Good morning, Mr. Goen," she greeted him pleasantly.

"We'll see," he answered. He was hunched over his desk looking intently at a map. "Know that orchard Joyce was yammering about?" he asked without looking at KC.

"Yes, I remember going there—"

"Talked with them this morning. They want a web page. I want you to go talk to Marilyn Snider. She's the owner's wife. She does all the publicity. Here's the directions." He handed her a map.

"Uh, Mr. Goen, there's a bit of a problem," she stammered.

"Spit it out, girl," he demanded.

"I don't have my driver's license. I was going to get it this afternoon after work."

"Oh, for cripes sake," he grumbled as he threw up his arms in disgust. "Joyce, get in here!" he bellowed down the hall.

*I know it's only been four weeks, but I've never seen him like this,* KC worried.

"Joyce, d'ya think you could take her to the DMV to get her license?" he asked demandingly.

"Sure thing, boss," Joyce answered with a smile. She leaned close to his ear and added, "You better stop acting like such a creep or I'm going to go on a spending spree."

He spun around and looked at the two women. "Have I been rude?" he asked incredulously.

KC wasn't going to answer, but Joyce wasn't fearful of answering. "Have you been rude? Let me count the ways. First, you ..."

For the first time that morning, KC saw him smile. "Okay, okay. I apologize. Would you please take her to get her license?" He turned to KC. "I bet you haven't a car either, right?"

"Yes, that's correct," she was still suspicious of him. "But I'm going to as soon as I save enough money. I still have to pay back—"

"Restitution, yes, I know." He leaned back in his chair. With his fingers entwined together behind his head, he chewed on his lips for a moment or two. "Tell you what, you get your license and I'll lend you a car."

KC started to protest, but he put up his hand to silence her. "Get your license and I'll take care of the car situation until you can buy one. And I'll call Marilyn and let her know you can't make it 'til tomorrow." KC and Joyce stood as if glued to the floor. "Get out of here. Now! Joyce, no spending spree."

The two hurried to the outer office, pulled on their coats, and left the office before Richard had a chance to change his mind. As they closed the door, Stewart, the guy from the children's museum, walked past. He turned and glared at KC.

CHAPTER 13

J oyce looked curiously at KC. Although she'd never been a mother, she noticed that something was amiss with KC. She didn't want to intrude on KC's thoughts, so she kept her suspicions to herself.

"I didn't realize you'd been practicing for your test, KC," Joyce casually mentioned.

"Oh, I haven't," she flippantly answered. "I figure it's a lot like riding a bike. You get on and take off. The difference is that I needed to study the "rules of the roads." I suspect some rules have changed since I've been in prison. I don't think I'll have any problem with the written exam. I'll need to study where everything is on your car, so give me a few minutes behind the wheel and I'll be good to go, okay?"

"Whatever you say, girlfriend," Joyce smiled. "You can do anything you put your mind to, KC." They pulled into the parking lot of the DMV. "Okay, lady, switch places with me," Joyce instructed her passenger.

Nervously, KC slid behind the steering wheel. Joyce showed her how to turn on the wipers, turn signals, and emergency blinkers. KC asked where the proof of insurance and registration were kept, and Joyce graciously showed her everything.

"Are you ready?" she asked.

"As ready as I'll ever be," KC replied with a nervous giggle.

KC gave Joyce the thumbs-up sign when the test was graded. They walked outside together with the examiner.

"This car yours?" he asked with no inflection in his voice. "Where's the registration and proof of insurance?" he continued in an automaton manner. It was obvious he'd done this routine for years. "Okay, let's go," he directed.

He climbed into the passenger seat, and KC slid behind the steering wheel. He sat with his clipboard. As KC suspected, he asked her to show him where the wipers, directional signals, and emergency blinkers were located. She didn't miss a command.

"Okay, I want you to turn right," he instructed her.

Before she put the car in gear, she fastened her seat belt. She waited for a few seconds and asked, "Is this a trick? Aren't you supposed to fasten your seatbelt too?" She watched him snap his belt snugly across his waist. She put the car into gear and watched him check off something on the clipboard. After turning right, he asked her to drive downtown. There, she demonstrated her ability to parallel park.

"Okay, let's go back to the office," he remarked in his monotone voice.

She parked the car. He reached across the console and announced, "Congratulations, you passed the test. Let's go in. You'll get your picture taken, and then you're good to go."

When she saw Joyce waiting for her, KC beamed. She was so happy. It was as if she'd been given her independence. All she needed was a car, and Richard was going to let her use his extra one.

Waiting her turn for her picture, KC heard the guy ahead of her joking with the other examiner, "Am I supposed to have numbers to hold in front of me? Do I turn to the right or left first?" KC knew he was teasing, but it reminded her of the night she was booked. It was so traumatic just thinking of it that KC began perspiring profusely.

"Next," she heard the woman announce.

She jumped and then stood to her feet. "Kimberly Christine Elliott, is this the right name? Please sign here," she pointed to a line. "Step back, please. Look at the camera." Flash! It was over in a matter of a minute or two. KC had to wait 'til the license came out of the printer and cooled. The woman handed her the license and in one grand motion shouted, "Next!"

Joyce saw KC approaching. She stood and gave her a fist bump. "Oh, I'm so proud of you! It's almost as if I'm your mom."

"And you're probably more fun," KC answered with a hint of sarcasm in her voice.

"We'll see about that," a smile spread across her face. "Before we go back to the office, let's have a bite to eat, okay?"

"Where have you two been?" Richard inquired. "We've been going out of our minds, tryin' to do our jobs and yours too, haven't we, fellas?" He looked back at the other two guys.

"Yeah, we've been real busy!" Jason quipped.

The two women looked at the guys and then at each other. They burst into laughter as they pulled off their coats.

"Really?" Joyce quizzed. "If you've been so busy, why do I smell pizza?"

"Oh, man, she's got a good sniffer," Jason directed his comeback toward Richard. "Bet you can't get away with much at home, huh?"

"No way! If I came home with even a hint of perfume, she'd know I'd been with another woman. Women are like that, guys, so watch your backs." Richard loved to tease. He'd been married for twenty-three years and never once looked at another woman in a lustful way. "Sorry, ladies, but the pizza is all gone." He held the box up so they could see for themselves.

"She passed her test, got her license, and said she feels like she's truly experiencing her independence," Joyce told her husband. "So," she began with her eyebrows raised, "what car are you going to let her use? You know we only have the two cars we drive."

"Yeah, I know. I'm going to buy one for her, and then she can pay me back," he explained.

"Richard, I know you're a good man, but aren't you putting a little too much trust in this girl?"

He looked intently at her.

"Okay, I know we need to show her God's grace," Joyce continued. "But another car? We'll have to buy insurance, and now we'll have car payments. Are you sure we can afford it?"

"Joyce, settle down. Take a deep, cleansing breath and listen to me." He showed her to a chair. "If we let her use the car for business, we can write off some of the expense. After she's on her feet, we can give her the option of buying the car. Face it! She's got to have a way of getting around."

"But won't she want to use it for personal stuff?"

"Probably," he answered with a tilt of his head. "Do you have a better suggestion?"

"No," she regretfully admitted. "But why do we have to be the banker all the time? Remember that one guy that worked for us? What was his name? Michael something—you loaned him a thousand dollars to get current on his child support, right?" She watched him nod his head. "And what did he do?" She didn't wait for an answer. "He went to the casino and spent every bit of it gambling, didn't he? Did you get any back? *No!*" She was getting angrier by the minute. "Honey, I love you, but you can't rescue every ex-con!"

She walked out the door and to her desk. Sitting in her little cubicle, she fumed. The problem? She liked KC. She knew her mother and stepfather from church. Joyce knew they could afford it, but she was really tired of being the bank. Sitting with her back to the door, she did some number crunching. Content with her figures, she marched to Richard's office.

"Okay, here's the deal. KC has to repay thirty thousand dollars within five years. It's a lot of money, but it can be done. She needs to budget the money. I suspect she's going to want a place of her own soon. So, let's do this: We buy the car and let her use it for business and personal outings. We pay for the insurance, and she pays for the maintenance, oil changes, and so forth. I'll only go along with this if she takes that financial study class at church. After the restitution has been paid, then she can begin paying us for the car—what it's worth at that point plus interest. How's that sound?" She waited while he processed her idea.

"What if she refuses to take the class?" he replied.

"She won't. She needs the car for work, and it represents her independence. She won't like the classes, but it's the only way I'll agree to this."

Richard knew his wife, and she wasn't going to budge on this. "Okay, who's going to tell her" he asked.

"We are. You're going to tell her the terms, and I'm going to be with you. It's not that I don't trust her. You know I do. But I think she needs to see a unified front."

"Okay, call her in."

CHAPTER 14

"Hey, Mom," KC bounded into the house. "Mom, I got my driver's license! And ..."

Suddenly, KC was aware of the silence in the house. She walked through house looking for her mom. Returning to the kitchen, she browsed through some papers on the table hoping to find a note from her. Nothing. *Well, crud! I finally have some exciting news, and no one's home to share it with,* she mused. *Well, guess I'll get some hot tea. Wish I knew how to turn on the fireplace. Looks like a great place to curl up with a nice book.* KC filled the tea kettle and placed it on the stove. While the water heated, she roamed around the living room. Even though it was a cold November day, KC leaned against the door frame, looking over the lake. She found it surreal. After five years in prison, KC found comfort and peace as she viewed the serenity of the lake. The enormous fireplace drew KC's attention. She plopped down in her mother's chair.

Sunset was beginning to color the sky. The lighting in the large, cathedral-ceiling room was dimming. Looking toward the ceiling, she noted the track lights. She glanced around the room looking for the light switch and located a bank of switches. One switch turned on a light on the deck, and another turned on the breezeway light. *One of these has to turn on those track lights,* she concluded. She flipped the next switch. Although she didn't see an area brighten, she heard a soft *whooze* and the fireplace came to flame. *Oh, that was simple. I didn't expect that,* she thought with a gentle laugh. She continued flicking on and off switches. It was the next-to-last switch that turned on the track lighting. As she did, she could hear the annoying whistle of the tea kettle. *Good timing,* she smiled as she thought of steeping a cup of tea.

KC spooned a couple of teaspoons of sugar and poured a tiny bit of cream into her tea. Carefully she walked to the living room. *Goodness, it's been so long since I've had such privacy. Mom always said a good cup of tea helped the body relax. Mom said a lot of things, much of which were harsh words, but I must agree—a good cup of tea does help the body relax.* She yawned as she remembered her mother's comment. The old throw blanket sold by the chamber of commerce commemorating area landmarks was folded and tossed over the back of the sofa. KC placed the saucer and cup on the well-polished mahogany end table. With the help of the bookmark, she found the place where she'd stopped, wrapped herself in the throw, and began reading. She was so engrossed in the story that she didn't hear her mom and Charles come in.

"KC, I'm home," her mother announced. "Do you have company? Is Lisa here?" Questions, questions, questions. Rose always seemed to have questions. She shrugged off her winter coat and hung it in the hall closet. "Hi, honey," she said when she found KC in the living room. "Charles and I went to Bible study this evening. We're studying the book of Revelation. It is difficult to follow, but Pastor Thompson is very knowledgeable. He's given us a wonderful outline to follow," her voice trailed off as she thought of KC's accusations. "Oh, I'm sorry, dear. I didn't mean to ramble on. Do you have company?"

KC yawned. She slowly stood, meticulously folded the throw, and placed it over the back of the sofa. She smiled broadly. "No, Mom, I don't have company. I got my driver's license today—"

"But whose car is—" she began.

"It's mine," KC answered before her mom could finish the question.

"Where—"

"Mr. and Mrs. Goen bought it for me," she replied. "Well, actually it's the company car, but they told me I could use it until my restitution has been paid. Then I can buy it from them." A slight scowl crossed her face. "Mom, have you been talking with them?" she asked almost accusatorily. Her voice dropped, yet there was a hint of relief. "They told me I had to attend some class at their church and set up a budget. If I live by my budget, then I can buy it from them if I want it."

Rose stood with her hands opened, eyes opened wide, lips clamped tightly together, and eyebrows raised. She shrugged her shoulders as she answered, "No, honey, I didn't talk with them." She turned to leave the room. She didn't want to start another argument, but added, "I know you won't like this, but I'm glad they want you to attend the financial class. I've heard only good things from people who have attended." Changing the subject quickly, Rose asked, "Did you get something to eat?"

"Joyce and I had a late lunch after I got my license."

"Joyce? You call her Joyce? It's a bit presump—"

"She *asked* me to call her Joyce, Mom. Give me a break. I know how to show respect." Before another spat began, she decided to change topics. "I'm going to the orchard tomorrow morning. Have you been there recently?" She noticed her mother nod and continued, "Tell me about it."

Much of what Rose shared, KC had heard from Joyce. "And they have a petting zoo and playground equipment. They've really improved it since you were a child."

"Sounds like it. I'm looking forward to going. Know anything about Marilyn Snider?" KC was pretty sure she did.

"I don't know much about her. She's in Altrusa Club with me, but I haven't been in quite a while," her eyes darkened slightly as she looked at KC.

It was the way she'd said it that made KC suspect that her mother had dropped out of many activities because of her conviction. It had all happened so quickly, but the words tumbled out of her mouth like milk out of a jug.

"Let me guess. You haven't been since I went to prison. You dropped out of all of your clubs, didn't you?"

Rose didn't need to answer. She knew KC already knew.

Remorse filled her heart, and she said, "I'm sorry I embarrassed you so much." She kissed her mom.

Rose couldn't deny the truth. She didn't want another spat between herself and KC, so she changed the subject.

"Is it too late to take me for a ride in that car?" she asked lightly.

"I'm tired, Mom. I think I'll go to bed. See you in the morning. G'night, Charles."

"You're getting better," Charles noted.

"Better at what?" his wife asked nonchalantly. She felt confidently that she knew what he meant, but she wanted him to explain himself.

"You know what I mean." His face lit with a smile.

Rose was in a playful mood and began teasing. "Better at cooking? You always told me I was an excellent cook. Better at keeping house? Better in bed? I'm getting better at what, Mr. Smarty?"

CHAPTER 15

*What a beautiful day,* KC thought. The leaves were turning a variety of red hues. With the reflection of the morning sun, the leaves were gorgeous. Walking slowly yet determinedly toward her car, KC inhaled deeply the crisp morning air. She sniffed the air and caught a whiff of burning leaves. The acrid odor provoked a sneeze. *I don't care. I still love the smell of burning leaves.* With keys in hand, she grasped the car door handle and opened it. She placed her red leather notepad folio on the passenger seat and slid behind the steering wheel. *I'm beginning to feel like a working girl,* she mused. She adjusted the rearview mirror and backed out. *God, help me to give a good presentation and be successful today,* she prayed silently. *Did I just pray?* She was mystified at the thought. She hadn't prayed since she was imprisoned. A smile spread across her face, and her eyes twinkled.

Her hands gripped the steering wheel at the ten and two o'clock positions. KC was nervous she'd do something wrong and get pulled over by the police. Gradually, the death grip she had on the steering wheel began to relax. She pulled smoothly into a parking spot at the office. She reached across the car to retrieve her notepad folio, exited the car, and walked confidently toward the office. Butterflies seemed to have taken control of her stomach. *I didn't realize I was nervous,* she thought. *I'll go over the procedures again with Joyce and then go to the orchard.* She swallowed hard, trying to allay her nervousness.

"Good morning, Joyce. How are you this morning?" she greeted jubilantly. Her face exuded excitement, but her eyes didn't reflect joy. Her shaking hands betrayed her friendly greeting.

"Mornin' to you too. Does this joyful greeting you're exhibiting indicate how you really feel, or are you covering up some nervousness?" a very perceptive Joyce asked. A broad smile spread across her face. "I suspect you're a little nervous about your first official appointment, right?"

KC felt her face warm as the blood rose to her cheeks. "I should have known I couldn't fool you. But Mom always told me that eyes are the window to the soul. Guess she was right," she laughed anxiously. Placing her notepad folio on the desk, she asked, "Joyce, would you mind going over the procedures once more? I want to make a good impression on Mrs. Snider." She paused slightly before continuing, "And"—the word was emphasized—"I want to seal the deal." She looked down the hallway toward Richard's office. "I need to prove myself to Mr. Goen too."

Joyce reached across the desk and ever so lightly touched KC's shaking hands. "My dear, you will do fine." Her soothing voice was just what KC needed. "Here, let me look at what you have here." She perused the information for a couple of minutes. Every so often, KC heard Joyce mumble a *hmmm* or *good.* "KC, this is excellent. You've done a very good job." She looked pleased. "Now go out there and knock her socks off," she said with a snicker.

"You really think this is okay?" The question was indicative of KC's lack of confidence.

"You're really nervous about this, aren't you?" God had blessed Joyce with the gift of discernment. It was a gift that was both a blessing and a hindrance at times, but Joyce had long ago learned to respond to the God nudges she experienced. "Before you leave, would it be okay if I prayed for you?" All the employees knew Richard and Joyce were Christians and always attended church services, but the Goens didn't push Christianity. It was the way they lived their lives and the kindness they showed to others. "If you'd rather I didn't, it's okay." She sensed hesitation on KC's part.

The blush of embarrassment had risen in her cheeks again. "You mean here? Now?"

"No, dear, we'll go to my office. I wouldn't do anything to embarrass you," she answered, genuinely concerned for KC's peace of mind.

"Oh, okay. I'm okay with you praying for me." A hint of hope was in her voice.

Joyce led her to her office, where they prayed together.

"Okay, you'd better get out of here. If Richard opens his door and finds you still here, he might fire both of us," Joyce joked. Her eyes twinkled. "God's with you, KC." However, the phone was ringing, and she didn't think KC heard.

# CHAPTER 16

"**I** got it, Joyce! I got it. She signed the contract!" KC was barely inside the office when she announced her success. Her face was beaming.

"I knew you could do it, KC!" Joyce responded with enthusiasm. "Let me take a look."

KC gave her the contract and looked over Joyce's shoulder.

"Hey, what's going on here?" Richard's booming voice startled KC.

She spun around, her hand clutched at her throat. "Uh, we were j-j-just l-l-looking over a contract," KC sputtered.

"Richard! You scared the daylights out of her. You apologize, now," Joyce demanded. "You can be so intimidating sometimes." Her face was red with anger.

"I am sorry I frightened you, KC. Sometimes I don't realize how loudly I speak." He held out his hand in apology. "I take it Marilyn Snider inked the contract. Congratulations!" He returned to his office.

"Honestly, KC, he can be so irritating sometimes. It's hard to believe he's really quite shy when he behaves like this. Let's have a cup of tea to celebrate your success." Joyce was already heading toward the little kitchenette.

"Are you sure Mr. Goen won't mind if I take a break?" KC asked hesitantly. "I mean, I do have work to do."

"You need to relax, KC. You don't have to prove yourself. You've already done that. We are going to sit down and have a cup of tea. I don't care what Richard says." She grabbed KC's hand and pulled her down the hallway. "Besides," she said with a smug look, "I own this business too."

"KC, it's time to go home," Richard announced. "I don't pay overtime. Now, get." He smiled. "Seriously, KC, you've done a good job today. After that little cup of tea," he turned and winked at Joyce, "you've had your eyes glued to the computer. Go home and rest. There's plenty of work to keep you busy tomorrow." He held her coat for her. "Come on, I'm not going to let my female workers walk to their cars alone. Now, go." Richard waited while KC slipped on her coat and grabbed her purse and notepad folio. The three walked out together. Helping Joyce into her car, Richard watched KC climb into her car. "Lock the doors, young lady!" he shouted. KC gave him the thumbs up.

*He's like a dad,* she thought. *Well, I think he's like a dad. He's like the dad I would have liked to have had.* She revved the engine, backed out, and went home.

"Mom, I'm home," she announced while taking off her coat. "It was a great day! Marilyn Snider signed a contract. Mr. Goen was happy ..." Suddenly she realized she was talking to an empty house. "Oh, great! Exciting news and no one to share it with," she complained. KC walked to the kitchen to fix a cup of tea. She saw a note on the counter. Picking it up, she read, "KC, Charles and I have reservations at Kenyon's Palace. We want you to join us. Please don't say no. We really want you to come. Love, Mom." *So much for a quiet evening at home,* she thought as she turned to get her coat.

She arrived at the restaurant fifteen minutes later. The hostess greeted her, announcing, "I'm sorry, but I haven't any tables available."

"My mother is holding a place for me. Rose Ell—No, I'm sorry, she's remarried. Rose Phillips."

"Oh, yes, here she is. Follow me." The hostess smiled, but it lacked warmth. "Your mother must be pleased to have you home." She led KC to her table. "Enjoy yourself!"

*Do I know that woman?* KC thought. She greeted her mother and Charles but kept looking at the hostess. *She was almost hostile.*

"Mom, do you know who the hostess is? What's her name?" KC asked, trying to disguise her discomfort.

"Oh that's …" Rose tilted her head, touched her forefinger to her temple, and patted it. "I can't remember her name." Glancing toward the hostess's desk, Rose tried to recall the name. "I don't know, honey. Let's order our meal."

The three ordered their meals, and KC shared her news. "Mom, Mr. Goen and Joyce were so excited for me. I was so invigorated that I could hardly contain myself. I really had to keep my eye on the speedometer. I wanted to show the contract to the Goens." KC was talking so quickly that she almost missed the spark of light in her mom's eyes. "What's wrong, Mom?" she asked, her voice dropping almost to a whisper.

"I think I know that woman, the hostess." Her face blanched. "I think she works at the courthouse. Oh, no, KC, I forgot to tell you about the phone call."

CHAPTER 17

"What phone call, Mom?" KC whispered through gritted teeth.

"There was a phone call from Logan Parsons," she fidgeted with her napkin.

"What d-d-did he s-s-say?" KC stuttered. Her face ashened.

"You were supposed to call him by 5:00 p.m. today," Rose lifted the napkin to her eyes. "Oh, KC, I'm so sorry. I forgot."

Charles cleared his voice. "Ladies, there isn't a thing we can do about this now." He turned to KC. "Your best bet is to call him first thing in the morning and explain that you didn't get the message until too late to call him back." He was calm. "Rose, next time, explain to Mr. Parsons that he should call KC directly." It was a statement, not a demand or an accusation.

"Charles, I only hope he is as understanding as you think he should be." KC picked at her food. Silence fell among them.

"May I speak with Mr. Parsons?" It was 8:00 a.m., and KC had called promptly to talk with her parole officer. Her stomach was in knots.

---

"Parsons, here!" Not exactly rude, but definitely not a polite greeting.

"Mr. Parsons, KC Elliott speaking. I'm sor—"

"You should be! Don't you know I can send you back to the joint?"

"I know, I know, but I didn't get your message until after your office was closed." She swallowed the lump in her throat. "Please don't send me back. It was an honest mistake."

Parsons allowed several seconds of silence. It was a technique he used to cause his parolees the greatest amount of discomfort as possible.

"Mr. Parsons, please!" Her voice trembled, and tears stung her eyes.

"Okay, this one time. Don't let it happen again, hear?" Parsons derived satisfaction when he could make a parolee squirm.

"I won't, Mr. Parsons. If it isn't a violation of parole, I think I'll get a cell phone and then you can call me directly. Is it a violation?" KC bit her lip in anticipation of his answer. She was still learning her way around the parole system and all of its regulations.

"I'll let you know at 4:45 this afternoon. We have an appointment then. Understand?" It wasn't just a statement. It was an order.

"But I don't get off until—"

"I said 4:45. Be at my office at 4:45!" He let five seconds tick off the clock and added, "I'm sure your boss will understand since he hires felons." Parsons didn't wait for a response.

KC stared at the silent phone handset.

"Everything okay, KC?" Joyce touched KC's shoulder lightly.

Startled, she responded, "What? Oh, yeah. Everything's fine." Her voice was barely audible. Joyce was not letting it drop.

"You sure? Wanna talk and have a cup of tea?"

"No, I've got a lot of work to do." Her eyes didn't move from the computer screen.

"Okay, if you decide you want to talk—"

KC cut her off. "I'll let you know."

At about ten o'clock, KC poked her head into Joyce's office. "I'm sorry about earlier. I shouldn't have interrupted you. If you're ready for a cup of tea, I'm ready to talk," she said, her eyebrows raised in speculation.

Joyce swirled about to face KC. "It's okay. I knew something was bothering you. Let's have that tea." She stood and led KC to the break room. "We'll talk, if you're ready."

While the water was heating, KC paced. "For goodness' sake, sit down, KC. You're making me nervous." Joyce pointed to a chair. "Sit!" Then she laughed. "Sounds like you're a dog. I'm sorry. Please sit." She smiled and asked, "Is that better?"

"Woof, woof," KC said with a laugh and sat down.

"Now, what's bothering you?" Joyce was very forthright.

KC circled the lip of her cup with her finger. "Well, my parole officer called late yesterday afternoon and left a message on our machine. I was to call him yesterday by 5:00, but Mom forgot to tell me. I called him first thing this morning. He wasn't very understanding. He demanded that I meet with him at 4:45 this afternoon. Joyce, that means I have to leave by 4:15." She looked down. The nervousness was apparent as she wrung her hands. "I don't get off until 4:30. I hate to ask Mr. Goen for special favors." KC stopped complaining to sip some tea. "What's he going to think if I have to keep taking time off to talk to a parole officer?"

Joyce guffawed. She laughed so hard she had tears streaming down her face.

"What's so funny!" KC demanded.

"KC, who do you work for? Remember where you were when you began your internship? And remember Richard told you our company has a history of giving ex-cons a second chance? Of course, Richard understands you have to meet with your PO." She wiped her eyes with a napkin. "Now, go tell Richard you have to meet with your PO." She scraped the chair along the tiled floor and stood. Joyce pointed toward Richard's office and announced, "Go! Now!"

KC could still hear Joyce laughing as she walked away.

Around four o'clock, Joyce approached KC's office. She could hear soft crying and sniffling. *Oh, God, please give me the right words to comfort and assure KC. She's emotionally so fragile.* Tapping lightly on the door, she walked in. "KC, God is with you. And remember, Richard and I are here anytime you want to talk." She reached for a tissue and handed it to KC. "Go wash your face. Don't let that parole officer know you're nervous. Hold your head high. You've served your time. And you're doing a good job."

"Thanks, Joyce. I appreciate—"

"No more. Just do what you have to do, do a good a job, and that's all we expect."

KC arrived at Logan Parsons's office at 4:40. From the bench where she sat, she could see that he didn't have anyone waiting. It didn't appear that he was working on anything, but he took his time finishing a drink. At five minutes to five, Logan acknowledged her presence.

"Well, Elliott, I see you made it on time." He enjoyed being condescending to his clients.

"How's your adjustment to society going?" Logan continued grilling KC. He asked about the job and problems she might be having.

KC kept her answers brief and to the point.

"Okay, I see you've paid back about fifteen hundred dollars. You've got a long way to go. Think you'll make it?"

"Sir, I'll make it." She oozed confidence even though she didn't feel confident.

"One more bit of business." He opened a desk drawer and pulled out a specimen jar. You need to pee in the jar. We'll see if you're drug free."

He turned around and shouted, "Need a woman to administer drug test!"

A woman appeared and led KC to the restroom. KC opened the stall and started to close the door. "Oh, no, you don't. I have to make sure it's your urine," the woman declared.

Wide-eyed and red-faced, KC blurted out, "You mean, you're going to watch me pee?"

With her lips pursed together, the woman tilted her head to the right and said, "Looks that way. It's my job. Sorry. Do it and get it over with."

KC did as she was ordered and handed the jar to the woman. "How long do I have to wait?"

"We'll let you know in a day or so." It was a matter-of-fact answer. "If the police show up with cuffs, you failed," she answered with a smug smile. "If not, you passed." She looked at KC and added, "I hope, for your sake, it's clear. Parsons has the record for sending the most parolees back to prison. He looks for violations. It's his deviant nature"

KC turned pale. It wasn't that she was using drugs. She never had done drugs. It was the knowledge that Logan Parsons liked to send parolees back to prison.

She didn't hear anything the next day and assumed the test was negative. It was a safe assumption since she knew she wasn't doing drugs. But she wouldn't put it past Logan Parsons to tamper with the test results.

She did, however, purchase a cell phone and knew she should

call his office to give him the phone number. With a cell phone, Logan could contact KC directly, although she really didn't want to hear from him.

Dread filled KC, and her stomach cramped. She almost tasted vomit as she punched in Logan's phone number. *I hate that man*, she thought, and with anger she pushed the send button.

"Parsons, here!"

Before she could stop it, she heard herself responding, "Elliott, here!" She grimaced, knowing he would think she was mocking him.

"Think you're funny, huh? Well, let's get together next Wednesday at 6:00 p.m. We'll see how funny you are then."

"Oh, I'm sorry, Mr. Parsons. I'm so accustomed to answering 'Elliott, here' at the office," she lied. "It just popped out." She stuck out her tongue at the phone, knowing it was a childish act. "Yes, Wednesday at 6:00 p.m. will be fine. Oh, by the way, here's my cell phone number. I'll be at the office then."

"No, meet at One Buck Coffee shop." The line went dead.

*Okay, Mr. Congeniality.* Her mouth twisted to the right and her eyes bulged.

CHAPTER 18

Wednesday morning came, and the day proceeded as any other Wednesday. However, as the day neared an end, KC became quieter. Joyce had become accustomed to KC's moods. Her instinct told her that KC had a meeting with her PO. She walked to the break room and prepared two cups of tea. For KC's cup, she dropped in two sugar cubes and a little cream. She carried the tea to KC's office and announced, "Tea time" with a fake English accent.

"You always know when and how to cheer me," KC laughed, reaching for the tea. Joyce sat down.

"I s'pose you have another appointment with your PO." She paused as she looked tenderly at KC. "Honey, it's going to go okay." She handed an envelope to KC. "Go ahead. Open it." Her shrewdness shone as she sat in silence, glowing with satisfaction.

KC read,

> To Whom It May Concern:
>
> KC Elliott completed an internship with Advanced Web Designs over two years ago. Upon her release from prison, she was hired as the website designer. Her employment has been beneficial for

our company. My husband, Richard, and I, as the owners of this business, are pleased to have her as an employee. We realize we cannot change the terms of her parole. However, we wanted to assure you that she appears to have become a successful and productive citizen.

Thank you.

It was signed by both Richard and Joyce. Tears stung KC's eyes.

Her finger wiped away the tear sliding down her cheek, and she choked back a sob. "Oh, Joyce, thank you so much. Parsons won't care, but I do." Her chair flew across the room as she stood to give Joyce a hug.

"Oh, there's more." As KC reached for a tissue, Joyce pulled another envelope from behind her back. Joyce's face glowed with excitement. She placed the envelope in KC's hands and announced, "Since you've been here, KC, our business has increased by 25 percent. Richard and I are giving the employees a raise and promoting you to office manager." Joyce watched KC's response.

Her eyes widened, her brows lifted, and her hand trembled as she held the envelope. "J-J-Joyce, I d-d-don't know what to say." The envelope hadn't yet been opened as she kept turning it in her hand. "I was only doing my job." KC lowered her voice, and her head bowed in humility. "I had no idea things were going so well."

Joyce reached toward KC. "KC, you have done a wonderful job. Richard and I wouldn't have promoted you if we didn't feel you were deserving." With her thin, long fingers, she lifted KC's chin. "Child, you've become part of our family. I know this sounds hokey, but we love you as if you were our daughter." She looked around the office. "We accept all the employees as family. Some do disappoint us." She cocked her head to the left, and her compassionate eyes moistened and narrowed. "Sometimes we've had to dismiss employees. But when someone shows him- or herself to be exceptional, we try to compensate accordingly."

"But—," KC started.

"There are no *buts*. You have served your time, and you've earned our trust." She patted KC's hand. "Now, I know you've got an appointment with your parole officer. Freshen up your face, and get out of here. Don't want to keep him waiting, ya know," Joyce asserted with an equal amount of humor and trepidation.

Following Joyce's counsel, KC went to the restroom to splash cold water on her face and reapply makeup. Frowning at the image in the mirror, she thought, *I'm certainly not fixing my face for Logan Parsons. However, I don't want to be seen in public with smudged mascara and a tear-streaked face.* The task was done in fewer than five minutes, and she returned to her office to gather her belongings. Sitting on the desk was the envelope Joyce had given her. She picked it up, but her hands trembled so that she dropped it to the floor. She knelt over to retrieve it.

"You're not throwing that away, are you?" a gruff voice behind her said.

Jolting to attention, she turned and saw Richard. "No, sir, Mr. Goen. It slipped out of my hands." Her face flushed and felt afire.

"Well, are ya gonna open it or not?" The harshness of his voice belied the respect he had for the young lady standing before him.

She opened the envelope. Opening the letter, she read,

Dear KC,

Joyce and I have been pleased with your work here. Our business has increased over 25 percent since you've come on board. As a token of our appreciation for a job well done, we are giving you a

promotion and increasing your salary. You are now
the office manager. Your next paycheck will reflect
a raise of two hundred dollars a month.

KC already knew she'd been promoted to office manager, but
she had no idea she'd receive such a large pay increase. "Oh, Mr.
Goen, thank you so much. I don't know what to say." There was a
part of her that wanted to give him a big hug and another part that
knew it was inappropriate.

"Well, KC, with that promotion comes more responsibilities.
Think you can do the job?" He was serious but tried not to be stern.

"Do you have a job description? I'd like to review the new
duties," she asked, so anxious to please.

"Honestly? We don't have a job description. Here's what's going
on. Joyce has been having some medical issues. I wanted to give her
a break from office responsibilities. Tomorrow, I want you to talk
with her. She'll tell you what she does"

KC glanced at her watch.

"KC, get out of here," Richard said, suddenly realizing the
time. "You have an appointment. If you're late, tell Parsons it was
my fault. Now get!"

KC hurriedly grabbed her purse and left.

*Medical issues?* KC thought. *I wonder what's goin' on? I hope it isn't
serious. God, I really like Joyce. Don't know what I'd do without her. She knows
my moods. Please don't let anything be seriously wrong. Hmm! I think I just
prayed again.*

She swung her car into the parking lot of One Buck Coffee
shop and walked toward the doorway. She saw Logan parking his
car. KC was greeted by a mild-mannered young man. "Smoking or
nonsmoking?"

"Well, I'm not sure. I prefer nonsmoking, but I don't know

about my par …" She'd almost said *parole officer.* "I don't know about the other party." She glanced around nervously.

"Well, then let's make it a nonsmoking table, okay?" He was already walking away.

"Works for me," she responded. *It's nice being the one to make the decision in this relationship.* Her disdain for Logan Parsons could almost be tasted. It was the taste of bile. Every time she met with him, she was uncomfortable. She sensed depravity in him.

"Good to see you are on time, Elliott," he announced with his usual air of superiority. KC had been waiting just a couple of minutes. "Wouldn't want to send you back to the pen," he added. *There's nothing I'd like better than to send you back, Elliott. You really don't deserve a second chance.* He sat across from her in the booth. "So, how's it going?" KC reached for her purse to retrieve the letter from Richard. "I asked you a question." Logan spat the statement through gritted teeth. "Answer me immediately. Do you hear me?" He spoke louder than he realized. Patrons near them gawked at them.

"Excuse me," KC replied in a quiet, determined voice. "I was trying to get the letter Richard asked me to show you." She looked intently at Logan. "I'm doing fine, thanks. I report to work daily and on time. Now, may I give you the letter Richard asked me to deliver?" Determined but still aware of the power Logan held over her, she pulled the letter from her purse. With deliberateness, she placed the letter on the table in front of Logan.

Sipping his coffee, Logan ignored the letter but placed her file on the table to review. "Says here you passed the last drug test. That's good to hear."

"Should be. I've never done drugs," she answered unashamedly.

Logan glowered. "Right. How'd the marijuana get in your cell? Still claiming you're innocent?" His voice dripped of sarcasm.

KC straightened her back, pulled her shoulders back, clasped her hands together, and leaned forward. "I'm not only *claiming* to be innocent. I *am* innocent of that charge," she rebutted. "Yes, I know I can't prove it, but I know I am innocent." She sat back in the chair. *What was I thinking? I shouldn't talk to him like that!* Her heart was thumping wildly as if she'd done ten rounds with a prize fighter. The butterflies in her stomach felt like they'd become hummingbirds. *Calm down. Don't let him know he's rattled your cage.*

Logan unfolded Richard's letter. He was silent as he read. His left eyebrow lifted as he read.

"Hmmm," he muttered, his only reaction. He slipped the letter into her file. Clearing his voice, Logan responded, "You already know I think Richard Goen is an idiot for hiring ex-cons. This only proves it. I'm going to recommend he have an audit done before you assume your duties." He slapped her file into his briefcase and rose to leave. "If any money is missing, I'll see that your parole is revoked and you'll go back to the big house. You will go directly to jail, you will not pass 'Go,' and you will not collect two hundred dollars. Is that understood?" He left without waiting for KC's answer and without paying for his coffee. The server brought the check, and KC was left to pay the tab.

CHAPTER 19

*Well, that went well,* KC mused. *What an arrogant airhead! And to think I had to pay for his coffee. Not only is he a jerk, but he's a cheapskate too.* KC pulled her wallet from her purse to retrieve a ten-dollar bill. Although out of prison for only a few months, she'd already learned that coffee was expensive, especially specialty coffee. One Buck Coffee shop was only a name. Coffee was costly there as well.

It was too late to return to her office, so she went to the lake to relax and review the events of the day. It was there that KC always found solace. She pulled into her favorite area. She didn't realize that her muscles could tense up so much. It wasn't her job; it was knowing she had to meet with Logan Parsons. She did some shoulder and neck rolls to lessen the tightness between her shoulders. *I really enjoy this spot. As soon as I arrive here, I feel myself relaxing. Thanks for making this so beautiful, God.* KC giggled aloud and announced to no one in particular, "Guess, I'm learning to pray again." She pressed her lips together and added, "But it isn't the same kind of prayer Mom prays."

Since she had never had a brother, KC was surprised that she knew the Boy Scout motto: Be prepared. She was always prepared for a visit to the lake. She walked to the back of her car and unlocked the trunk, where she pulled out a pair of tennis shoes and her camera. Quickly, she slipped her slender feet out of her dress shoes and into her tennies. "Ah, that feels good," she sighed.

"What feels good?" A voice startled her.

"What?" She turned abruptly, following the sound of the voice. Her heart rate increased.

Standing not more than thirty feet from her was Logan Parsons. Fear raced through KC's body.

"I asked, 'What feels good?'" he repeated himself. "The fresh air, the wind blowing in your face or"—he paused, looking menacingly toward KC—"could it be that having a good-looking man look at you feels good?"

"Getting out of my dress shoes feels good," KC answered matter-of-factly. She slammed the trunk shut and walked back to the driver's side. She'd turned her back to place the camera on the seat when she heard Logan approaching.

"In a hurry? I thought you came here to relax." He leaned against her car and smiled. The smile never reached his eyes. His eyes remained hard and narrowed.

"I'm sorry. I just remembered I have work to do at home," KC answered with more confidence than she felt.

"Oh, come on." He touched her shoulder. "Let's go for a walk."

She jerked away and calmly announced, "No, I have work I need to do. Besides, I thought our professional meeting was over." She didn't wait for an answer. Climbing into the car, she closed the door and locked it before Logan could pull it open. She snapped her seat belt closed and pulled away. Her heart was beating so quickly that she thought it was going to beat out of her chest. She wanted to speed away but knew Parsons would accuse her of speeding. Glancing at the rearview mirror, she saw him laughing.

*How in God's green creation did he know I would be there?* KC thought. *I've never seen him here before.* Her heart was still thumping, and she knew she was hyperventilating. *Calm down, KC! He's gone,* she reminded herself. *Go home. You'll be safe there.*

As KC pulled into town, she needed to quiet herself. Checking her mirror, she didn't see anyone following her. *Where can I park so I can settle my nerves? Mom doesn't need to see me this tense.* She spotted a group of women going into a church, so she pulled into the parking lot. Ignoring the fact that she wearing a professional suit and tennis shoes, she followed the ladies in.

Sighting the discrepancies in KC's dress and shoes, a woman approached her and asked, "Miss, can I help you?"

Taken aback, KC quipped, "Uh, no, no. Uh ..." Looking around, she continued, "I was looking for a restroom. Been on the road and really needed to visit."

"Ma'am, are you sure? You passed two gas stations as you came into town." The woman lowered her voice. "What do you really need?"

Looking at the floor and trying to appear contrite, she answered, "I needed to find a place to pray."

"Oh, I see. Let me show you to our sanctuary." She paused a few seconds and continued, "I'll tell my friends. I'll be right back."

KC was stuck. She had to go to the sanctuary and at least pretend to pray. She waited for the woman to return.

"I'm glad you felt you could stop in for prayer. We are a church that believes in forgiveness and answered prayer. Is there something I can pray for? Illness or something?"

KC felt like the woman was fishing for information. Yet at the same time, KC decided to be honest. "Someone was following me. I stopped to pray for protection."

The woman clutched her throat. "You're in danger? Husband abusing you? I can take you to the women's shelter," she offered.

"No, it isn't a husband, but I thank you for your concern. I don't need to go to a shelter. I need to get myself together before I go home. I don't want my mom to know. She'll worry about me."

"Are you sure? I'd be happy to help you." The woman didn't even seem concerned for her own safety.

"No, just let me pray for a few minutes. Then I'll be out of your way."

"It's okay. You're not in our way. Our meeting is downstairs in the fellowship hall. If you don't mind, I'll sit in the back of the sanctuary while you pray. I want to be sure you're safe. When you're ready to leave, I'll see you out to your car. I'll not bother you. Okay?"

"That's fine. Thank you." KC didn't know what else to say. She walked to the altar and knelt in prayer. After about ten minutes, she rose to leave. The woman was still there as she'd promised.

"Thank you for your kindness, Miss. Next time I'm in need of prayer, I think I'll come back here. Your hospitality is appreciated." KC glanced about the sanctuary and added, "I'd appreciate your confidentiality too."

"Of course, you can count on it. Now, let's go to your car." As the women left the sanctuary, the *click, click* of the woman's high heels could be heard as KC's tennis shoes squeaked along the ceramic tile.

CHAPTER 20

Despite the disconcerting event of the night before, KC woke in a positive mood. Hurriedly, she dressed for work and bounced down the stairs.

"Morning, Mom. Grabbin' something to eat later. Got work to do. See you tonight," she announced. "Later."

"Well, I never ..." Rose said caustically.

"She's not a child anymore, Rose." Charles's hands rubbed Rose's shoulders. He turned Rose around to face him. "She needs to make her own decisions. She'll eat when she's hungry." He kissed her forehead and added, "Besides, you've got to give up control. Understand?"

Rose didn't respond.

"Rose, did you hear me?" His voice was firm but gentle. He lifted her chin with his fingers. "You've got to give up control." He didn't wait for an answer but covered her lips with his.

"I know you're right, but she's my little girl, and she's been through so much and—"

"It's nice to hear you talk like that. I know she's had a tough few years, but she's an adult. You've got to let her go. You know, one of these days, she's going to walk in here and announce that she's found an apartment. Then what are you going to do?" He waited for that to sink in and then added, "Better start thinking about it, honey. She's doing well at the office. Once restitution has been taken care of, she'll have all the money she needs for an apartment." He kissed her hand and said, "Think about it. It's going to happen."

Rose watched as Charles grabbed his key and put on a cap. Not another word was said. He blew her a kiss and went out the door. Silence. The *tick, tick, tick* of the old grandfather clock was annoying. *Some praise music will help with the silence,* she thought. But after five minutes, she discovered nothing was going to drown out the ache in her heart. *Charles is right. KC is doing so well, she will be moving out on her own soon.* To her surprise, tears stung her eyes and the cascade flowed down her cheeks. *I'm glad Charles isn't here to see me blubbering. God, what am I going to do when that day comes? It will be like losing her all over again.* Rose was so accustomed to short, immediate prayers that she often found herself praying when she didn't realize she was.

"Rose." She turned quickly to see who had come into the house. No one was there. Walking to the kitchen to pour herself some tea, she heard it again. "Rose, listen to me." Instantly, she knew it was the voice of God. Dropping into a chair at the table, she lowered her eyes and answered, "Yes, Lord, what is it?"

Seconds passed. In her heart of hearts, she heard God answer, "She will be all right. Haven't I always said I would be with her? I was with her during the trial. When she was in prison, I protected her. It was I who encouraged the Goens to offer her the internship and the job she has now. Rose, don't you believe I will be with her? Charles is right. You've got to let her grow up. And, Rose, you've got to forgive her. I mean really forgive, not just mouth the words. You've got to really forgive her."

"But, God …" Rose had a habit of arguing not only with others but also with God. "No buts, Rose. KC knows she sinned. She's aware she embarrassed you. You've made that abundantly clear to her. Now, I'm telling you, you need to forgive her. And you need to ask her to forgive you."

"I know, but it's hard," she continued to debate with God.

"Rose, remember when Sari, Abram's wife, laughed when I told Abram they would have a son? Remember?"

"Yes, I remember reading it."

"What did I say to Abram? Do you remember that?"

"Yes, Lord, I remember. 'Is anything too hard for the Lord?' But what's that—"

"What I'm saying is that you will need to ask me to help you forgive. Doing it alone will be hard, but with my help you can do all things. Now, my dear, will you trust me? Will you really trust me to mend the rift existing between you and KC?"

The tears flowed readily as she choked out, "Yes, Lord, I will trust you. I will trust you to mend my broken heart and heal our relationship. Please be patient with me, dear God."

"Yes, my child, I will. Remember, I love you." A soft breeze touched Rose's cheek, and she was convinced God had kissed her.

The brief encounter with God had energized Rose. She prepared potatoes, carrots, and celery for stew and browned the meat. She threw it all together into the slow cooker, added some seasoning, and began the household chores. She was like a hurricane but left nothing destructive in her wake. She got the windows washed and shining; the furniture polished; and the laundry washed, dried, ironed, and put away. It had been a productive day. The aroma of beef stew permeated the house.

*Smells so good. I should bake some biscuits too,* the quintessential homemaker thought. With the expertise of a professionally trained chef, Rose got all the ingredients out, mixed them together, and put homemade biscuits in the oven when Charles came home.

"Oh, Rose, you fixed my favorite. It smells so good." He twirled her around to face him. "After my lecture this morning, I thought I might be eating beans and hot dogs." He gave her an affectionate swat on the rear and started upstairs to clean up.

"Wait just a minute, Sir Charles." Rose tried to sound as if she were upset. "You come back here and sit. I have something to say to you."

Charles stopped with his right foot on the first riser. "What did you say?"

"I said I have something to say to you. Now sit!" She pointed to a chair.

"Woof! Woof!" Charles joked. "Am I a dog? Where is my treat?"

"Charles, please. Be serious! I do have something to tell you and it's important. Want some coffee?" He nodded his head, but Rose had already poured him a cup.

"This morning you said some things that upset me. I was lonely and really feeling sorry for myself when I heard my name called. I turned to see if you were still talking, but no one was here. I decided to turn on some praise music, but I heard the voice again. It was God, Charles. God was talking to me." She waited to see if Charles was going to question her sanity. He sat, rubbing his index finger around the top of his cup. Rose wasn't convinced he had heard her and asked, "Did you hear me, dear?"

He nodded.

"Do you want me to tell you what he said?"

Charles shrugged his shoulders.

"God told me KC was going to be all right."

Charles began to smile.

Rose put her finger on his lips and continued. "He told me I needed to forgive KC. Well, honey, you know me—I couldn't stop. I started to argue. I asked if he knew how hard that would be. God assured me he would help me." She stopped so Charles could think about that. "So? What are you thinking?" She demanded.

"I'm thinking I serve and love an awesome God," he said and stood, wrapped his arms around his lovely wife, and kissed her. "Loving God, thank you for visiting with my Rose this morning. I know forgiving KC isn't going to be easy, but I know you will be with Rose. With your help and constant encouragement this will be accomplished. Now, thank you, God, for this wonderful woman I hold in my arms and for the talent she has in preparing a delicious meal. I'm hungry. Would it be okay with you, God, if I get cleaned up so I can eat?" He felt Rose giggle, and he added, "Amen."

Charles hurried toward the stairs as Rose playfully tried to swat him with a towel. "You better hurry. Dinner will be ready in twenty minutes."

Rose smiled. *I don't know when I've felt so relaxed with a man. And, thank you, God, for bringing such a godly man into my life.* The oven timer buzzed. She checked the biscuits and was pleased to see that they were lightly golden brown on top. *Perfect. KC always likes my biscuits with honey, and Charles will cover them with stew.* With a quick glance in the refrigerator, Rose discovered that there was no honey. *Not a problem. I'll call KC and ask her to stop by the store for some.* She punched in KC's cell phone number. The smile she'd worn most of the day faded some when she reached KC's voice mail. Still, she left a message: "Hi, honey, it's Mom. On your way home, would you stop at the store for some honey? Thanks. See you at supper."

CHAPTER 21

Rose and Charles finished eating, but KC hadn't arrived for dinner. A tear slipped down Rose's cheek. She had looked forward to sharing the meal with her. Rose turned her back toward Charles. *Sniffle! Sniffle!* She didn't want him to know how close she was to tears, but her subterfuge didn't work. Charles slipped his strong arm around her waist and gave her a slight hug.

"Remember, honey, you surrendered KC to God. God is going to take care of her."

"But," she began, her sniffles giving way to tears, "she could have at least called." Her tears gave way to heaving sobs. She tried to choke them back, but that only made it worse. "She has a cell phone, so she should have called."

Charles gently turned Rose to face him. He kissed her forehead and held her tightly as she cried. The sobs wracked her body. Deep, heart-wrenching sobs tore at Rose.

"I'm so afraid I'm going to lose her, Charles."

"Honey, maybe she had extra work to do and lost track of the time." He caressed her shoulders and offered this as a logical explanation.

A long, pregnant pause hung between the two.

"Really? Do you really think that's what happened?" she asked with a look of expectancy in her eyes. "After all the mean-spirited things I've said, I guess I wouldn't blame her if she didn't want to come home." The tears began to flow again. She dabbed her eyes.

"Honey, you go lie down. I'll take care of the dishes," Charles suggested. "It might help you if you get some rest." With his hands on her shoulders, he pointed her in the direction of the stairway. "Besides, I know you usually get headaches after a good—or, in this situation—a bad cry." She started to protest, but she slowly climbed the stairs.

As the clock struck eight o'clock, Charles heard the back door open. It was KC. For the first time he could remember, he was really angry with her.

"Where have you been? You mother prepared a nice supper for you, and you didn't even have the common courtesy to call and say you'd be late. She's upstairs. I sent her to bed. She'd cried so much that she had a headache." His anger was relentless. "Whatever has happened between you and your mom in the past needs to be buried." He turned and walked away.

KC stood dumbfounded in the kitchen. She'd never seen Charles in such a rage. She knew she should have called, but circumstances hadn't allowed her. She was torn between going to her mother and confronting Charles. Given that her mom was resting, she decided she would unload on him.

"If you had given me half a chance to explain, you would know it wasn't my fault." He turned to respond, but KC continued. "Mom called and asked me to get some honey on my way home. I did. As I walked to the car, I thought I heard footsteps behind me. I glanced around, but I didn't see anyone. When I got to the car, I discovered someone had slashed my tires." She paused to catch her breath. Retelling the story caused the blood to drain from her face.

"Are you okay?" Charles quizzed.

"Yes, I ran back to the store to call the police." As quickly as the blood had drained from her face, it flowed back and made her face beet red with anger. "You know, as soon as they discovered I'm a convicted felon, they accused me of doing it myself. I was so angry. They wouldn't even file a report. I had to call a tow truck to take me to a tire shop to buy new ones. It cost so much that I don't have enough money to make my restitution payment this week." Thinking of the consequences of missing a payment caused tears to fill her eyes. "Logan Parsons said that if I missed one payment, he'd file a request to have me sent back to prison. Charles, you can be angry if you want, but it wasn't my fault, and now I have to figure out what to do about getting money." After spilling her guts, she plopped down on the nearest chair and cried.

*Oh, great! Now I have* two *women in tears. What am I going to do?* Charles thought. *Rose needs to understand why KC didn't make it home for supper, but at the same time, I'm afraid to tell her. Oh, God, what am I to do?* It wasn't profanity; it was an instant prayer. He was angry with KC but certainly understood given the circumstances. He was torn between telling Rose that KC had a reasonable excuse and not telling her because he knew the reason would worry her.

"KC, I'm sorry I yelled at you. I should have waited to hear your explanation. It's just that I love your mom so much. I hate to see her so upset. Forgive me?"

"Of course, I forgive you." KC poured herself a cup of coffee, which she rarely drank. "Now if we can only think of a way to explain my tardiness without having to tell Mom."

"Tell Mom what?" KC heard her mother ask.

"Hey, man. I did exactly what you told me. Gimme my money!" the scruffy guy demanded.

Logan handed him a C-note, enough to get about a half dozen oxytocin pills. He provided just enough money to keep the creep addicted. Logan knew whom he could manipulate to his own purposes.

"You promised me two C's. I want it, now!" he demanded.

"Ya know I could turn you in, don't you? You just confessed

to a misdemeanor," Logan Parsons responded. "You think you can get more money from me?" He laughed, "Ha! You've got another think comin'. Now get out of here!" Logan knew he had the upper hand on this guy. He was nothing but a drug addict. *When he needs more pills, he'll come looking for me. I've got him over a barrel. I need him, but he needs me more. What a loser!*

"I asked you a question! What is it I should or shouldn't know?" Rose was like a dog with a new bone when she wanted or needed to know what was happening. "You know I'll find out, so you just as well tell me now." Her hands were on her hips. It was apparent she wasn't moving until she learned what KC and Charles were talking about.

"KC was just telling me about having flat tires and needing to get them replaced. It cost so much that she's going to be short money for the next restitution payment," Charles calmly answered. He grabbed Rose's hand, winked at KC, and added. "Now, was that worth getting all upset?" He smiled. "Rose, you wouldn't mind if we loaned KC the money for this week's restitution payment, would you?"

Rose was satisfied with the answer. "Of course not, but KC, it *is* a loan. You will repay it, right?" She said it with compassion.

"Yes, Mother, I will. How can I possibly thank you and Charles?" Teasingly she added, "I'll even sign a promissory note."

"No, dear, you will not." Rose drew her cheek a little to the left in disgust. "You will not sign a promissory note. However, as you can afford it, we would appreciate repayment."

"That goes without saying. Now, will you two leave me alone. I'd like to warm up my supper." She turned toward the refrigerator and quickly back to her mom. "Mom, thanks for the biscuits, and yes, I stopped for the honey. That's when I discovered my tires had been—"

Charles coughed as he tried to covered KC's mistake.

# CHAPTER 22

"What do you mean, her tires were slashed?" Rose challenged. "Why am I just now learning this?" Rose was furious. "You lied to me!" Her nostrils flared.

"Now, Rose, calm down," Charles said softly. "It was probably some hoodlums. I'm sure it wasn't malicious." He poured his wife a cup of coffee and told her to sit down. "Now listen to me: you can't go around assuming things. You know, it's been in the paper that sometimes tires are slashed as initiation into gangs. You've got to admit—it's better for tires to be slashed than people. Right?"

Rose paused and let his words sink in. Gradually, her breathing slowed and returned to normal. She looked down, and then her gaze met Charles's. "You're right, honey. It was better that the tires were slashed and not a person, especially since that person might have been KC." She shuddered as if she was chilled. "Oh, my goodness! What if KC had been there?" Her breathing became rapid again as if she were hyperventilating, and the color drained from her face. She turned from Charles and stared out the windows overlooking the lake. Hugging herself, Rose thought of all those years she had been angry with KC and embarrassed because her daughter was in prison. She realized that her stubborn pride had caused a rift between her and KC. *Oh, God, I've been a fool. I've been a stubborn old fool.* Tears flowed freely as she continued to pray. *Forgive me, dear Jesus. Forgive my foolish pride. I beg you: please help KC forgive me too. I have several years to make up. God, my heart tells me KC is in danger. I know Charles and KC are trying to protect me, but I know she's in danger. Please protect her. I don't know what I'd do if I lost her again.*

KC was still shaken up when she went to work the next day. She was jumpy and short with her coworkers and Joyce. She had a difficult time focusing and was often mentally absent. KC hadn't teased or joked with Joyce all morning, and Joyce noticed that she hadn't taken her lunch break either.

After all the years that she and Richard had been employing ex-cons, she knew that each person adjusted to freedom differently. Most had mood swings, but usually it was soon after they were released. Some developed alcohol problems, and others became abusive with their families. Joyce was totally thrown off by KC's behavior. She seemed as if she'd adjusted to life quite well. By the middle of the afternoon, Joyce decided she needed to confront KC. It wasn't going to be an ordinary conversation but one of a supervisory manner. She hated those conversations, but she preferred to deal with employee issues and let Richard handle the rest of the business.

"KC," she began, "I need to see you in my office." Looking around to be sure the other employees didn't hear, she added. "I need to see you now."

KC followed her into her office.

"You seem to be a little off today. Are you ill?" Joyce wanted to give KC the benefit of a doubt.

KC sat with her head down and wrung her hands. She rubbed the palm of her hand with the thumb of her opposite hand.

"KC, I asked you a question." Joyce's voice was stern. "You aren't sick, are you? But something's wrong. You've been impolite toward your coworkers and rude to me and Richard. You've got to be honest with me, or, as much as I don't want to, I'll have to write you up, and that will go into the report to your parole officer. I don't want to, but I will if I have to." Joyce paused for several seconds. She leaned forward, put her elbows on the desk, folded her hands together, and with her thumbs between her upper lip and nose, she asked again, "What's going on, KC?"

"I apologize." Her voice was flat. "I'll apologize to the others." KC stood as she was ready for the conversation to be over.

"KC, sit down. We are not done!" Joyce was abrupt. "Now, I asked you what's going on. I want an answer. Please, don't make me tell Richard about this meeting."

"I thought I would get over this ominous feeling, but I've been haunted with it all night," she whispered. "I didn't want to say anything. I don't want to you be a burden to you. Joyce, I love working here. You and Mr. Goen have made me feel so welcomed. I've tried really hard not to cause you problems." She swallowed hard. "If you want, I'll resign effective immediately."

Joyce stood and placed her hands flat on the desk. "KC, we do not want your resignation. For goodness' sake, you've been a good employee. You know we trust you. Something happened. What happened? Nothing you tell me will surprise me. But if I can help, I will. Please! Now! What's going on?"

With her right index finger, KC wiped away a tear that slipped down her cheek. "I stopped at the grocery store last night. When I was in the parking lot, I thought I heard someone following me. I turned but didn't see anyone. But when I returned to the car, I found my tires slashed," she whispered. "Every tire was slashed," she spit out. "Every tire was slashed!"

Although Joyce wasn't a mother, her motherly instinct kicked in. She reached across the desk and touched KC. "I'm so sorry, KC." She walked around the desk and sat in a chair next to her. "It must have been terrifying." Joyce handed KC some tissues. A minute or so went by before Joyce felt KC was ready to continue.

KC blew her nose and shoved the tissue into a pocket. "I called the police, but as soon as they found out I had a record, they refused to file a report. They were convinced I had done it." She twisted her bracelet. Her mouth was drawn to the side and her lips smashed together. "They said I did it," she emphasized each word. KC lifted her head and looked into Joyce's eyes. "Why in the world would I do a thing like that?" Shaking her head, she sat looking into her lap. "I am so sorry, Joyce. I thought I had everything under control. I didn't mean to be a ..." She decided not to use the word she was going to use. "I didn't mean to be a problem."

"Listen to me, KC. What happened wasn't your fault, and the police were wrong—dead wrong—for treating you that way. I understand why you've been on edge today. You don't need to say anything to the others. I'll take care of it." She inhaled deeply and added, "However, you must understand, I don't mean to frighten you, but you could be in danger." Joyce paused to let KC comprehend her words. "I really think we should call the police."

"No!" KC almost shouted. "No, the police are useless. Remember? They thought I slashed the tires on my own car. They will be absolutely useless. Please don't call them."

Joyce sat resting her chin in her hand with her elbow on the chair arm. "Okay, I won't call the police this time. However, KC, look at me. I will tell Richard what happened. I assure you, he will have something to say about this. One thing you must remember: From this day forward, you are not to work overtime unless Richard or I are here too. Is that understood?"

"But, how am I to—"

"I'm serious, KC. When we leave at the end of the day, you will be walking out with us. Do you understand that?"

"Yes, ma'am, I understand. May I go back to work now?"

"No, you may not. We are going to the break room to have a cup of tea. The other employees won't have any idea we've had an employee/employer type discussion."

"Do you have to write up this discussion?"

"I should. But given the circumstances, I'm not going to. Let's

116

get our tea." She led KC to the break room where they spent another ten minutes together. KC then returned to her office.

"Okay, everyone!" Richard shouted. "Time to go home. No overtime tonight." He helped Joyce get her coat. "KC, Joyce and I will walk you to your car."

"You don't ha—" she started to say.

"We will walk you to your car. This is not negotiable. Now grab your coat and purse and whatever else you need. We are leaving for the night."

Richard waited while she gathered her belongings. They all walked to their cars. She pulled out of the parking lot first, and the Goens followed her out. As she turned the corner, she saw a guy wearing a black hoodie and a ball cap. The hoodie was pulled over the cap, disguising any logo it might have had. Although it was dusk, KC felt him stare right at her. He lifted his right index finger to his brow as if saluting her. He turned and walked away.

A chill ran up and down KC's spine. *Oh! He's scary. He reminds me of ... Oh, no!*

CHAPTER 23

"Lisa, it's KC. Could we do lunch or supper? I really need to talk, and I'd prefer it not be at the museum. I'll even treat you to supper. Choose the time and place." She hit the "send" button on her smart phone. *My, how these things have revolutionized communications. I could get use to this.* The right side of her mouth lifted as if smirking. As quickly as the smirk appeared, a scowl replaced it. She reread her message and knew it sounded a bit ominous. Yet she didn't want to go into details when someone else might see the message. Plus, KC didn't want Lisa to feel awkward being seen with her again. *Will I ever feel normal again? Will the stigma of being a convict ever go away?* KC stared blankly as the sun began to set. *God, will it ever get easier? Will I ever really feel free? Is it possible to live a productive life and never again be known as a convict?* She was lost in sadness when the lights of a passing car startled her. *Oh, I didn't realize it had gotten so late.* She started her car, backed out, and headed toward home.

She hadn't driven too far when she realized a car was following her. It was dusk, but it seemed as if it was the same car that had been at the lake. *KC, stop being so paranoid. It's a car. Besides, who would want to follow you? Calm down!* Self-talk might work for some folks, but no matter how much she tried to slow her heart rate, her heart still thumped rapidly. She decided to test her theory. Turning to the left when she reached Walnut Street, she glanced into the rearview mirror; the car turned too. *Ah, it was happenstance.* She drove three blocks and turned right onto Kirkwood Avenue. The car followed. Her heart was beating faster than a drummer playing a drumroll. Her fingers grasped the steering wheel with a death grip. She wanted to speed up but didn't want to get stopped for speeding. Slowing down didn't seem to be an option. Maintaining her speed, she tried to elude her pursuer. KC finally decided to drive straight to the police station. Flipping on the right turn signal, she pulled into a parking space in front. The car continued on.

KC sat in the car for minutes, calming her nerves. *Can't exactly go in and report this. No one will believe me. I can't drive home. I don't want whoever was following me to know where I live.* Trying to decide on her course of action, someone tapped on her side window. Her right hand flew to her chest and her mouth gaped open. It was a police officer.

"Can I help you?" the woman asked. "I noticed you've been sitting here for several minutes. Are you okay?"

"Oh, thank you. I'm fine, but I do need some advice." She sighed heavily. "You see, I think I was being followed."

"Do you know who it was?"

Shaking her head, KC said, "No. No, I have no idea. I didn't want to drive home. Whoever it was, I didn't want him to know where I live."

"That was a smart idea. Do you want to file a report?"

"No, that won't be necessary. Besides—" She stopped.

"Why?" the officer asked.

"Well, no one would believe me. They didn't when I reported that my tires were slashed," she retorted as a tear slipped down her left cheek.

"Why not?"

KC turned, looked into the officer's eyes, and flatly announced, "Because I'm a convicted felon. They thought I was lying."

"Oh, I see. Well, I don't think you are lying. What's your name? Let's go file a report."

"No, I won't. But I do need a suggestion on how to get home."

"Well, I think I can handle that." The officer turned her head to the left, reached up with her right hand, and clicked a button on her radio. "Officer Roberts, I'm 10-7, Code 8 for a few minutes."

"Copy that, Roberts," the radio dispatcher responded.

"Now," Roberts replied. "Get into my squad car, in the back seat, and keep your head down. If the perp is still around, we don't want him or her to see you. Okay?"

"That's really nice of you, but what am I going to say to my mom?" KC was surprised she said it aloud.

"You might start with the truth. If that's not possible, tell her you ran out of gas."

"Oh, that she would believe. Think I'll try that."

The two of them got into the squad car and began heading toward KC's home.

Officer Roberts cleared her throat. "You know, I really shouldn't be doing this. I suppose I should have asked what you were convicted of before I give you ride."

"Well," KC said and then paused briefly. "It was embezzlement."

"Whew, at least it wasn't a violent a crime," the officer said. She wiped her index finger across her forehead. "But still ..."

"I know. I broke the law. I just hope I can find some redemption and become a productive citizen."

"Are you working?"

"Oh, yes. I received my bachelor's degree in computer web design while in prison. The Goens of Advanced Web Designs let me do an internship while in prison and hired me. They recently promoted me to office manager."

"It sounds as if you are on your way to reaching your goal." The car stopped in front of the Phillips's home. "Here we are. You take care now. If you ever need help, call the station and ask for Officer Sandy Roberts. Hear?"

"Yes, thank you. My car won't be towed away, will it?"

"Don't worry. I'll handle it. Now go in and get warm."

KC closed the door as softly as possible, but the porch lights went on immediately.

*Oh, great. I'm going to get the third degree.*

CHAPTER 24

"Oh, for heaven's sake, Mom. It's the first time I've ever run out of gas." KC's hands were on her head. "I need a ride to work. Is that too much to ask?" She turned on her heels, twirled around, and added, "Forget it! I'll walk!" KC grabbed her coat, gloves, and purse. She was out the door before her mom could reply.

*I really hate lying to Mom, but she'd just worry about me. I do hope God will forgive me.* It was a crisp day, so KC picked up her pace. She was afraid she'd be late. *I think I left my cell phone in the car too, so I can't call Joyce. Better hurry!*

It was 8:25, and KC pulled off her coat as she entered the front door and threw it on her chair. Slipping into the break room, she heated some water for tea. She rubbed her hands together, hoping to warm up. KC looked in the mirror and saw that her face was red from the cold. As soon as the microwave buzzed, she pulled the cup of water out and dropped a tea bag into it. She added a sugar cube, grabbed a spoon, and headed toward her office cubicle.

"Cuttin' it a bit close, aren't you?" Joyce quizzed.

"I'm sorry. I didn't mean to be late. I'll make it up."

"For goodness' sake, KC, can't you take some teasing?" Joyce followed her. "I noticed your coat on your chair. You're usually quite neat."

KC shivered, and her teeth began chattering.

"My dear, you're chilled to the bone. Doesn't the car's heater work? Rich—"

"No, don't tell Mr. Goen. I'm fine." KC hung her coat on the coatrack in the corner and sat down. Booting up her computer, KC wrapped her hands around the mug of steaming tea, brought the cup to her lips, and sipped a little. Setting the mug on her desk, she hugged herself.

"Listen, young lady, if something is wrong with the car, let me know. It is a company car. It's up to us to get it repaired." Joyce stood in the doorway with her hands on her hips.

"The car's fine, Joyce. I had to walk to work this morning."

"I don't understand. If the car is fine, why did you have to walk?" KC hoped Joyce would drop the subject when she didn't respond. It seemed as if time had stopped. Finally, Joyce began again. "KC, what's going on? I'm not only your employer, but I want to be your friend, a confidant. You can tell me anything. If it isn't illegal or immoral, I'll not tell another soul." She waited. Joyce's God-given gift of discernment annoyed KC.

"Joyce, you've been so kind. I hate to always be unloading on you." KC didn't even look at her.

"I don't mind being a sounding board. If I didn't want you to unload on me, I wouldn't ask. God has given me a gift for listening, and I'm not afraid to use it. So, whenever you want to talk, you know where you can find me." Joyce touched KC's shoulder and added, "KC, I really do care for you. I'm glad you're here. You're a real asset." She returned to her office.

KC's computer had booted up, and she was ready to tackle the next job. She had a proposal all together that she needed to show to a client. As much as she hated it, she was going to have to talk with Joyce. She needed her car and hoped Joyce would help her. She rolled her shoulders forward several times and then backward as if unwinding. KC stood and pulled in a deep breath. *Let's get this over with. Joyce will understand, but I don't want her to worry. Bad enough that Mom worries.*

Joyce sat at her desk with her back toward the door. KC tapped lightly on Joyce's door. "Come in, KC," Joyce announced.

"But how did you know—" KC began.

"I know the scent of your perfume. What can I do for you?" She spun around to face KC. She nodded her head toward the chair. "Have a seat."

"First of all, I want you to know that I'm grateful that you and Mr. Goen insisted that we all leave at the same time. But last night . . ." She paused. Wringing her hands together, blood drained from her face. "Well, I think I saw the guy who may be stalking me."

Joyce's eyes grew wide, and her heart began to thump faster. She kept silent, waiting for KC to tell her story.

"As I pulled to the corner, I saw a guy wearing a hoodie and a ball cap. He looked at me and tipped his index finger toward me. Then he turned and walked away."

"My dear, that doesn't mean—"

"That's not all. I like to go to the lake and relax before I go home. Last night, a car drove past me and turned around. As I pulled out of the parking lot, the car pulled out too. At first I didn't think anything about it, but then I realized that every turn I made, that driver made too. On the outside chance that I really was being followed, I decided not to go home."

Joyce interrupted, saying, "That was smart, but where did you go?"

"Well, that's why I need a ride. I drove to the police station."

"You filed a report?"

"Are you crazy? They wouldn't take a report when my tires were slashed." She spoke louder than she meant to. "No, I thought that if I stopped there, whoever was following me would drive on past." She bit her lower lip. "I was sitting in the car waiting for my heart rate to slow. A female officer tapped on my window and wanted to know if I was okay. She wanted me to file a report, but I wouldn't.

However, she insisted on giving me a ride home. She thought if I was being followed the stalker might be waiting down the street. Officer Roberts was very kind. Long story short, the car is at police headquarters. I need a ride there so I can get my car and then present a proposal to a client. So, Joyce," she said, paused. "would you give me a ride to get the car?"

"Of course, KC." She grabbed her coat and purse and told KC, "You know, I must tell Richard I'm leaving." She winked at KC, adding, "I'll probably have to tell him the whole story."

"Please don't, Joyce. I don't want to be a bother. You and Mr. Goen have been too accommodating for me. I don't want to be a burden."

"Oh, poo! I'm leaving the office in the middle of the day. He's going to want to know why. I can't lie to him."

"Okay, but I really don't want any special favors."

Joyce poked her head into Richard's office, spoke softly, and closed the door. "Okay, let's go, young lady."

Joyce dropped KC off at her car. She watched her take a piece of paper from under the windshield wiper. *Great! She got a parking ticket. I'll take care of it when she gets back to the office.*

KC whipped the paper off the window and climbed into the car. The engine roared to life as she turned the ignition key. Sitting there for a few seconds to allow the engine to warm up, KC looked at the paper. *I wonder how much I'll have to pay for this.* It was then that she realized it wasn't a ticket at all. It was a note, and as she read it, her stomach seemed to drop to the tips of her toes.

> You can try to hide from me, but I know where you work and where you live. You don't know me, but I know everything about you. Watch out! You'll never know where or when I'll appear. And you'll never know what I'm capable of either.

KC slammed her fists against the steering wheel. *I can't believe this. Who's doing this? God, if you're real, you've got to help me.* Silence filled the car. She jumped out of the car and looked around. She didn't see anyone. Her stomach was tied up as tight as a hangman's knot. *Get it together, girl! You've got an appointment. This is important so pull it together. Breathe in through your nose, slowly exhale through your mouth. Do it again.* KC repeated her advice several times. Finally, she was convinced that she could handle the appointment. She backed out and drove down the street. However, she constantly glanced at the rearview mirror.

Pulling into the client's parking lot, KC looked around. Everything seemed all right. She reached into the back seat for her portfolio and laptop. Taking a deep breath, KC squared her shoulders and tried to look confident although all she really felt was fear and anger.

Thirty minutes later, KC bounced out the door. A signed contract was in her hands, and her confidence was soaring. Then she saw it—another note. "How'd your meeting go? Told ya you couldn't hide from me."

CHAPTER $25$

L isa checked her voice mail and heard, "Hey, Lisa, it's KC. I'm available for supper anytime this week. Give me a call. Bye." *I'll call her later. She sounded worried.*

KC was still shaking and on edge when she returned to the office. With the contract signed and the website proposal approved, KC proceeded to activate the account and smiled weakly. Though pleased with her work, KC was jumpy. It was almost time for a break, so she walked to the break room. No one else was in there.

Joyce had caught a glimpse of KC as she passed her office and followed her into the room. She heard KC's deep sigh.

"Well, what was that all about?"

KC jumped, grasping her chest. "You scared me to death!"

"I could see that, but I wasn't exactly quiet when I came in. What in the world is going on?"

She shrugged her shoulders, shook her head, and pulled her sweater tight. "Here's the contract." Her voice lacked any excitement. Her eyes were dull.

"And here's your tea," Joyce announced as she handed the mug to KC.

Hot tea splashed out onto KC's fingers.

"Ouch! What a klutz!" She almost dropped the mug. She quickly placed it on the table and ran cold water over her fingers. Joyce sprinted to KC's side.

"My dear, let me see your fingers."

"I'm fine, Joyce. Really, I am." Her voice was terse, but her mannerisms belied her voice.

"Stop it! Right now! KC, something is bothering you and you must tell me. Now!" Although a patient woman, Joyce had watched KC's confidence slipping for about a week. Her work was still up to par, but she seemed emotionally fragile. She was pleasant with clients, coworkers, and her employers. However, she was sullen when alone in her office. KC seemed to be frightened. "Does this have anything to do with the note on your windshield this morning?"

KC nodded.

"Was it a ticket? If it is, we'll pay for it."

"No," she answered, detached.

"Okay, let's start over." Joyce tried to keep her voice calm. In truth, she was very worried for KC's safety. "Let's sit down." She soaked some paper towels with cold water and placed them on KC's fingers. "If it wasn't a ticket, what was it?"

Despondent, KC sat quietly. She stared at her hands and aimlessly rubbed her thumbnail. Joyce waited for an answer. She was a patient woman and would wait for KC to speak. In the silence that screamed to be broken, Joyce was praying for KC. *Oh, dear Jesus. It is as plain as the nose on her face that something is disturbing her. I feel certain it isn't anything here, but I am concerned about her life at home and outside of this place. Whatever it is, Jesus, please give me wisdom. I beg you to protect her. I know it must seem strange, but oh, God, I sense that KC is in danger. Please assure her that she can talk with me. I've grown to love her like a daughter. I don't think I could bear to lose her. Place your hand of protection over her.*

"Joyce, I'll explain, but I need to get my purse. Do you want to wait here or in your office?" It was spoken quietly.

"Well, my dear, let's take our tea to my office. You get your purse, and I'll take our tea to the office, okay?" It was more of a statement than a request.

"I'll be right there."

Two minutes hadn't ticked off the clock before KC appeared at Joyce's office. Two chairs were facing each other, and Joyce had their mugs on her old, gray, metal desk. "KC, close the door when you come in. I've asked Richard to answer the phone so we won't be disturbed."

"Okay," KC answered dully. She handed Joyce the note she had found on her windshield. "This is it."

Joyce took the paper from KC. She slipped her bifocal readers on and began reading. As soon as KC was sure she was done reading, she gave the second note to her.

"I found this one when I left the client's office today."

Joyce read it quickly and then said, "That does it, KC. We have to do something. Stay here. I'm getting Richard."

"Please ..."

"No, KC! Richard must know what's going on." Joyce was out of the office before the last word was uttered.

Once again, KC was left to stew about the situation. It reminded her of the night she was arrested. The officers left her in the interrogation room. Her stomach ached, her mouth was as dry as cotton, and she couldn't concentrate on anything other than what was going to happen.

"KC!" Richard boomed from down the hall. "In my office, now!"

*Oh, no. I'm going to lose my job. I'll go back to prison to serve the rest of my sentence.* Tears began welling up in her brown eyes. She took her glasses off to dab the tears away and then replaced them.

KC was barely in his office when he began, "Do you have any idea who would be stalking you?" He was genuinely concerned, but his voice was accusatory. He motioned toward a chair. "Sit. We've got to talk."

"No, Mr. Goen, I haven't any idea. I think that's what scares me the most. The other night, the night after my tires had been slashed, I saw a guy wearing a ball cap covered by a hoodie standing at the corner after we left the parking lot. He kinda waved at me."

She put her index finger to her eyebrow, showing Richard how the mysterious man had waved at her.

"Is that all?" He quizzed her. But he already knew she had been followed. Richard was testing her ability to be candid with him.

"Well, no, but I think you already know that. I was followed to the lake. And then around town. I didn't want the person to know where I lived, so I drove to the police station." She knew Joyce had told him the whole story. She didn't mind, but she added, "I know you know the rest. Please spare me from reliving it." She stared at the floor. *All I wanted was to return to a normal life. Guess I'll never have a normal life.*

"Have you told your parole officer?"

"Are you kidding?" She almost jumped out of the chair. "Logan Parsons would assume the same thing the police assumed. That man doesn't have an ounce of compassion." She looked at Richard. "I'm sure you think he's a decent guy, but there's something about him that I don't trust. You probably think I'm paranoid, but I simply don't trust him." KC spoke softly but with confidence.

"Thank you for your honesty and your candor. Sometimes one should trust one's instincts." He sat with his elbows on his desk, hands clasped together, thumbs resting just under his lower lip. It was his way of thinking. "I cannot have an employee fearful, especially when that employee is constantly in the public eye. I know you don't want to involve the police, but we've got to report this."

"They aren't going to believe it. I'm a felon, remember?"

"It's their problem, *and* it is their responsibility to keep the citizens safe. You are a citizen, a taxpaying and productive citizen of this wonderful city."

*Taxpaying, productive citizen.* That's exactly what she wanted and needed to hear.

Richard reached for his phone and dialed a number. "Yes, thank you. I'd like to speak to Detective Michael Shafer." He tapped his fingers on the desk as he waited. "Hey, Mike. It's Richard Goen. Remember when you said you'd help me whenever I needed help?

Well, I need that help right now." Richard explained what had happened to KC. "I have the notes here, but if you think you need to dust for fingerpri— Oh no, I'm not trying to tell you how to do your job. Guess I've watched too many cops and robbers shows on television.... And, Mike, the victim is an employee, recently released from prison. Her name is Kimberly Christine Elliott, but she goes by KC.... I know, but she's a citizen. By golly, you will take this report and you will follow up on it or—" Richard's voice was getting louder. "You will take this report, or I'll report you to the chief and city council. I expect you here within thirty minutes." He slammed the phone on its base. "Imagine that! He thought—"

"I know. He thought I'd made it up, right?" The dam broke. The tears didn't slip down her cheeks; they flooded. She dropped her head into her hands and sobbed, "I knew they wouldn't believe it. That's why I didn't want to report it." For the first time since she'd started working for the Goens, she was really angry. She wiped her eyes and face and almost shouted, "Just give me the papers! I'll throw them away."

"KC, I can't do that," Richard responded. "Stalking is against the law, and we're going to find out who did this."

KC's cell phone rang. "Do you mind?" Her brows lifted.

"No, go ahead. If it's ..." He didn't finish.

"It's my friend, Lisa."

He nodded.

"Hi, Lisa. Call you back in 'bout an hour, okay? Gotta talk to you about that guy at the museum.... No, I don't like him, but I think ... Later."

"KC," Richard's voice was stern, "do you know who's stalking you?"

CHAPTER 26

Lisa tried to keep her voice upbeat. However, she knew in her heart that something was wrong. She and KC had been best friends since grade school. Rarely had they squabbled. Smiling, she thought of the time she and KC had had a crush on the same boy. It had almost destroyed their friendship. Then the object of their affections suddenly asked another girl to a dance. Lisa and KC found solace with each other as they shared a banana split at the Dairy Barn.

KC stared blankly at Richard. How could he think I could possibly know my stalker! He was her employer, he'd given her the internship, he had promoted her, and she supposed he trusted her. His question concerned her. Did he think she was making up all this intrigue?

After twenty seconds has passed and the profound silence was more that she could tolerate, she answered.

"Mr. Goen, I sincerely appreciate all you've done for me. I've been honest with you. I'm almost offended that you'd think I would know who is stalking me. It's as if you think I've made it up. I assure you, I have not made up any of this. I do not know who is stalking me. All I know is someone is threatening me." As she turned to leave, she stumbled. Blinded by tears, she fell over a chair. She hurriedly picked herself up. Smoothing her jacket, she announced, "I'll see myself home. Thank you."

"No, you will not leave this office," Richard replied. "I'm sorry if you feel as if I was questioning you. But mark my words: when the police come to question you, they will be more insistent than you think I've been." He walked around the desk, reached for Joyce's hand, and continued, "KC, we don't doubt for a minute that someone is following you. But, with your record, the police will assume you've made up the story."

"For what purpose? Why in the world would I make up such a story? What could I gain from that?" KC dropped into the chair and sobbed freely. Her shoulders shuddered and shook. Her breathing was erratic. Fear was palpable.

Joyce could not stomach the scene any longer. Dropping Richard's hand, she went to KC. She placed her hand ever so lightly on KC's shoulder. Stillness filled the office. Joyce patted KC's shoulder with tenderness and understanding.

"KC, please. Give us, give our police department a chance to serve you properly. We believe you. It is apparent someone wishes to do harm to you." She placed her fingers slightly under KC's chin and lifted it. "My dear, trust us. We will always be here for you. Okay?"

The love KC saw in Joyce's eyes was so apparent that she could feel it. Her heart softened. Slowly, she nodded her head. "I will trust you, Joyce. If it wasn't for you and Mr. Goen, Mom and Charles, and Lisa, I'd have no one to trust." She dropped her head again.

"You're wrong, KC," Richard replied. "You can always trust God."

KC nodded her understanding.

"How about a prayer before the authorities arrive?" He waited. Richard was not going to force KC to pray.

"Oh, yes! Mr. Goen, I do need that prayer. Please!"

The three formed a small circle as they joined hands. Richard began, "Loving and trustworthy God, we need you now. KC needs your protection, and she needs assurance of your love and forgiveness. Someone wants to scare or harm our friend. Because of KC's criminal record, the police are less likely to believe her. But you, O God, can intercede, and that is what we ask. Help the police to see beyond her past and see the present and the future. Give us wisdom as we go through this difficult time. In the powerful name of Jesus, we pray."

As they opened their eyes, they saw the police standing in the doorway. How long they'd been there was unknown. Richard stretched out his hand to shake their hands and introduced himself. "Good afternoon, officers. I'm Richard Goen, and this is my wife, Joyce. We are the owners of Advanced Web Designs. This is KC Elliott, our office manager. Please come in."

"It's our understanding someone needs to file a police report?" the older of the two replied. "What's this about?"

Richard nodded toward KC. "I think you'd better talk with her." He looked compassionately at KC and added, "Would you like us to leave?" She shook her head. "Very well. We will stay if it's okay with the officers."

"Officers, I found these papers under my windshield." The papers shook in her hands as she offered them to the officers.

The two officers read the notes and looked at each other. The older officer asked, "Miss Elliott, there's more to this story than the notes. Tell me the whole story so I can file a report." He asked the Goens if there was a room where they could talk privately with KC. Richard showed them to the break room. The officers and KC sat around the table. Joyce offered the police officers coffee. She prepared tea for KC and excused herself.

"Now, Miss, tell us what happened."

"Well, you probably won't believe me—" KC began.

"Why would you say that?" the second officer inquired.

"Because I'm a felon." She bit her lower lip. Her hands, folded on the table, trembled. She rubbed her right ring finger with her left index and thumb. It was a habit she'd never broken after losing her class ring when she was incarcerated. "I suppose the police are always suspicious of people like me." KC's voice was barely audible.

An officer cleared his voice. "Why don't you let us hear your story. If it is believable, we'll follow up on it. You've served your time. Now, tell us what happened."

For the next few minutes, KC told them the story. Everything she reported matched with what she'd told the Goens.

"Well, Miss Elliott, it seems apparent you are being stalked. Any idea who it could be? An old boyfriend? Someone you met in prison, a guard, or another employee? One of your clients?"

KC pressed her lips together and shook her head. "No, I can't think of who it might be. I haven't seen anyone following me." She leaned back in her chair. Her eyes narrowed and her brows knit together. "But the night after my tires were slashed, I saw some guy at the corner. I couldn't see his face, but I sensed he was looking at me. He put his index finger near his eye as if saluting and then pointed it at me." She shuddered. Fear backed up into her throat. It tasted like vomit. "You don't think—."

The officers looked at each other, the Goens, and then KC. "Miss, we can't be sure. Can you give us a description? Anything?"

Tears glistened in her eyes. "No. All I remember is what he did. He was wearing a ball cap with a hoodie pulled over it."

"Ma'am," the older officer began. "Without a description or a name, there isn't much we can do. However, it appears you are definitely being stalked. Understand, we can't do anything until he is identified. Then you can petition the court for an order of protection. Until then, I suggest you get some pepper spray and carry it with you. Park in lighted areas, and if possible, always have someone accompany you."

"You don't understand," she retorted. Fear encompassed her. Her heart throbbed faster than rumors in the prison system. The room began to spin. KC jumped, staggered to the trash can, and threw up. The officers recoiled. After heaving up everything she'd eaten and more, she turned to the officers. Joyce heard KC retching and rushed into the office. She heard KC remark, "I can't have people accompany me wherever I go. I've got to work. I have to make restitution payments. I can't lose this job. I'll go back to prison."

Joyce, who had been standing beside KC, put her arm around her. "Honey, you're not going to lose this job. We will figure out how we can make this work for you." She placed her index finger under KC's chin and lifted it so she could look straight into her eyes. "KC, I want you to go home now. Try to get some rest. Richard and I will figure out a way to make this work for all of us." She turned to address the officers. "Are you gentlemen done? I want to follow her home."

"Yes, we'll be in touch," the older one answered. They closed their report book, nodded, and left.

"KC, get your things together. Let's go."

"But, Joyce, what about—"

"No, there are no what abouts today. You're going home."

Joyce followed KC home. Sitting in the car, she watched KC enter the house. She glanced around before driving off and noted she didn't see anyone or anything threatening.

KC dropped her work folder on the kitchen counter and began to brew herself a cup of tea. The silence in the house only intensified her fear. She carried her tea into the great room. As she flipped on the switch for the fireplace, the phone rang. It startled her. She dropped the cup, which shattered on the hardwood floor. Pulling herself together, she answered, "Hello? Phillipses' residence. Hello? Hello?" She heard heavy breathing, and then a computerized voice said, "I know you are home alone. Think I'll come over." KC slammed the receiver down. *Oh, my God. What can I do?* She'd become accustomed to breath prayers.

She remembered the business card the officers had given her. Her fingers trembled as she pulled it from her wallet. Picking up the phone, she realized the line was dead. She raced to her coat, grabbed her cell phone, punched in their number, and waited for them to answer.

Car lights flashed through the windows of the great room before she could complete the call. KC grabbed a broom from the closet. Raising it over her shoulder like a baseball player, she prepared to swing it when the door opened. Her heart was thumping so hard that she thought she was going to have a heart attack. The garage door motor started. Rationale told KC she was safe, but fear and apprehension won over rationale. She was ready to fend off her stalker. The door opened.

# CHAPTER 27

K C swung the broom with all her strength. It struck Charles's right wrist, and she heard a crack. Instantly, she knew it wasn't the broom handle. Charles dropped his Bible and grabbed his wrist, writhing in pain.

"What in the world?" Rose was torn between caring for Charles and yelling at KC. "What were you thinking, young lady?"

"Rose, deal with this later. I need to go to the hospital. You'll have to drive."

"I'll go with you," KC declared. Her eyes were wide. "I'm so sorry."

"Not now! Let's get him to the hospital," Rose glared at KC. "I do expect an explanation." She grabbed a plastic bag and filled it with ice. Charles jerked his wrist back in pain when Rose laid the ice on it. "I'm sorry, honey." They all got into the car, and Rose fastened his seat belt. She scurried to the driver's side. The engine roared to life. KC rode in the back seat. Not a word was spoken. The only sound was the car's engine and a slight moan from Charles when the car hit a bump.

After his wrist was x-rayed and casted, the three returned home. Although Charles was still in pain, he asked Rose for a cup of coffee, and the three sat at the table. Charles looked at KC.

"I think some baseball teams could use a slugger like you!" He needed to break the tension in the room. Despite the effects of the drugs, he managed a smile. "I know there's got to be a reason why you did that. I really thought you liked me," he remarked with a smirk on his face.

Rose wasn't quite as understanding. She hadn't said a word to KC since the incident happened.

"I'd like to know what in the world you were thinking, KC."

Silence remained for several seconds. KC didn't look at her mom or Charles. She kneaded her ring finger with her jaws clamped together tightly. Her stomach knotted. KC swallowed deeply; she felt nauseated. She took a sip of water. "I didn't mean to hurt you, Charles," she said, touching his uninjured arm. "I really didn't." She glanced at her mom. "Mom, I've done everything I could to prevent telling you this because I know you would just worry." She took another drink of water before she continued. "Remember when my tires were slashed?" Rose nodded. "Well, there's more to it."

KC explained what had happened. "I hadn't been home long when I got a phone call. It was a computerized voice, and the caller knew I was home alone." Tears welled up in her eyes. She didn't want to cry so she cleared her voice. "I was getting ready to call the police when you came, but I was afraid—"

"You call them right now!" Charles demanded. The medication slurred his speech, and his eyes struggled to focus. "Call them, n-o-w!" He fell asleep at the table.

"Let's get him to bed, Mom." She reached for Charles's uninjured arm. "I'll call the police as soon as he's in bed."

"I think we'd better get him to the sofa and let him sleep there tonight," Rose answered.

Once they had him settled on the sofa, KC reached for the phone. She punched in the phone number that the officers had given her and waited.

"Officer Roberts, it's KC Elliott. You took a report about me being stalked late this afternoon. Please call me. I have more information. Thank you."

Sitting at the table, Rose spoke softly. "I'm sorry I was so curt with you earlier." She dabbed her eyes. "I haven't been very kind since you returned. You must think I'm horrible. I have to plead guilty to all your accusations of being unforgiving and lacking grace. Yes, my pride was hurt when you went to prison. Charles and I have been talking about it." She glanced toward her husband, sleeping soundly. Rose continued, "I've decided to see a counselor to help me work through my anger." She swallowed the apple-sized lump in her throat. "Honey, would you be willing to see—"

"What? You think I need to see a counselor?" There was a hint of frustration in KC's voice. She stomped toward the patio door. Silence! To an outsider, it appeared the ladies were at a standoff. But KC slowly turned toward her mother. She folded her arms around her midsection and responded, "Well, if you can recommend a good counselor, I'll go. I have nightmares almost every night. The guilt eats at me when I'm alone. The fear of being stalked has only compounded it." KC hugged the hot cup of tea in her hands and said, "Yes, Mom, I think it would be a good idea." She chewed on her lips, first the right side and then the left. "It would be a good idea, but I haven't any insurance, and it would cost a mint." KC looked shattered. "Almost every penny I earn I use to pay off the restitution. I can't afford a counselor."

The second hand of the kitchen clock ticked off several seconds. Rose didn't want to solve all of KC's problems. However, she had a suggestion.

"You got a degree in what?" she asked, but she already knew the answer.

"Mom, you know I got my degree in webpage designs. That's why I'm at Advanced Web Designs. Why? What's that got to do with counseling and being stalked?"

"Think about it, honey." Rose stepped into the great room to check on Charles. Returning to the kitchen, she filled a mug with water and put it in the microwave to heat. "What is it you do for Richard and Joyce?"

"I do marketing and design webpages for clients. You know that. I don't know what you're getting ... what a great idea!" She jumped up, scraping the chair across the tiled floor. "Mom, you're a genius." Relief spread across KC's face. *Mental note to self: ask Goens if they'd be willing to allow her to do a trade-off—counseling for reduced billing for a certain number of hours.* However, as quickly as she experienced relief, it was replaced with fear and despair as her phone rang.

"KC Elliott here," she answered. The right side of her upper lip rose slightly. Her eyes narrowed. Looking at her mother, she opened her mouth and stuck her index finger in as if gagging herself. "Yes, Mr. Parsons. I'll be there tomorrow afternoon at 4:30." She ended the call and looked at her mom. "I don't believe I'm going to say this, but I'm really disappointed it wasn't the police." She laughed briefly as the phone rang again. "KC Elliott. Yes, Officer Roberts. Could you stop by? My stalker called this evening. In fifteen minutes? That'll be fine. Thank you."

KC looked at her mom, her mouth curled to the left. "Well, whether they believe it or not, it is going to be reported."

Rose smirked. "They'll believe something happened. The evidence that you were frightened is snoring in the living room." They laughed and hugged each other.

Fifteen minutes later, the officers arrived to take the report. "Miss Elliott," Officer Roberts said, "we believe your report of the stalking. We don't have enough officers to stake out your home, but I have a suggestion. Check the caller ID before answering your calls. If the number is unfamiliar to you, let your answering machine or voice mail answer. Maybe he will be stupid enough to leave a message. You might want to talk with the district attorn—"

"Oh, I don't think so. They won't believe me," KC retorted with uncompromising confidence.

"They'll have our report. They'll believe it." Roberts turned to leave, but spun around. "At any rate, they'll have to do something."

CHAPTER 28

"Well, Elliott how's it goin'?" Logan didn't even look at KC as he flipped through her paperwork. "Hmm? What's this?" He slammed a piece of paper on his desktop. "You made a police report? What's that all about? Says you hit your stepfather with a broom. You know that's assault, right? You could be sent back—"

"Yeah, I know," she interrupted. Her lip quivered. "I can be sent back to prison." She felt fear gripping her like a vise being tightened.

Logan spun around in his swivel chair and spit out, "Shut up! Just shut up! I didn't give you permission to talk, did I? No, I didn't! So be quiet!" He turned away. *I think I've got her rattled.* In a couple of weeks, she's gonna break. He stole a glance in KC's direction and saw her wipe her eyes. He smirked. It was time to begin to show some kindness. "Oh my, why didn't you tell me you thought you were being stalked?" He raised his head and paused before speaking. "Tell me what happened."

KC recited for Logan all the events that had occurred. He sat soundlessly and thoughtfully with his fingers steepled together and elbows resting on the chair arms. His eyes contracted, and he massaged his temples. *I wish she'd just shut up!* KC paused to take a breath, and Logan jumped in.

"So, Elliott, how can I help? I know it seems as if I'm kinda hard-nosed, but if you think you're in danger, I can run interference with the cops."

KC gazed at him. *Can he possibly mean that? He's never shown sympathy. Still don't think I can trust him.* "Thank you, Mr. Parsons. I don't think I'll need your help. If I do need help, I'll call you."

"Okay, let me give you my business card." He reached inside his suitcoat pocket and pulled out a leather card holder. He picked up a pen and added, "I don't give my personal cell phone to all my parolees, but if you ever need help, call." He stood and walked around the desk. "That will be all. I'll call you for our next meeting. Understand?"

KC nodded. She stood and started toward the door, but Logan blocked it. "You'll call if you need me, right?"

The hair on her arms stood on end, and KC's heart thumped against her chest. Fear rose in her throat. She reached for the business card. Logan stretched out his hand to shake hers. KC hesitated.

"It's okay. You don't have to be afraid to touch me," Logan stated. He held her hand a couple seconds longer than necessary.

"Mr. Parsons, I'll call you if I need to, but I really need to go. I have another commitment—one I can't miss."

He stepped aside and allowed her to leave.

*I don't like that man. He simply cannot be trusted. I don't know whether his offer to help is genuine or if he has an ulterior motive.* KC tried to shake the ominous feeling. *Hopefully supper with Lisa will lighten my mood.*

Pulling into the parking lot at Kenyon's Palace, KC looked for a spot near a light post and near the door. She found one near a light, but she had to walk several yards to the door. She carried a small canister of pepper spray in one hand and kept her finger on the panic button of her car keys. She could hear footsteps behind her, and she quickened her steps.

"KC, wait up! I just got here!" It was Lisa.

KC exhaled a long, slow sigh. The death grip she held on her keys and pepper spray relaxed. She forced herself to slow her pace. Lisa came up to walk alongside her.

"Hey, girlfriend, what's the hurry?" Lisa had always been observant. "You act like you're afraid of something. Whatcha got in your hands?" She grabbed KC's hand and forced it open. She gasped and breathed out a whisper, "You're carrying pepper spray! What's goin' on?"

"Inside. I'll tell you inside." She glanced around. "Please, let's go in." KC's fear was palpable even to Lisa.

Lisa glimpsed over her shoulder too. Yet she didn't know what or who she should be looking for. The two friends hurried into the restaurant.

"Good evening, ladies!" The hostess greeted them warmly.

"Good evening," KC responded warmly. "If it's possible, could we have a table in a corner? Preferably one where we can watch the door." She forced a smile and slipped the hostess a five-dollar tip.

"Yes, I'll see what I can do. Thank you." She returned in a couple of minutes and showed the ladies to their table.

With their drinks ordered, they scanned the menu. The two decided on their meals and placed their order. Lisa leaned across the table to talk quietly.

"KC, tell me what's going on. I haven't seen you this jumpy since you were arrested. What's going on?"

KC didn't want anyone to hear their conversation. She spoke in whispered tones, pausing when someone walked near. But she told Lisa everything.

"But do you have any idea who—?"

"Lisa, I'm not making any accusations, but I think I saw that guy you've been having trouble with. What's his name? He wanted to talk with you the day we had lunch together."

"Oh, you mean Stewart?" She dropped her head. "I'm afraid he can be rather menacing, but I don't think he'd ever hurt anyone.

Besides, I had to let him go." She tipped her head to her left and scanned KC's face. "Why do you ask about him?"

"Remember I told you I saw someone lurking around the office? There was something about him that reminded me of that guy." She rubbed her ring finger. "I couldn't see his face, but he gestured just like that Stewart." She put her right index finger to her eyebrow and saluted. "I saw him do that to you."

"KC, that doesn't mean it's Stewart. Lots of people do that." Lisa reached across the table and tapped the back of KC's hand tenderly. "Listen, my friend, I know you're scared, but you can't accuse Stewart of stalking without more proof."

"I know," she responded. She chewed on her lip. "I just don't know what to do. But on the outside chance it is him, watch your back. Okay?" She gazed into Lisa's eyes. "I don't want anything to happen to you because you're my only real friend."

Lisa nodded her head. "I understand. You be careful too. I just got my friend back. I don't want to lose you again." The server brought their meal. "Now, let's try to forget all this stuff and have a nice meal, okay?"

"Great idea," KC responded. For the next forty-five minutes, the two women chatted as if nothing was wrong. Both declined the offer of dessert and requested their check. Before they left the restaurant, they hugged each other and agreed to meet for lunch another day. KC reached into her purse for her keys and the pepper spray. She smirked at Lisa and whispered, "Police told me to carry it, just in case, so now I'm ready to go to the car."

KC watched Lisa drive away. She started her car and put it in drive. Someone wearing a black hoodie stepped in her path, saluted her, and then ran across the parking lot. Her nostrils flared, and her blood pressure soared. She stomped on the gas. *I'm not gonna take this anymore!* But he disappeared into the darkness.

Not more than three blocks from the restaurant, Logan sat in his car. He'd listened to talk radio and munched on cold pizza. After almost two hours, he saw a shadowy figure approach. The gait of the figure assured him it was his contact.

"Well, how's it gonna, buddy?" Logan handed a C-note to his parolee. "Doin' everything I've told you to do?"

"Yeah, man. I don't wanna go back to the joint! You gonna back me if I get caught, right?" He flicked his cigarette on the ground and crushed it with his hiking boots. He grabbed the money and stuck it into the pocket of his sweatshirt.

"Yeah, of course," Logan replied. *You think I'm a fool? No, I'm not gonna back you. I'd rather see you go to the big house.* "You just do everything I tell ya, hear?" He didn't wait for an answer. He revved the motor and left. He sneered and then snickered. *Ol' Stu isn't gonna know what hit him when the cops get him. I didn't know this was gonna be such easy pickin's. What an idiot!*

# CHAPTER 29

K C pulled into the garage, relieved that Charles and her mom were home. "Hi, folks. I'm home. Had a nice supper with Lisa," she announced with enthusiasm. "We went to—"

"Kenyon's Palace, right?" Charles asked with no emotion.

"Yeah, how'd you know?" KC detected a problem with her answer. "You jealous we didn't invite you?" she joked with him.

"You better come in here." He nodded his head toward the great room.

Rose sat quietly on the leather loveseat. With tissues wadded in her hand, she padded the space next her. "You better listen to this." She pushed the play button on the telephone recorder.

"Hi, sweetheart. Hope you and your girlfriend had a nice dinner at Kenyon's Palace. Told you I had my eye on you. You can't hide from me." It was the computerized voice again.

KC sighed heavily. Adrenalin surged through her veins. "I ... I can't take it anymore." She doubled over, convulsing in tears.

"Enough! I will not tolerate someone terrorizing the people I love." Charles's face was red with anger, and he pounded the table. "I will not!" He grabbed his cell phone and punched in 9-1-1.

"9-1-1, what's your emergency?"

"I'll tell you what the emergency is. My stepdaughter is being stalked, and I want an officer out here now."

He paced from the back door to the windows in the great room. With his wrist in a cast, he kept slapping his leg. With each step, his anger deepened.

Rose, never at a loss for words, sat quietly. She twisted the tissues in her hand. Occasionally, she'd wipe away a tear that escaped down her paled face. KC sat next to her mom and patted her hand.

"Mom, I'm sorry. I should never have moved back here."

"This is not your fault." Charles's thunderous voice could be heard from across the room. "What's takin' police so long to get here?"

"Charles, calm down!" Rose stood indignantly. "You have every right to be angry, but it won't do you any good if your blood pressure goes sky high. Settle down!"

The flash of headlights filled the windows. Charles was at the door before the officers had a chance to ring the bell. "'Bout time you got here." Charles held the door for them. "My stepdaughter is being stalked, and your department seems either unwilling or too inept to find the idiot."

"Mr. Phillips, please calm down. Let's sit down." The officer took Charles by the elbow and led him to a chair. They all sat around the dining room table. "We have the copy of a report filed by KC Elliott yesterday." He paused, looked toward KC, and asked, "You are the complainant?" KC nodded. "Is your stepfather telling me there is more to what you told the officers yesterday?"

"Yes, sir." She swallowed the large lump in her throat. "I got home a while ago and—" She turned to Charles. "Why don't you play the recording?"

"Officers, can we go to the living room? I don't want the ladies to listen to this again." He stood and led them to the room, where they listened to the call. "Now, I expect you to do something. I will not tolerate my girls being threatened."

"I certainly understand your anger and concern, Mr. Phillips. It is going to be difficult to trace the call, especially since the perpetrator is using a computer device to disguise his or her voice."

The officers listened to Charles rant but finally asked to speak with KC.

"KC, please tell us everything you can remember." She looked puzzled, so the officer explained. "When did the calls begin? When did you discover you were being stalked? Any idea who it might be?"

KC looked at her hands folded in her lap. Her mouth twisted to the left as she thought about her answer. "No, officers, I have no idea who it might be. If you have the original report, you know as much I as do." She fell silent. "I don't know what to do. I can't go anywhere without being followed." She stood and began walking about. She stepped to the windows and looked outside. "I can't live like this! I can't!" Tears dammed in her eyes began overflowing. She glared at the officers. "Look! You guys didn't have any problem finding me and arresting me. Why can't you find this guy? I did my time! Now I want some peace. I want to become a productive citizen. If this guy isn't found, I'll never feel safe."

"Ma'am, we'll do all we can to find this guy. Let us pool our resources and review our notes." They stood to leave. The older officer turned toward Charles, Rose, and KC and added, "I have a daughter about your age. I would do everything in my power to protect her, and I'll do everything possible to resolve this issue." He handed Charles his business card and gave another one to KC. "If you think of anything or anyone, call. If you need anything, call."

Charles felt better after talking with the officers. "Ladies, why don't you two go on to bed. I need to spend some time in prayer, praying God's hand of protection over this house and over KC. He kissed Rose on the cheek and gave KC a hug. Rose and KC climbed the stairway hand in hand.

Charles did pray. However, he also checked and rechecked the locks on the doors and windows. He thumbed through the phone book looking for a home security company. *First thing in the morning, I'm going to get security for this house. I don't care what it costs.* His eyes narrowed. *Never wanted a gun in the house, but I'm going to get one.* He patrolled his house all night. He looked out the windows hoping to see KC's stalker.

As the sky turned from inky black to brilliant yellow-orange, Charles poured himself another cup of coffee. He hadn't slept all night. His five o'clock shadow was very distinct. The security of his wife and stepdaughter was foremost on his mind. His eyes darted toward the stairway as he heard a noise from upstairs.

"Charles, dear, are you up already?" Rose asked quietly. She looked at her husband when she entered the kitchen. "Oh, dear, you never came to bed, did you?" She wrapped her arms about his neck and kissed the top of his head. "You haven't slept a wink, right?" She walked around to face him. Her forehead creased, and her tired eyes widened. "You're really worried, aren't you?"

He pulled Rose close and answered her questions. "Yes, I'm up already; no, I never came to bed; no, I didn't sleep a wink; and yes, I'm worried." He kissed her tenderly and held her to himself. "When I married you, I married your family. I vowed I would take care of you. I intend to do just that." He released her and poured a cup of coffee for Rose. "I'm worried about the safety of my two girls. I'm going to have a home security system installed as soon as possible." Looking over the lake, he announced, "I may not be able to provide twenty-four/seven protection for the two of you, but you can bet your last dollar, I will do my best to keep our home safe."

Rose concentrated on Charles's face. His jaws were clenched tightly together, and his lips formed a thin, straight line. She could see his determination.

"And I'm going to teach you both to shoot a g—"

"There will be no guns in this house, Charles! Do you hear me? No guns." She pulled her robe closed. "I'm afraid of those things, and—"

"But how can you protect yourselves?" His voice was getting louder.

"How about we take some karate lessons?" KC asked. She'd

slipped into the kitchen. "Charles, I don't think I can have a gun. But karate lessons would be a good thing."

Angrily, he set his coffee cup on the counter. Coffee splashed onto the counter. He smacked his forehead and replied, "I hadn't even thought of that, KC." He ran his hands through his hair. "I love you both so much. I want to protect you, and I can't be with you both all the time." He grabbed the phone book and began thumbing through it. "Okay, karate lessons for both of you. But we are going to have a security system installed."

"Anyone for waffles?" Rose queried. No one answered. "Yeah, me neither."

"Think I'll get ready for work," KC announced. "You two can decide what to eat, but I think I'd upchuck anything I ate." KC climbed the stairs. With each step, she felt a sense of foreboding. *I had to watch my back in prison. Never thought I'd have to watch it after I was released.* She browsed through her clothes, trying to decide what to wear. Deciding on a black skirt and tailored blazer with peaked lapels, three pockets, and buttoned cuffs, she added a silk, yellow, short-sleeved top. *Black seems to reflect my mood, but the yellow hopefully will offset it. I don't want the Goens or my coworkers to know how frightened I am.* She laid her clothes on the bed and headed to the bathroom for a quick shower.

The shower relaxed her tensed muscles but did nothing for her emotions. Dressed for her business day, KC descended the stairs. She grabbed her red portfolio and purse. With her keys in hand, she started toward the garage, but Charles stopped her.

"KC, I think it's time to get your oil changed. Take your mom's car. She'll take your car for the day. Okay?"

"I hadn't even thought of car maintenance. Thank you. If it isn't a problem, it would be really helpful. Mom?" She turned to her mom's approval.

"Not a problem. I've got to go to the grocery store. If you'd like, I'll drop it off at the office when it's done. Sound okay?" Rose asked.

"Yeah, that's fine." KC started to leave but turned to add,

"You might want to call to be sure I'm at the office. I still have appointments to keep. I can't let all this nonsense interrupt my job." She smiled at her mom, but the smile didn't reach her eyes.

"I'll do that, honey. See you later, and have a good day."

KC pulled out of the garage and didn't see anyone lurking about. She drove around town for a while. Glancing in the rearview mirror, she tried to determine if anyone was following her. Convinced she was safe, KC drove to the office and parked the car.

With the car maintenance done, Rose was on her way to the grocery store. She didn't have a long list, so it wasn't going to take long. But Rose met a lady from church, and they visited in the grocery store for quite a while as the groceries were scanned, bagged and placed in the cart. Then, Rose went to the car and found a paper under the wiper. She pulled it off and read, "I thought you were supposed to be at work. Wonder what your PO would say if he knew you were shopping during the day rather than working."

Rose crumpled the paper in her hand and leaned heavily against the car. She wept, "Is this never going to end?"

# CHAPTER 30

A lady noticed Rose's distress and approached her. "Ma'am, are you okay?"

Rose turned quickly and lost her balance. She crumbled to the asphalt. Tears flowed. "I simply can't take it anymore."

The lady knelt beside Rose and tried to determine what was wrong. Rose was inconsolable. Finally, the lady called 9-1-1. "No, she doesn't seem to be injured, but she's clearly distressed about something.... No, I don't see another person with her. Please send someone to help.... Okay, I'll stay with her 'til you get here."

Rose managed to choke out, "Call my husband." She punched in his phone number, and the lady relayed the information to Charles.

The police arrived and looked at the note Rose had found under the wiper. "Do you have any idea who it might be from?" the officer asked.

"No!" she shouted at the officer. "Can't you guys get it into your thick skulls that my daughter is being stalked? This is her car. I took it for an oil change and was going to return it to her after I was done grocery shopping."

"Rose, are you okay?" Charles shouldered his way to his wife's side. "What's going on?"

The tears began again, and she hiccupped sobs. "Another note, Charles. I can't take it. I'm so afraid I'm going to lose KC again."

Charles didn't understand. He turned to the officers. "What's she talkin' about?"

They showed him the note, which they'd placed in a plastic evidence bag. His rage reached his face. He felt his blood pressure rising and his heart throbbing faster. He lost his senses and grabbed an officer by the collar. "You guys have got to find this lunatic! I'm tired of the threats being made against KC. Do something! Or I—"

"Settle down, mister," the officer retorted. "I'm still trying to determine what's going on."

"Well, it's as plain as the nose on your face. My family's in danger, and you yokels don't know what to do about it!" He pulled his hand back as if to strike the officer, but the officer grabbed Charles's arm.

"Don't do anything stupid! I don't want to haul you back to the station."

Splaying his fingers through his hair, Charles apologized to the officer and added, "I just don't know what to do. Whoever is stalking KC is real shrewd. I'm afraid for her."

KC's phone rang. She hoped it was her mother calling but was disappointed to see Logan Parsons name on the caller ID.

"Hello?" KC tried to sound upbeat.

"I think we are overdue for a meeting, Elliott. I'll meet you at the office at 4:00. Don't be late."

"Wait, Mr. Parsons. I can't get there at 4:00. I don't have a car today. It won't be available 'til later."

"Fine," he conceded. "I'll see you at 5:30. Don't be late. Understand? Don't be late. Remember: I'm accommodating you."

The day seemed to drag for KC. She hated meeting with Logan. *That man gives me the creeps. I feel like he's undressing me. I'll be so glad when this parole period is over. I so need my freedom.*

The office door opened, and KC's mouth fell open. She stood grasping her throat. "Why are you here, Charles? Is Mom okay?"

He glared at her. "As a matter of fact, your mother is a mess. Whoever is stalking you left a message on the car while your mom was grocery shopping. After we were done with the police, I had to take her home. She was crying. I tried to get her to lie down, but she can't get the note she found on the windshield out of her mind. This has got to stop, and I mean right now!" Charles's voice began soft but increased in volume the longer he spoke. By the time he was done, he slammed his fist on the counter. "It has to stop now!" He turned to leave. Reaching the door, Charles spun around and added, "I expect you home at 5:30."

"I can't! I have to see my parole officer then."

"Fine. You be sure to tell him about being stalked." Charles slammed the door as he left.

The door crashed loudly, and Joyce rushed out of her office. "What's goin' on here?" She glanced at KC. "What happened? And who was that?"

The blood drained from KC's face. "I'm sorry, Joyce. *That* was my stepfather, Charles, and—"

"I know Charles, but I've never known him to create such a ruckus. What in the world's going on?"

Tears filled KC's eyes and she ground her teeth, willing herself not to cry.

"You already know about the stalking. Well, whoever is stalking me left a message on my windshield this morning. Only it was Mom who found it. Charles said Mom is a mess. She can't sleep. She's crying and pacing the floor. Joyce, I don't know what to do."

Joyce placed her hand on KC's shoulder. "I know what to do." She bent down and added, "First, *we* are going to get ourselves a cup of tea, and then we are going into my office to pray about it." She paused, looking into KC's brown eyes, and continued. "I believe we all need God's guidance on this. Don't you?"

KC had lost her faith in God when she went to prison. "It's clear

I can't do anything about it, so I guess I had better learn to trust someone who can. And you seem to think that someone is God. So, yes, let's pray about it."

KC wrapped her fingers around a hot cup of lavender tea.

"Dear, lavender tea is supposed to be good for calming one's nerves. Take your time, but we are going to pray about this situation. Now, tell me what happened."

With her fingers wrapped around the cup, KC slowly repeated what Charles had told her.

"But how did your mom get the message?"

"Well, the only thing I can figure out is that it was an accident. I needed the oil changed and the tires rotated, so Mom offered to take my car and let me use her car." As soon as the words were out of her mouth, she knew what had happened. "The stalker thought I was at the grocery store. He had no idea Mom and I had switched cars for the day." KC jolted out of the chair and started for the door. "Oh, my goodness, he's watching us all the time. How can that be?"

"KC, sit down, honey. We really need God's direction. We are going to pray about this."

Reluctantly, KC returned to the table. Joyce reached for KC's hand. "Let's pray." KC listened as Joyce talked.

*It's like she's talking with God. It's like she's having a conversation with God. Oh, she really believes in this God stuff.*

"Amen." Joyce patted KC's hand. "We are going to trust God to solve this problem. Right?"

KC nodded her head but wasn't entirely convinced that there was a God or that God could solve this problem. She glanced at her watch. "Joyce, thank you, but I've got to leave. I have to see my PO at 5:30."

"Okay, dear. It will be okay. God is protecting you."

*I hope so, Joyce. I hope so. But I don't trust Logan Parsons.*

# CHAPTER 31

Logan was in his usual foul mood. All day he grumbled about something. He slammed file drawers closed and threw down the handset of the phone. He kicked chairs, tables, and his desk.

"Hey, man, what's your problem?" a coworker asked. "You've done nothing but make our lives miserable all day. Some girl turn you down or somethin'?"

Logan crossed the room in four quick steps. Grabbing the man by his shirt, he shoved him against a file cabinet. "Shut your mouth, or I'll shut it for ya! Ya hear me?" He then pushed the man toward his chair. "I'm outta here! Gotta couple of meetings with some cons." He turned to leave but glanced back. "You guys better hope I'm in a better mood tomorrow."

"Yeah, we hear ya! Hope you find a woman tonight. Might help that attitude of yours," the other parole officer bit back.

After Logan left the office, he slid into his car and reached into the glove box. Pulling a manila envelope out, he opened it and pulled out a handful of bills. He fanned the bills and smiled. *Boy, Stewart has been worth every dollar I've given him. Gonna have to warn him what will happen if he doesn't do everything I say.* His eyes narrowed, and his lips formed a thin line. *Tonight, I begin phase two of my plan.* A smirk crossed his face, and he nodded his head. *Yeah, got a plan. It's worked before; it'll work again.*

Logan sat in his car for thirty minutes listening to country music. In the distance, he recognized Stewart moseying toward the courthouse. Logan whistled and nodded to him, and he walked to the driver's window. "Get in, buddy!"

"What's up?"

"I said get in. Just do as I said."

Stewart knew what the next statement would be. Logan took pleasure in lording over the heads of his parolees his power to send them back to prison. Stewart had heard stories of convicts going back to prison for being fifteen minutes late for an appointment. He didn't doubt Logan would send him back too.

"Hey, buddy, you doin' a good job for me?"

"Yeah, I always let a couple days pass before I send her another note or call her." Stewart stuck a cigarette between his lips and inhaled deeply. Blowing out a long flume of smoke, he added, "Kinda like that voice distorter." He chortled, "Yeah, it's a nice touch." He looked at Logan. "I can only imagine the fear it causes." When he didn't get a response from Logan, he sighed and continued, "I'll do a good job for ya, Mr. Parsons. Ya can count on it."

"Well, here's your next payment. Keep up the good work, ya hear?" Logan gave Stewart a wad of money. "Make sure you don't get caught. Hate to send ya back, ya know?" He threw his head back and laughed loudly. He watched Stewart stuff the money in his front right pocket. "Now, get out!"

Stewart carefully got out, closed the car door, turned to Logan, and raised his finger to his eyebrow in a salute.

Logan watched Stewart slink away into the darkness. *Ah, she's weakening. It is definitely time to go to phase two.* He pursed his lips together and nodded his head, and with narrowed eyes, he said aloud, "Yep, time to move to phase two."

He turned the key in the ignition, and the engine roared to life. Headlights briefly illuminated his co-conspirator. Logan watched as Stewart exchanged money with another lowlife. He knew Stewart was buying drugs. *Drive away*, he thought. *I know I should report illegal activities. I could send that idiot back to prison in a New York minute, but I need him right now. When I don't need him any longer, he'll be gone like that.* He snapped his fingers.

Logan drove to the drive-through at a fast-food restaurant and ordered a cup of coffee. He paid and then drove to the lake. In the darkness and the cold, damp weather, he began planning his next move. Minutes ticked off. As he sipped the last of his coffee, he slapped the steering wheel. *Yeah, that'll work. I know she's afraid. She's one smart cookie. I know she doesn't trust me, but I think I know how to change that. Phase two begins the next time we meet.* His lips pursed to the right as he shook his head with an air of satisfaction.

Logan started the car and headed toward his home. Pulling into the garage, he swore. *I hate this dumpy apartment. Mom should give me more money from that stinkin' trust fund, but she's such a tightwad.* He walked to the garage door and manually pulled it down.

*God, I don't know how Mom could work this job all her life. She drove all over the state, constantly meeting with felons. Those idiot men and women belonged in prison, and she had to listen to their lies every day. Even when she was home, she was always doing paperwork. She never had time for me. She knew I wanted to become an actor, but she threatened to cut off my trust if I didn't take this job. I didn't even apply for this stupid job; she arranged it. It's like she's got an "in" with the state director.*

Fumbling for the apartment key, he dropped all the files, and papers scattered everywhere. "Oh, for Pete's sake!" he roared. "I hate the thought of spending more time working tonight." He picked up all the papers scattered on the cement garage floor and dropped them on the tiny kitchen table. Two steps from the table, he reached the refrigerator. Logan grabbed a bottle of beer, popped open the lid, and gulped down a couple of swigs. Then he began sorting through the paperwork.

It was after one o'clock in the morning when the files were in order. Logan slipped his shoes off, slung his Dockers over the chair, and threw his shirt on the chair arm. He lay on the sofa. "Ahhh! I just need a day when I don't have to do anything," he said to no one, just needing to say something. "Yeah, I need to get that witch." *Thump*—he slammed his fist into the sofa. *Tomorrow begins phase two. Phase two, to ... mor ... row.*

# CHAPTER 32

A fter the scene in the office, KC wasn't sure she'd have a car to drive. Charles was so angry that she thought he might have forgotten to leave her the car. He *had* forgotten to give her the keys. Lucky for her, she had an extra set in her purse. She walked out and was pleased to find the car there. She slipped behind the steering wheel, put the keys into the ignition, and brought the engine to life. With her seat belt buckled, she glanced down and noticed she had a text message. "Can't meet 2nite. Call 2morrow for appt. Parsons" KC banged her hand against the steering wheel. "Oh, how I hate that man. He's messin' with my mind. I know he is." *Phew*—a long breath of air slipped through her lips. "I hate that man. Yeah, I know. I brought it on myself. If I hadn't … No, I am not going beat myself up for the rest of my life. I'm going to focus on the future and become a productive citizen. I'm going to become the person my mom can be proud of, and I'm going to put the past in the past and live in the present." A smile slowly spread across her face. KC nodded her head as her resolve settled in her mind. "I'm not the person I was five years ago, and I'm going to be a better person today than I was yesterday." She pumped her right fist as she asserted her resolution. "I may have to see Logan Parsons, but I am not going to allow him to control my life. I'll report as he requires; I'll give him a urine specimen as is required. But he is not going to pull me down." KC drove to the lake and parked where she loved to park. She slipped a classical CD into the player and allowed the music to soothe her spirits.

KC noticed it was past five thirty and decided she'd better go home. Charles had been livid that afternoon. *I hope he's in a better mood,* she thought. Backing out and steering the car in the direction of her home, KC felt a wave of bile filling her stomach and esophagus. It wasn't that she was afraid of Charles, but she suddenly realized how terrifying the experience must have been for her mother. KC felt her face burn as fear changed to anger. *How dare he scare my mother! It's one thing to stalk me, but leave my mom out of it!* She slammed her fist against the steering wheel. *I don't know who's responsible, but I'm going to find out!*

Pulling into the driveway, KC felt a strength she hadn't experienced for years. It was clear that the stalker wanted to control, demoralize, and terrorize her. Whoever the stalker was, he or she didn't know the power that those actions had released in this young woman. KC was governor of her life; discouragement was not going to be her companion. Nor was she going to allow the stalker to intimidate her.

KC burst through the kitchen door. Throwing her purse onto the kitchen counter, she shouted, "Mom? Where are you? Mom?"

Hearing KC's grand entrance, Charles exploded from his chair and sprinted to the kitchen. "Shhh!" he snapped. His index finger covered his lips. "Your mother is sleeping." He poured hot water into a coffee mug, handed KC a tea bag, and added, "You and I are going to talk." He turned swiftly on his heels and retreated to the living room.

KC rolled her eyes, and her lips pulled to the right. She plopped the tea bag into the cup and dunked it several times. *Charles is still steamed about the note,* she thought as she reached for the sweetener, and a smirk crossed her face. *Boy, I can see he really loves Mom. I take some comfort in knowing that!* Grabbing her mug, she walked into the living room. She put her mug on the coaster and sat down, sighing heavily.

"Charles, I'm sorry about what happened this afternoon. I really am. I've been trying to deal with the stalking myself. I'd hoped I could spare you and Mom from even knowing. Obviously, I wasn't successful." Charles licked his lips as if he was preparing to say something, but KC put her hand up to stop him. She sipped some tea and returned the mug to the coaster. "I've been hesitant to talk with my PO about it." She looked across the room and fell silent. Charles remained quiet. Several seconds went by before KC turned her face toward Charles. "I don't trust that man." KC puckered her lips as she thought. "I told Mom that first night that there was something about Logan Parsons that I didn't trust." She glanced away from Charles for a couple of seconds. Then she continued, "I know you love her, Charles." She smiled. "I'm really grateful for the way you've taken care of her." She exhaled and looked at her hands folded in her lap. "I have to call Logan tomorrow to reschedule an appointment. I'm going to tell him all about the stalking. Maybe he can help me."

Charles nodded his head. "That's a good idea, KC. I know this isn't your fault. When I yelled at you this afternoon, I was just so angry. Rose was so upset. I really do love her. She's my life." He stopped and pulled a handkerchief from his back pocket to wipe his eyes. "I waited a long time to find the woman God wanted for me, and I've found that in your mom. I'll do everything I can to protect her." He took a long drink of coffee. "If you'd like, I'll go with you to see Logan."

"I don't know, Charles. He isn't very nice and seems to be a real stickler for rules." She paused, puckering her lips again. "He's always reminding me that he can send me back to prison like that," she said, snapping her fingers. "It's like he's a bully." She shrugged her shoulders. "But he's in charge so I have to do everything he says."

Charles heard the upstairs toilet flush. "Your mother's up. I think I'll walk down to the lake so you two can talk." He stood, crossed the floor in five or six steps, and added, "KC, I'm always here for you. If you need anything, please let me know." He looked toward the hallway. "She'll be here any minute now. You two talk as long as necessary. Call for me when you're done." He touched KC's shoulder. She tried not to move, but Charles felt her shudder. *Guess I shouldn't do that again*, he thought as he shoved his hands into his pants pockets and left the house.

KC rummaged through the refrigerator. She pulled out some chicken breasts and mixed together the ingredients for sweet and sour chicken. She put the frying pan on the burner and heated it. When it was hot enough, she put the chicken breasts in the pan.

"Oh, I smell something cooking," Rose said, announcing her presence. She slipped on her apron. "How can I help?"

KC turned around. "You can sit down and let me fix supper." She cleared her throat and added, "It's the least I can do." She pulled her mother into a hug. Tears slipped down her soft cheeks. "Mom, I'm so sorry for what happened today." She sniffled, reached for a tissue, and blew her nose. "Charles and I had a talk." She washed her hands and then continued to fix the chicken. She turned the chicken breasts. While they fried, she grabbed the head of lettuce and pulled apart the leaves. She pulled out three salad dishes and fixed each of them a nice lettuce and tomato salad. She then sprinkled shredded cheese on top of them. "I know you think Logan Parsons is a nice young man," she said, and then a slight smile spread across her face. "I bet you'd like me to marry someone like him." She watched as her mom's lips puckered. She shrugged her shoulders and a grin softened her features. "I knew it!" KC exclaimed. "But, Mom, it's not going to happen." She hesitated. "Remember? I said that first night there was something about him I didn't like. I didn't trust him." She crossed her arms and added, "I still don't trust him, but I'm going to talk with him about this stalker. I'm hoping he'll help me, give me some advice, help me find out who's doing this." She turned and added the sweet and sour mix. She opened a package of broccoli and dumped it into a pan of hot water.

Rose stood and walked to KC. "Honey, I know this hasn't been easy. I haven't made it easy for you. But whoever is stalking you could be dangerous. You've got to report this. Charles and I have hired a private investigator." KC started to interrupt, but Rose stopped her. "No, honey. This is not negotiable."

KC sighed loudly. "Okay, if you insist. But would you do a favor for me?"

"Anything, honey."

She turned, facing her mom. With no smile or expression, she asked, "Would you call out by the lake and tell Charles supper is ready?"

Rose grabbed a dishcloth and threw it at KC. "You still have that wicked sense of humor."

"Go on, Mom. I'll set the table."

CHAPTER 33

KC left Logan's office feeling upbeat. *Maybe I've misjudged him. He seemed genuinely concerned. I'm surprised! He does have a heart.* KC laughed at the thought. *I know he has to maintain a professional distance. He has to be the one in control. It just seems as if he enjoys the control way too much. Guess I need to start seeing the good in people.*

It was the end of the day, so KC headed to the lake to relax. It was there she began to unwind from both work and the stress of meeting with correctional officials. She still had several years of probation. KC slipped out of her dress shoes and reached for her walking shoes. She leaned over to tie her shoes when her cell phone rang.

"Hey there, beautiful. Care if I join you for a walk?" It was the computerized voice. KC dropped the phone, fell into the car seat, slammed the car door shut, and locked it. She started the car and she sped down the street. Her heart was beating a drum cadence marching double time. She was within a couple of blocks of home and didn't see anyone following her, so she stopped the car and tried to calm down. *The last thing I need to do is upset Mom. Calm down, KC. You're a big girl. You can handle this.* She inhaled a long breath of air, held it a few seconds, and slowly exhaled. It was an exercise she'd learned in yoga class. It always seemed to calm her nerves. She repeated the exercise several times. Each time, she could feel her heart slowing to a normal rhythm. *Okay, now I think I can go home, and Mom won't have any idea anything happened.* KC pulled her car into the garage and closed the door.

"Hi, Mom, I'm home," KC announced cheerfully. There was a lilt in her voice, but it betrayed her true emotions. "Mom, I'm home. Where are you?" She tossed her car keys on the counter. No answer. KC felt her heart beginning to beat rapidly again. She hurried up the stairs, but her Mom and Charles were not there. KC's breaths came rapidly. *Calm down—their car is here. They've got to be here.* She ran downstairs and searched again. Finally, she looked on the deck. She found her mom and Charles sitting there. Charles had his arm wrapped around her mom's shoulders. KC sighed. *Thank you, God, for bringing Charles into my mom's life. I can see how much he loves her. You knew how much she needed someone who'd really show her what love is. I know this mess is really upsetting for her—for me too. Please help Mr. Parsons find out who the stalker is. I know I messed up my life, but I'm really trying now. Mom and Charles shouldn't have to deal with this ugliness.* KC backed into the kitchen and decided to prepare supper.

*Chicken breast is always a healthy choice.* She pulled out the frozen chicken. While the chicken cooked for several minutes, she mixed together mushrooms, onion, and garlic powder. She reduced the heat and added the mixture. The water was boiling, so she dumped the egg noodles in. She deftly added the cream of mushroom soup and milk. When it came to a boil, she reduced the heat again. When the chicken mixture was ready, KC drained the noodles and added it to the mixture. She was putting the vegetables in the microwave when she heard her mom and Charles come it.

"Well, something smells good," announced Charles. "Do you suppose the chef fairy came?"

"KC, I didn't know you were home. You didn't need to fix supper."

"I saw you and Charles enjoying some time alone and thought I would let you have that time together. This," she said, sweeping her hands over the meal, "was nothing." She pulled open the cupboard doors to get the dishes. There was an envelope standing against the plates with her name on it. She slipped it into her pocket. "Mom, could you set the table for me? I need to go to my room for a minute."

"Sure, honey. Take your time, but don't forget about this luscious meal you've prepared."

"I'll be right back—trust me."

KC hurried upstairs. She suspected it was a card from her mom or perhaps Charles. She sat on the bed and slid her finger under the flap of the envelope. She pulled out the card and opened it. The blood drained from her face. "Hi sweetie, you never know where I might show up. Wanted you to know: you can run, but you can't hide." KC's heart thumped like a piston on a train racing down the track. *Breathe, KC. Breathe. Inhale slowly, exhale slowly.* She repeated the instructions several times.

"Honey, the food is going to either burn or get cold if you don't come down soon!" her mother shouted.

KC pinched her cheeks to get some color in them and declared, "I'm coming. Don't you do a thing. I've got everything under control." *Everything's under control except my life.*

KC put the meal on the table and Charles said, "I'd like to offer a prayer, if you don't mind."

"Mind? Not at all."

"Gracious and loving God, thank you for your blessings, for this wonderful food, and for your protections. Help us to live lives that always honor you. Amen."

After the meal, Rose insisted that KC and Charles relax in the living room or out on the deck. "KC prepared a lovely meal; it's only right that I clean up." She looked at the two still sitting at the table and added, "Now, go. Go relax." It didn't take them more than ten seconds to scrape their chairs along the tiled floor as they stood to leave.

"Well, we certainly know when we're not welcome," Charles

replied mockingly. "Let's go, KC. We'll just enjoy ourselves while your mother slaves away."

KC laughed at the way Charles teased her mom.

"The sunset is pretty here. Want to watch it from the deck?"

"I'd love to, but I'd better get a sweater. I'll be right there."

KC hurried to her room to get the sweater but also the card. She'd show it to Charles but didn't want her mother to see it.

"Charles, I'm glad you wanted to come to the deck. I've got something I want to show you." She handed him the card. His face turned red and felt hot as he read it. With his teeth clenched tightly together, he asked, "When did you get this?" he demanded.

"That's what scares me. It was propped against the plates in the cup—"

"Wait! You mean this man was in our house? How? When?"

"Charles, please keep your voice down. I don't want Mom to know."

He paced the deck for a minute. "You're right. Rose shouldn't know about this. But how did he get in? I'll have to have the locks changed."

"If you change the locks, Mom's going to know something is wrong."

He balled his fist and struck the palm of his hand in frustration. "You're right, KC. You're right." He splayed his hand through his hair. "What am I going to do? KC, what am I going to do? I have to protect Rose." He realized that it sounded like he did not care for KC and added, "And of course, I will protect you too."

He and KC sat in the deck chairs watching the sun disappear behind the trees across the lake. Silence hung between them as dusk fell.

"Charles, I think I should find an apartment. This is my problem. You and Mom have been dragged into it."

"I understand what you're saying, but I really don't think that's the answer. If you were alone, you'd be in more danger." He stroked his chin. "After your Mom goes to bed, I'm going to call that private investigator again." His eyes narrowed. "KC, look at me. We must do everything we can to protect your mother from knowing all this. So mum's the word, right?"

"Totally agreed. Mum's the word." She paused. Touching his forearm gently, she added, "Charles, I can see how much you love Mom. If I haven't thanked you before, I want you to know that I really appreciate how you care for her. We've had our differences, but I love her with all my heart."

"Mum's the word," they said together and then laughed.

"Mum's the word about what?"

Charles and KC turned to see Rose standing in the doorway with her hands on her hips.

# CHAPTER 34

"Why, honey, if we told you, you'd know." Charles thought so quickly, he added, "It's a surprise. Please don't spoil our surprise." He grasped her hand, brought it to his lips, and kissed it. "We both love you, and we've planned a surprise for you." He embraced her and winked at KC. *And Lord, please forgive me for lying to my devoted wife.*

"Well, when will I learn what this surprise is?" she quizzed.

"When all the details have been worked out, then and only then will you know," KC announced. She glanced at her watch and added, "I've got a book I want to spend time with. You'll excuse me if I go to my room, won't you?"

"Of course, dear. Thank you for the lovely dinner," Rose replied. "Honey, I think you are doing very well. I'm so proud of you." She kissed KC's left cheek. "You go to bed now, and I hope you enjoy the book. When you're done with it, perhaps I'd enjoy reading it. Good night."

Charles wrapped his arms around Rose after KC left the deck. "Sweetie, you've made wonderful progress in your relationship with KC." He kissed her forehead and continued, "She's really trying hard to redeem herself. She's still going to have difficulties. People are suspicious when they learn someone is a convicted felon. KC needs our support."

Rose looked into Charles's dark eyes, kissed him, and quietly answered, "And my pride really got in the way, didn't it? I hope KC can be as forgiving as God is."

Charles nodded and led her to the deck railing, where they stood watching the sun slip below the horizon. As it did, the warmth of the sun lessened, and Rose snuggled closer to him.

"Perhaps we should go inside," he suggested. He placed his hand in the middle of her back and directed her toward the door. Once inside, Charles hinted that he'd like a cup of coffee. Rose caught the hint and went to the kitchen. As she left the room, Charles locked the door, and as he pulled the window dressings closed, he checked the window locks. Everything was locked, and he felt he'd done everything he could to protect his family.

He joined Rose at the counter bar in the kitchen. Silence hung between them for several minutes. "Charles, I know you're going to think this is foolish, but I think KC is in more danger than we realize." Saying it aloud caused a shiver to chill Rose, and she sipped some hot tea. "I don't know what we can do." She reached for Charles's hand, "And I don't know why I have this feeling." Charles didn't confirm or deny her suspicions. His silence spoke volumes to Rose. "You think so too, don't you?" she asked softly.

"Honey, we're doing all we can to protect her. Since we are doing all we can, we must trust God to protect her when we aren't with her." He reached for his Bible, opened it to Psalm 32, and read, "You are my hiding place; you will protect me from trouble and surround me with songs of deliverance" (NIV). "I know it is difficult to trust God when we don't know what's ahead, but let's pray together now, okay?" Rose nodded. Charles began, "Lord God, You are our hiding place. Sometimes we fail to run to our hiding place. We think we can handle whatever issues are troubling us. Help us to trust you where we cannot see. We ask you to protect KC from the person or persons who are terrorizing her. Surround KC with your divine shelter. KC has to work, and that means she is among the public, which means she is vulnerable. You protected

David when he was running from King Saul. Please keep a bubble of protection over KC wherever she might be. Lord, I pray for my dear wife. I can only imagine the anguish she feels as she watches KC struggle with the fear she has. I thank you for her efforts to forgive KC. I know it hasn't been easy for Rose to swallow her pride"—he squeezed Rose's arm—"but oh, God, I've seen Rose grow closer to you as she grows closer to KC. As we go to bed this evening, I ask you to give us all a good night's rest. I offer this prayer in the precious name of our loving and caring savior, Jesus Christ." He pulled Rose into a tender embrace and kissed her cheek. "I love you, Rose Phillips. We will trust God, and we will learn to obey God, right?"

With her index finger, Rose wiped a tear from her cheek and answered softly, "Yes, I'll do my best to trust God. But, Charles, I'm really afraid for KC."

He led Rose upstairs to the bedroom. She sat in her rocking chair while Charles readied his clothes for tomorrow and turned on the shower. He pulled off his jeans and tossed them into the clothes hamper before slipping into the shower.

*Oh, tomorrow is laundry day. I'd better get the clothes ready.* She dumped the clothes on the floor to sort. *Whites, colored, heavy clothes.* Ever since a ballpoint pen went through the laundry and the dryer, she always checked Charles's pockets. *What's this?* She pulled out a piece of paper. It was the card KC had found in the cabinet. Her hand flew to her heart, and she felt light-headed. "Charles!" she shrieked.

Charles, wearing only a towel, hurried from the bathroom. "What is it, Rose? Are you okay?"

"I am *not* okay. What is this?" She held up the note. "When did KC get this?"

Charles struggled to come up with an explanation. He decided that honesty, though not necessarily all of the truth, was required. "KC gave it to me this evening when you were cleaning up." He looked down like a little boy being scolded. "We didn't want to worry you." He slipped on his robe and held her closely. "Honey,

I'm going to talk with the investigator tomorrow. I'll do all I can to protect KC. This has gone on long enough."

The color was beginning to return to Rose's face. "Will you go downstairs and be sure all the doors and windows are locked?" she asked. "I know he hasn't been in the house, but I want to be sure we're safe."

"Yes, honey, I'll take care of it," Charles agreed. "You go ahead and get ready for bed, okay?" She nodded her head.

Charles put his slippers on and descended the stairs. *She has no idea the note was found in the cabinet. He was in the house. I'm glad she insisted I check the doors and windows.* Charles was downstairs for five minutes and then returned to his bedroom. "All doors and windows are locked. We're safe, Rose. Now go to sleep." He kissed her lightly on her lips. "I'll take care of this tomorrow."

Rose lay close to Charles, her arm draped over his torso. He lay quietly, praying for direction from God. Several minutes ticked by, and Rose's breath became slower and more even. He knew she'd fallen asleep. He gently moved her arm from his chest and quietly slipped out of bed. Not wanting to awaken anyone, he left the hallway light off. His foot touched the last step just as he heard a window break and the squeal of tires as a car sped away. He turned on the light, and at the same time he heard Rose scream.

"Stay there, Rose! Call 9-1-1." He looked upstairs and saw both Rose and KC standing together. The color had drained from their faces. "Call 9-1-1, now, Rose!" he shouted through clenched teeth.

CHAPTER 35

K C's cell phone marimba tone sounded. She looked at the caller ID and cringed. "Hello, Mr. Parsons." She rolled her eyes. *You're the last person I want to talk with today.* "Yes, that's correct. My stepfather called the police because someone threw a brick through the window.... Okay, I'll be at your office after work today."

*I don't know what or who is going to break me first: Logan Parsons or the stalker.* She slid the phone into her purse and prayed it wouldn't ring again. Work projects were behind schedule as her mind had wondered so much over the last few days. *Must focus! I must focus.* KC worked feverishly all morning. She vaguely heard the phone alert sound, reminding her of an appointment. She gathered her files, photos, purse, and laptop and was ready to leave when Logan Parsons walked in.

"Oh, I'm sorry, Mr. Parsons. I was leaving for an appointment. I thought we were meeting at your office this afternoon after I clocked out here." She was cordial but irritated.

"You'll remember I told you I could show up at your place of employment anytime I wanted, right?" His arrogance was as obvious as a firecracker. "Why don't you check with Goen and see if I can job shadow you today." It was a statement, not a question.

"You want to go with me on a business call?" KC questioned.

"That's what I said. Now go ask Goen if it's okay with him." She turned to walk away, and he added, "It will be. He's been through this with me and other felons."

KC explained the situation to Richard, and as predicted, he gave the okay.

"Okay, Mr. Parsons, let's go." KC put her briefcase and laptop on the backseat. She was surprised to see Logan open the car door for her. She sat down and pulled her long, slender legs into the car. "Thank you, sir. That was kind of you." *I still don't trust you.* He walked around and jumped into the seat beside her. *Okay, KC, he's waiting for you to do something wrong. Seat belt, mirror, no radio, don't speed.* Self-talk was the only thing that was going to get her through this afternoon. She backed out and headed toward her appointment. "Mr. Parsons, if you're going with me, how should I introduce you to my client?"

"You could say I'm your parole officer," he said with a smirk. "But," he said as he reached over and tapped her arm, "I suggest you say you're training me. I think that will be okay, don't you?"

He knew that touch on her arm was inappropriate, but he didn't care. He wanted to keep her off guard and at the same time wanted her to think he could be nice, if only occasionally.

Arriving at their destination, Parkside Fitness and Self-Defense, Logan walked around the car and opened the door for KC.

"Can I carry your laptop for you?" he asked.

"No, I'll be fine. Thank you for asking," she responded respectfully.

KC and Logan were greeted by the receptionist, and who asked them to be seated. Soon, they were shown into the manager's office. "Good afternoon, Mr. Hutsell," KC began. "Let me introduce you to a colleague, Logan Parsons. Mr. Parsons is job shadowing with me today. He'll just be observing." She glared at Parsons with a look that said, *Don't utter a word.*

The two men shook hands, and Logan sat quietly, watching KC make the presentation.

*Wow! She is good. She's good looking—no, she's great looking. And she knows her business. She is confident and knows how to close the deal. Boy, hate to admit it, but she might actually be a success story.* He watched as she completed the sales contract and slipped it across the table for Hutsell to sign.

*Yeah, she'll be a success story, and I can't let that happen.* Logan was plotting his next act of terror. *There are too many other POs who sign off on clients who eventually reoffend. I'm not going to let that happen. I don't care how attractive, smart, and efficient she is. She'll go back to prison if I have anything to do with it.*

"Thank you, Mr. Hutsell, I'll have the final draft of your webpage ready in a couple of days. I'll call and make an appointment, okay?"

"That sounds fine, KC. Thank you, and it was nice meeting you, Mr. Parsons."

KC and Logan walked to her car. Again, Logan opened her car door. After climbing in, he complimented KC on her presentation. "Good to see that the education you received at taxpayers' expense paid off. That was a good presentation. Keep that up and you will be a success in whatever field you choose."

"Thank you, Mr. Parsons." That was all she said. *I really don't want to talk with you, and I hope you'll get the hint with my silence.* They returned to her office. KC started to get out of the car, but Logan gripped her arm.

"Elliott, we still have some business to take care of. Please stay here."

KC sat back. The seat belt was loose across her chest. "Since gas prices are high, do you mind if I turn off the engine?"

"No, no. Go ahead. This shouldn't take long." He reached into his breast pocket and pulled out the police record. "Can you explain this?" He showed her the report.

KC scanned it. Everything looked accurate, and she responded, "The report says it all." She sighed. "Is there a problem?"

"As a matter of fact, there is. You or a family member have filed several police reports. It's almost as if you are—"

"What? Filing false reports?" She turned in her seat to face him. "How dare you make such an assumption! You have no idea how terrorized my mother has been. I've had to lie to her because I didn't want her to know the extent of the problem. But, of course, she found out. I'm being stalked, and I have no idea who or why." KC was so angry that her nostrils flared.

"Settle down, Elliott. I know you're being stalked. I want to offer you some self-defense classes. You think about it, okay? Let me know the next time we meet." He pulled the door handle and let himself out. He walked to his car, got in, and drove away.

*Well, I certainly didn't expect that. It's almost as if he cares.* She sat, reviewing their brief conversation. *I'll talk with Charles tonight. Maybe I should take self-defense classes.* Then she remembered the signed contract in her briefcase. *I'll contact Mr. Hutsell. It makes sense that I should go to Parkside Fitness and Self-Defense for lessons.* She nodded as she knew it was the right decision.

Logan drove around the block. *Yep, she'll learn some simple self-defense moves.* He laughed aloud as he sat in his car. *But she'll never know I have a black belt in karate.*

CHAPTER 36

"Charles, I know you're behind me," Rose stated softly. "Whatever do you want?" She spun around quickly and swatted him with the dish towel. "Why do you think you can sneak up on me? I know the fragrance of your aftershave." She smiled, slipped closer to him, and kissed him on his cheek. "You look like the cat that swallowed the canary." She kissed him again. "Charles, what are you up to?"

"Rose, I've got some news on the stalker." His gentle smile faded. "Could I have a cup of coffee?"

"Of course. Are you going to tell me what's going on?" She poured them both a cup of coffee. Handing Charles his cup, she added, "Now, sit and illuminate me."

He sighed heavily. "Okay, I hired a private investigator several weeks ago. Tracking this guy has been difficult because he's been using a voice-altering program and throwaway cell phones. The PI knew he'd make a mistake sometime, and he finally did. The only thing is the guy is a drug addict and doesn't have two pennies to rub together to buy the program or to keep buying throwaway phones."

"But if you know who the stalker is, why can't you have the police arrest him?"

Charles breathed deeply and shook his head. "I wanted to, but the PI said no."

185

"He what? Didn't want to report him to the police? Is he crazy?" Rose was incredulous. She shoved herself back from the table and walked out on the deck, slamming the door.

Charles let her go. He watched her pace the deck. Her lips were moving, but he heard nothing. He knew she was praying and he was not going to disturb her and God. He sat quietly, watching and offering his own prayer. KC had been being stalked since she'd been released from prison. He noticed that Rose had been losing weight and that dark circles had formed under her eyes. Gulping down the last of his coffee, he saw Rose fall. His chair fell backward as he jumped up. Running to the deck, he pulled her into an embrace. "Rose, honey, speak to me." She didn't respond. He laid her down, ran back to the kitchen, and grabbed his cell phone. Dialing 9-1-1, he also snatched a throw to slip over her. "Rose, honey. Rose, the ambulance is on the way." He looked up and prayed, "Please, God. Don't take her. I need her." He wept.

"Mmm, what happened?" moaned Rose. Her voice was quiet.

"Oh, God. Thank you!" Charles shouted. "Thank you." He kissed Rose on her cheek. "Oh, honey. I think you passed out. The ambulance is on the way."

"What foolishness! Help me up." She struggled to stand.

"No, lay still. You need to be checked out. I don't know if you hurt yourself when you fell."

"I'm cold."

As he pulled the throw blanket over her, he could hear the sirens and knew help was on the way. "Stay here. Help's comin'."

He met the paramedics at the door.

"She's on the deck. This way." He showed them the way. While they were tending to Rose, he called KC.

"No, I don't know what's wrong.... They're going to take her to the hospital to do tests to find out what caused her to collapse. She'll be going to Central Hospital. I'll meet you there. Drive carefully. Bye."

The paramedics had Rose ready for transporting to the hospital by the time he finished talking with KC.

"Wait!" he shouted at the paramedics. They stopped. "I need to see her." They stepped aside as he approached the gurney. "Honey, I'll see you at the hospital. KC's going to meet us there. I love you." He kissed her on the forehead and cheek. He whispered, "I love you more than I can begin to tell."

Stepping aside, he nodded to the paramedics. They slipped her into the back of the ambulance, slammed the doors shut, and jumped into the cab. Sirens blaring, the ambulance rushed Rose to the hospital. Charles hurried to the garage in such a hurry that he almost forgot to open the door. He tapped the steering wheel while muttering, "Hurry up, hurry up." Backing out, he squealed the tires on the pavement. As he sped down the road, he heard a voice say, "Cast all your cares on me. I care for you." He turned to the passenger seat but didn't see anyone. Yet he was certain he'd heard someone talk. Then he heard, "I care for you. Rose is in my care. She'll be okay. Slow down."

Charles brought the car to a stop. So much had happened so quickly, tears stung his eyes. "Oh, God, I know you care for Rose, and me, and KC. I love Rose so much. I was so afraid I'd lose her. Thanks for reminding me that you are caring for her. I've gotta get to the hospital, but yes, I'll slow down." He put the car in gear, pulled away from the curb, and drove the speed limit to the emergency room parking lot.

KC was already at the hospital. She met Charles at the door. "What happened, Charles? They won't let me see her." She had hurried to the doors but was denied admittance.

"KC, your mom is going to be okay. I've got it from a good source. She's going to be okay." He squeezed her shoulder.

"Then you've talked with the doctor?"

"No, I talked with the great physician." She turned to look at Charles. Her eyes narrowed and her brows knitted together, and she looked quizzically into his eyes.

"On my way here, I was speeding. I heard a voice tell me she was going to be okay. God told me she was going to be okay and that I should slow down." He saw KC roll her eyes. "Yeah, I know you think I'm crazy, but you'll see. There is nothing seriously wrong with your mom. Here, let's sit and wait for the doctor."

He bought KC a cup of coffee and then remembered that she didn't drink coffee. He returned to the soda machines and bought her bottled water. They unconsciously took turns walking to the emergency room door and peering inside. It seemed as if hours had passed, but it was only forty-five minutes.

"Mr. Phillips," a nurse said as she touched his shoulder. "Dr. Ali will see you now. Your wife is in cubicle seven."

Charles and KC almost knocked her down trying to get to the woman they both loved.

"Dr. Ali, I'm Charles Phillips, Rose's husband, and this is KC, Rose's daughter." They shook hands. "What's going on?"

Dr. Ali removed the latex gloves and tossed them in the trash. "I think she just fainted, but I want to take some additional tests." She pinched the skin on Rose's hand and added, "She is a bit dehydrated, so we're giving her fluids to hydrate her. I'd like to keep her overnight for observation." She turned to leave but stopped. "Rose told me she's had to deal with quite a bit of stress. She needs to have her life destressed or ..." She gave them a warning look and then left.

CHAPTER 37

*A*lleviate stress. *Oh, God, I don't know how to do that. I'm the one causing all the stress. How can I possibly alleviate Mom's stress?* KC paced the hallway, waiting for an opportunity to talk with Charles. He seemed to have a steadying calmness with Rose. KC's moving out was not an option as far as Charles was concerned. In his opinion, living alone placed KC in greater danger. *Perhaps this situation with Mom will change his point of view. He might be glad to see me go.* She stopped and, gazing out the window, began gnawing on her lower right lip. *Where would I go? I still have that huge restitution fine to repay. Oh, crud! I'll have to get a room at a flophouse.* Leaning her forehead against the cool window, KC sighed heavily. A tear trickled down her cheek, and she flicked it away.

Charles slipped up behind her. KC jumped and spun around when he placed his hand on her shoulder. "I'm sorry, KC. I didn't mean to scare you." The silence between them was so profound and tense that they could barely breathe. It was Charles who broke the silence. "I said your name several times. It was clear you were in a world of your own. I didn't want to intrude. The nurses say we should go home. Your mother is stable and needs rest."

KC nodded and started to speak when Charles continued, "I'm guessing you haven't had anything to eat, right?" She nodded again.

"Then let's stop and get something, okay? Name your favorite spot—anywhere but fast food."

KC smiled weakly. "It's too late to go for something heavy to eat. So"—she scrunched her lips together thoughtfully—"oh, I don't know. Let's go to Kelso's."

"Kelso's? That greasy spoon?"

"Yeah, the greasy spoon. They've got some great scones and a variety of teas, and they have hot coffee too." She smiled smugly. "See you there." She was down the hallway before he could reply.

KC was already seated when Charles arrived. She'd ordered her favorite flavored tea and a cup of coffee for Charles. "Hope you don't mind, but I asked them for decaf for you. Thought you might not need the full octane tonight." She tried to joke, but the smile on her face didn't reach her eyes. There was no twinkle. She sat quietly, twisting the paper napkin.

Charles reached across the table and put his large, calloused hand over her small, long fingers. "KC, we're going to get through this. I promise you." She pulled her hand away from his and quietly wrapped her hands around her cup. She sat soundlessly, peering at but not really reading the menu. The waitress arrived and asked if she wanted the usual. Nodding her assent, KC barely acknowledged her presence. After she and Charles had placed their order, KC finally broke the stillness.

"I really think I should move out, Charles." He started to speak, but KC glanced up. Her gaze, though not hostile, stopped him. "No, listen," she said, raising her right index finger. "You heard the doctor say that Mom's level of stress needed to be lowered. The only way I see that happening is if I move out." She stirred her tea aimlessly. The only noise came from the tables being cleared and other diners' conversations, but KC was oblivious to their presence.

The waitress brought the scones and the check to the table. Charles bit into a scone, and his eyes furrowed while he munched. He tipped his head first to the right and then the left. "Oh, KC, this is delicious. What do they use? It's not raisins." He ate a little more and announced, "It's cranberry, isn't it?"

A smirk crossed KC's lips. She nodded. "You're quite an aficionado, aren't you? But you're also trying to change the subject."

He swallowed his bite and sipped some coffee. "I don't think it's a good idea for you to move out until we solve this problem." He folded his hands together and steepled his index fingers. With his fingers over his lips, he added, "I've talked with the private investigator, and he thinks he's getting some good leads. He thinks it might be another month or so before he has all the evidence."

"But what about Mom?"

The last of the scone was in his mouth. He raised his finger while he finished it. Then he finished his coffee. "Your mother is going to a counselor and will be on some medications that will help calm her nerves. I've talked with the pastor, and we've made arrangements with some of her friends to keep her busy for the next few weeks. One woman is redecorating her house—"

"Well, 'nough said. That will keep Mom busy for weeks." KC's face lit up, and a smile now reaching her eyes broke across her face. She dropped her head slightly and added, "Charles, thank you for being so understanding. You are so good for Mom, and you are good *to* her, too." She reached for the check to pay it, but it was gone. "I was going to pay for the scones and coffee. Give me the check. I insist."

"I don't have it." He held up his hands, proving his innocence. He caught the waitress's attention. "Could we have our check, please?"

"Oh, the gentleman over there …" She turned and pointed to a booth on the opposite wall. It was empty. "I guess he wanted it to be a surprise."

Charles nearly knocked her down trying to get to the door. But whoever the man was, he was gone. Charles pulled his cell phone from his pocket and punched in a number. "Hey, it's Charles Phillips. I think the stalker followed us to Kelso's Café. Yeah, we were ready to pay for our coffee, and the waitress said another man had paid .... No, I didn't see anyone. You want me to do what... Okay, I'll see if they have a surveillance camera. Then what... Okay. I'll wait here. Listen, you better solve this quickly. My wife's in the hospital. The stress has gotten to be too much. Find this guy and do it fast."

Charles stood in the darkness of the parking lot and tried to slow his breathing. His heart felt like it was beating as fast as a drummer beating a marching cadence. He turned to see KC exiting the door. "No, KC, we're going back in there. The investigator is on the way over." They walked back in and sat in the booth they'd just vacated.

"What's goin' on?" she demanded. "Tell me, what's goin' on?"

Charles ignored her but called the waitress over. "Your manager in?" She nodded in the direction of the kitchen. "Tell her I need to see her, now." He barked the order. It was harsher then he intended. *I'll apologize later.*

"Sir, is there a problem?" A diminutive woman of about forty years and with slightly graying brown hair stood by the booth. She had on a white apron and a pencil stuck between her ear and the earpiece of her glasses.

"First, when we're done talking, would you please ask the server to return? I spoke sharply to her, and I'd like to apologize." Assured the waitress would return, Charles began to explain the situation but at the same time be as vague as necessary. "I've got a buddy coming over to check out your surveillance camera. You've got one, right?"

She nodded in the direction of the camera and interjected, "We've had people walk out without paying. This gets them almost every time. Do you need a warrant?"

"Not unless you decide not to cooperate." He paused a second or two. "Do you have any children?" She nodded. "Then if your daughter"—he raised his left eyebrow as if to ask if she had a daughter—"was in danger, wouldn't—"

"Absolutely! You've got my cooperation." She looked at KC

and touched her gently on the shoulder. "You're in here a lot, aren't you? You like that sweet wild orange tea, as I remember, right? I'll bring you a cup." She turned to Charles. "Another cup of coffee? It's on the house."

"Thank you. Now, about the server …"

"I'll send her over." The two ladies spoke in hushed tones. The waitress approached with coffee, hot water, and tea.

"I want to apologize for barking at you. I shouldn't have been so demanding, but it was important for me to speak with the manager as quickly as possible." The bell at the top of the door announced the arrival of another guest. "Oh, please bring another cup of coffee and tell the manager I need to talk with her again. And I'd like you to have this." He handed her a ten-dollar bill. She smiled as she walked to the kitchen.

"KC, this is Nate Conover. He's a licensed private investigator." They shook hands.

The manager returned. She had in her hands a VHS tape. "Hope this helps." She started to walk away but turned. "Hey, do you need to look at it right now? I've got a television you can use."

"Yeah, that'd be great," Charles announced. The three hurried to the office and watched the tape intently. Nate pushed the button to fast forward it to tonight. The seconds ticked off the clock, but it seemed as if it were minutes. When the tape showed KC entering, Nate stopped the tape.

"KC, I want you to watch carefully. Is there anyone on the tape that looks familiar?" The television was capable of playing the tape in slow motion, so they watched it that way several times. The manager poked her head in the office and asked if they'd seen anything. She had just closed the door when KC leaned in closer.

"Can you play that again?" she asked Nate. He rewound it and pushed the play button. "I think I know that guy." She pointed at a guy wearing a black hoodie and a ball cap. She quivered and rubbed her arms as if she were cold. "I've seen him a couple times. I'm almost certain."

"You know him?" Nate asked.

"Well, I don't really know him. I've seen him around."

Charles put his hands on KC's shoulders and looked deeply into her eyes. "Think! Where have you seen him? Think!"

"I'm trying, Charles." Tears began to flood her eyes. She covered her face and breathed deeply. "I *think*"—she drew out the word—"I think he used to work at the children's museum. I think Lisa called him Stewart."

"Are you sure?" Nate questioned. He was so excited that his heart was racing like a thoroughbred horse's. If KC was even slightly sure, it gave him something to work with. "Do you know his last name?"

She shook her head slowly and her eyes narrowed. "No, I don't know his last name, but Lisa would. Want me to call her?"

"No, that's not necessary. I'll get it. You two need to go home and get some rest. Okay?" Charles held KC's elbow as they left.

Nate stayed behind to talk with the manager. "Do you mind if I keep this tape?" he asked as he was slipping it into his coat pocket.

"Hey, if it helps catch that guy, go ahead."

CHAPTER 38

T he children's museum opened at ten o'clock, and Nate Conover was the first one to enter. He hadn't been supportive of the museum's being built, especially since it added to his property tax, but as he browsed the various exhibits, he was pleased with what he saw. He took his time looking around.

Nate noticed that every employee had a picture ID on a lanyard, which was worn around their necks. However, he didn't see anyone who looked like the man in the video. He walked to the gift store and purchased a toy. Glancing over his shoulder, he noticed that no one else was in the store except for the cashier. "Miss, could you tell me where I could find the administrative offices? I'd like to apply for a job." It was a lie; he didn't want a job. He hoped it would get him access to the museum curator.

"Sure, turn right and go to the end of the hallway. The elevator is to the left. Take the elevator to the fourth floor," she explained. "The elevator opens to the executive suite. Just tell the receptionist what you want." She turned to straighten some shelves. "Don't think there's any positions open, but it won't hurt to try."

Nate walked into the main part of the museum and browsed the exhibits again. Eventually, he walked to the elevator and took it to the fourth floor. As the doors opened, Nate walked to the desk.

"Hi, I'm sorry to trouble you, but I'm looking for the curator,

Lisa … I'm sorry. I don't know her last name." He reached into his vest pocket and pulled out his license. "I'm Nate Conover, private investigator." He smiled and added, "Would you please ask your boss if she'd see me? It's really important."

It was the receptionist's custom to call her boss on the intercom. However, this was an exception since Nate had flashed his PI license. "Please have a seat. I'll be right back," she replied. Her eyes were filled with questions, but she knew better than to ask.

Knocking lightly on the door, she waited for Lisa to respond. "Yes, come in." The door was opened enough to allow the receptionist to explain who was present. Lisa scooted her chair back and walked to the door.

"Mr. Conover, you're welcome to come in, but I'm sure I can't help you."

"Lisa—I'm sorry, I'd call you Miss but I don't know your last name."

"The name is Borders, Lisa Borders. You can call me Dr. Borders," she answered coldly. She glared at him. "What is it you think I can do for you?"

"Dr. Borders, I've been hired by Charles Phillips. He's the stepfather of a friend of yours." He paused to let it sink in. He watched as her eyebrow arched quizzically. "You do know KC Elliott, right?

Lisa nodded slightly. "Please be seated." She returned to her chair. "Yes, I know KC. Why are you investigating her? She's done her time, and I thought she was doing well, keeping her appointments with her parole officer. I thought she'd kept her nose clean." She glanced down at her desk. When she raised her head, there were tears in her eyes. "I really wanted KC to do well. I can't tell you how disappointed I am that she's in trouble again."

Nate cleared his throat. "Hmph, actually, Lis … I'm sorry, Dr. Borders, I'm not investigating KC. She isn't in trouble. But trouble seems to be following her." Lisa's head tilted to the right. "That's right. You see, KC is being stalked. We think the stalker is or was an employee of the children's museum." He pulled out a picture of Stewart. "Know this guy?"

Lisa nodded slightly. "Yes, he was an employee."

Nate stared at the photo and rubbed his index finger over his upper lip. "Don't s'pose you can tell me why you let 'im go?" It was more a statement than a question.

"No, I'm sorry. Legally, I can't. I'm sure you understand." She pulled open the file drawer, retrieved a folder, and put it on her desk. "You'll excuse me if I speak to my administrative assistant for a few moments, won't you. I'll be right back. I need to ask her a question."

"No, you go right ahead. I'll wait here."

She walked out, leaving the door open just a little. While she was gone, Nate pulled the folder toward him and opened it. His eyes narrowed as he scanned the report. He slipped it back into the folder and put the folder in its original location. He sat back and crossed his legs, arms folded on the chair arms and his hands pressed together lightly touching his lips. When Lisa returned to her office, she announced, "Mr. Conover, I believe our business is done. Please see yourself out." The frostiness in her voice was gone.

"Thanks for nothing," Nate announced loudly enough for the administrative assistant to hear. "I'd appreciate it if you didn't say anything to KC." This was spoken quietly. He winked conspiratorially and then closed the door.

As he left, he looked at Lisa's administrative assistant. "Tough lady!" He pressed the down button and waited. Stepping into the elevator, he smiled to himself. *I think we've got him. Gotta be sure though. Don't think he's smart enough to pull this off himself and don't know why he'd be stalking KC Elliott.*

CHAPTER 39

Lisa had been helpful in identifying the alleged stalker as Stewart Alexander. Nate immediately went to the circuit court office. He requested Stewart's file and set up shop at the far end of the counter. Stewart had a lengthy rap sheet; most were petty crimes. But Nate noticed that he had several allegations of stalking, all of which had been dismissed. As he scanned over the files, his eyes narrowed.

"Hey, how long to get a copy of this file?" he asked the clerk.

"Wow! That's a big file," she answered. Glancing around the office, she noticed it wasn't too busy. "I might be able to get it done before the end of the day. Will that help?"

"That'd be great! I'll be back by three o'clock. If that's a problem, give me a call, will ya?" He handed her a business card.

"Yeah, that'll work, Conover. But I've got hundreds of your cards. You can keep this one."

Nate glanced at his watch. His lip twitched as he realized that he didn't have enough time to accomplish anything before picking up the file on Stewart. His stomach growled, reminding him he hadn't eaten. Dodging cars, he walked across the street to the diner. It was a popular spot for police, attorneys, and courthouse employees. He sidled up to the counter. A pert, college-age woman asked for his order.

"Oh, I don't know," he said, scanning the menu. "Guess I'll try the special. It's good, right?" He winked at her.

"Yes, sir. It's good. Wouldn't be the special if it wasn't good."

There was a lull in business, so the server returned to chat with Nate. "So, what's your job? Attorney or cop? Ain't seen you in here."

"Well, I'm not an attorney, but I used to be a cop. I know the food here is always good." He stopped himself from adding what he was thinking. *And the waitresses are usually good-looking too.*

"Whatcha doin' now if you ain't a cop?"

"I'm a PI, private investigator."

She was curious. "Why ain't you a cop? You kill someone?"

"Yeah, but that's not why I'm not a cop." His answer was terse. "He tried to kill me. It was kill or be killed." A long pause followed, and then he added, "I turned to alcohol, and that's why I'm not a cop."

"Well, Mister," she said, dropping her voice, "if you're not police, can you still help people?"

"Depends," he answered.

"Well, don't look now, but that guy over in the booth near the mirror? He's been buggin' me."

Nate's eyebrows furrowed deeply. "What do you mean? How's he bugging you?"

"Keeps asking me for a date. I tell him no. He grabs my wrist and asks again. He won't take no for an answer. Sometimes he swats me on the butt."

Just then, the man said, "Hey, sweetie, how 'bout another cup of joe?"

"Be right with you." She turned to get the carafe.

"No, I mean now. I want coffee, now!" he demanded.

Nate had heard enough. He jumped off the counter stool and walked decisively over to the table. He leaned over the table, placed his hands flat on it, and firmly said, "The lady said she'd be right with you. She'll be with you as soon as she can. And you don't need to be demanding service … or dates. You keep your hands off her.

She doesn't want to date you." Nate glimpsed over his shoulder. "Now, I think you've had enough coffee. Pay the lady and get out of here. If I hear you have pestered her again, I'll have the cops arrest you."

"Yeah, you and who else?"

Nate grabbed the man by the collar, pulled him out of the booth, and led him to the door. "Don't come back, ever!" he shouted. He watched the man stagger down the street and out of sight. Returning to the counter, Nate sat down to eat his lunch.

The waitress was stunned. She stood open-mouthed as she watched the action.

"Hey, listen, lunch is free today, mister. Thanks."

Nate sat quietly as he completed his lunch. He tossed a five-dollar bill on the counter as he left.

Returning to the courthouse, he was approached by a young man. His employee identification indicated that he was Logan Parsons. Logan stretched his arm out to shake hands with Nate. "Word travels fast. Just heard what you did to that guy at the diner. He's been bugging that girl for weeks. Nothing we said to him seemed to deter him. I hear you really put him in his place."

"It was nothing. Might have been my size that got his attention," Nate answered.

"Whatever. Anything I can do to help you?" Logan asked, following him into the courthouse.

"Don't think so. Just getting a copy of some guy's file."

"Hey, Conover," the clerk barked. "I've got that file copied for ya." She shoved it toward him. "Ya owe the county fifteen bucks."

He opened his wallet, pulled out a ten and five, handed them to her, and replied, "Hey, I need a receipt, okay?" He put the receipt in his pocket and left.

Logan watched Nate turn to leave and then asked, "Whose file did you copy?"

"It was Stewart Alexander. Know him?"

"Yeah, he's a junkie and petty thief."

Arriving home, Nate changed out of his dress clothes and into his lawn working clothes. *I want to do some surveillance on this character. Don't want him to get suspicious of me.* He not only dressed like a bum, but he smeared dirt on his face and used some deer urine spray. Satisfied that he looked and smelled like a homeless person, he checked the address Stewart had given on his employment application. Nate tossed a couple of black plastic bags filled with clothes, a blanket, and a pillow into his 1990 Dodge Monaco. The dents, broken right taillight, and duct-taped back-up light were always a good cover-up.

He drove to Pigeon Hill, the sleazier part of town. Taking a swig of whiskey, he let it drip down his chin and spit the remainder on his blue jeans. Nate parked his car down the block from Stewart's apartment. Nightfall came, and Nate saw the lights go out in his quarry's apartment. He quietly left his car. He'd already selected the next spot where he could keep an eye on Stewart, and it wasn't long before a Ford Focus pulled up. Stewart climbed in and the car drove off, but not before Nate memorized the license plate.

Nate was satisfied that he'd gathered good information. He returned home and undressed in the garage. After he showered, he called Charles Phillips. No one was home, so he left a message.

"Hey, Phillips, Conover speaking. Wanted you to know I think we're on the right path. I've got a license number to look up tomorrow morning. I know this has been going on for months, but I think the end is coming. Later." He punched the end button.

Nate mulled over the evening. *I'm pretty sure Stewart is the stalker, but I'm no closer to figuring out the motive. As far as I can tell, he has no real connection to her. He didn't work with her, didn't go to school with her, and wasn't working or an inmate at the same prison she was assigned to. He doesn't and has never worked for Advanced Web Designs.* He opened a bottle of Diet Pepsi. *It is cases like this that make me wish I hadn't given up drinking.* He knocked back a gulp of his drink and belched. *What am I missing?* He mashed his lips together in disgust. He pulled out a small notepad and began making notes. He splayed his hand through his hair. *First thing in the morning, I've got to find out whose car Stewart got into tonight.* He finished the soda, flipped on the television for the news. As he listened to the weather report, he unbuttoned his shirt, took off his jeans, and dressed for bed. He tossed his dirty-smelling clothes into the garage. *Will have to use these again, I'm sure. No use washing them.*

Sleep came easily for Nate at first. Then, suddenly, he was sitting up in his bed with sweat beaded on his forehead and his heart racing. *Good grief! Will these nightmares ever stop!* He traipsed to the bathroom and splashed cold water over his face. It'd been three years since he'd woken with the barrel of a .357 Magnum pointed at him. He moved in time to miss the slug meant to kill him. A fight ensued, and Nate wrestled the gun from the intruder, but the perpetrator rushed him. Nate had no other option than to shoot him. The perpetrator died. Nate was cleared of any charges, but this episode drove him to drink. His alcoholism was the reason he was discharged from the police force. From time to time, the nightmare reared its ugly head, and tonight happened to be one of those nights. Nate fixed himself a cup of coffee and began scanning through Stewart's file again.

"Hey, who's the guy hangin' out in the stairway?"

"Man, I don't know. Some bum, I s'pose," Stewart answered. "Ya know, I don't live in the best area. Got bums hangin' in the stairway and park all the time. What's the problem?"

"I don't have a problem, but you might." A silence dropped between the two men. Stewart reached in his shirt pocket, pulled out a cigarette, and lit it. Logan slammed on the brakes. "Whaddya think you're doin'? You know I don't smoke and don't allow smoking in my car. Throw it out! Now!"

Stewart pinched off the end of the cigarette and tossed it out. "What's up your crawl?" he asked. "You're in a foul mood."

Logan ignored Stewart's questions.

"Listen, you need to lay off that Elliott broad for a while. She needs to think she's safe."

"I need money for a hit of coke," Stewart replied.

"Not gettin' it from me," Logan grumbled. "No work, no pay. You knew that from the start."

"But ya don't understand, I need a hit. Need it tonight," he demanded.

"Not tonight. Not givin' ya any money tonight. I've got your number. I'll call in a couple of weeks." Logan pulled to the curb. "Now, get out."

Stewart opened the door and slipped one leg out. Glaring at Logan he retorted, "Just remember, Mr. Bigshot, I got something on you too—aiding and abetting a criminal. Bet your boss would like to know all about your shenanigans." He stepped out of the car and shot back one more crack, "Don't think I won't do it, either." He slammed the door.

Logan drove away, but Stewart's threat concerned him. He would certainly lose his job and most assuredly go to prison. He slammed his hand against the steering wheel and swore. "I hate that man. I absolutely hate him. But he's right. He could ruin me." He drove around the block and looked for Stewart.

Standing with one foot against the building, Stewart appeared to be expecting Logan's return. He smugly waved as Logan pulled up and motioned to him to get in.

Stewart opened the door. "Think you can spare some money now?"

"Just get in, jerk!" Logan drove around for some fifteen minutes before stopping near a deserted parking lot. "Here's a hundred dollars. Try to budget it. Can't give you more right now. And stay away from Elliott. Got it?"

Steward knew something was going on and continued harassing Logan.

"So, what's really happening? Fallin' in love with the broad?"

"Are you crazy? I'm not in love with her. She thinks she's so smart, so uppity. No, but stay away from her—or else."

"Or else what?"

"You don't wanna know. Now get out of here." Logan revved the engine and pulled away.

CHAPTER 40

Logan slammed his apartment door shut and nearly pulled the refrigerator door off its hinges. He pulled out a beer and twisted off the lid. He almost finished the beer with one long gulp. With a loud thud, he put the bottle on the counter. Pulling open cabinets, he tried to decide what to eat. Nothing sounded good, so he ordered a pizza.

While waiting for the pizza to arrive, Logan mulled over the brief conversation with Nate. He pounded the chair arms in anger and frustration, asking, "Why in the world was Conover investigating Stewart?" Logan knew Nate's reputation. Although no longer a cop, Nate's expertise had helped solve several cold cases.

A knock at the door disrupted Logan's thoughts. Jerking open the door, he barked, "It's about time. What took you so long?"

"Sorry, sir. There are two Tharp Streets in town. I went to the wrong one. That'll be $13.50."

"You're such an idiot! There's only one Tharp Street; the other one is Tharp Road. Don't you have a GPS?" He thrust the money at the boy. "No tip tonight! Get out of here!" He slammed the door and flipped off the porch light.

Logan's foul mood continued. "Why'd that pizza joint hire such an idiot!" Pulling open the pizza box, he yanked off a piece and took a bite. "It's cold. I'm not surprised. Can't find decent, dependable help any longer." Spitting out the pizza, he reached for the phone and punched in the phone number for the pizza parlor. The phone rang about six times before it was answered. Logan didn't even wait for the lady to complete the greeting. "I want to talk with the manager. Now!"

"I'm sorry, but he's busy right now. Can I have him—"

"I said now! Or I'll report your joint to the health department," he threatened

He waited a couple of minutes before hearing the manager answer, "Can I help you?"

"I ordered a pizza nearly an hour and a half ago. When it was delivered, it was cold. Your delivery boy got lost. Can't you provide your drivers with a GPS? What kind of joint are you operating?" The longer he ranted, the more furious he became.

"I'm sorry your pizza was cold. We'd like to keep your business, so I'd like to give you a free pizza. Would that correct the problem, sir?"

"Not if the driver is going to get lost. Why don't you throw in a GPS for each of your drivers? That might entice me to continue ordering your pizzas."

"I can't guarantee a GPS for all the drivers. Tell you what, I'll give you five free pizzas." The manager paused. "If you give me your name and address, I'll make a note so your next five orders will be free."

Logan gruffly provided the manager with the information.

*There's nothing in this file that suggests why he's tailing KC. Oh, there are a couple of arrests for stalking, but they were dismissed.* He drew his lips to the side. *I wonder if I ought to follow up on those?* He finished off his coffee and flipped on the television. After watching the tube for five minutes, Nate was asleep again.

It was about eight o'clock in the morning when the phone jangled Nate awake.

"Conover here," he answered, rubbing his face.

CHAPTER 41

Nate met Charles at the diner across from the courthouse. "Well, Conover, whaddya got? Do you know who the stalker is?" Charles always got down to business "Nate, I like you, heard good things about you, but this is affecting Rose's health. KC's putting up a good front, but I can see it's distressing her too. It's got to stop." He paused for a sip of coffee.

"Charles, I think I'm onto something, but I still have to prove my assumptions. Give me another month, month and a half. I think I can solve this issue by then." Nate looked intently at Charles and added, "I'm really not dragging this out. I've got to be sure I've got the right person, and then that person will be charged and convicted. Okay?" Silence hung between Charles and Nate despite the clatter of plates and cups in the diner.

"Okay, but you've got to finalize this. Understood?" He gulped the last of his coffee, stood, and tossed down a ten-dollar bill. "That should take care of the check." He walked out without so much as a glance toward Nate or the server.

"You back again? Whatever you're workin' on must be pretty

important. Don't usually see you here this often." It was the clerk Nate had talked with the previous day.

"Well, I need some more information." He lowered his voice. "Ya know that case you printed for me yesterday?" She nodded. "Well, I need more specific information."

"Okay, whaddya need?" She dragged a writing pad over and pulled out the pencil she'd put behind her ear.

"Stewart Alexander had two reports of stalking lodged against him. I'd like to know who filed the complaints and why the cases were dropped. Think you can help me?"

"Gee, I don't know. I'll check with the clerk of courts—"

"No, I don't want anyone to know you're doing this. I'll give you a C-note if you can get this for me. Okay?"

"Well, I could certainly use that. I'll see what I can do."

Nate smiled, gave her a thumbs-up, and left.

*That went well. Hope my next stop is as successful.* He slipped into his car, started it up, and pulled out of the parking deck. He circled the parking lot at the police station until he found a space and checked his notes from the previous evening. Nate walked into the station with an expected cockiness. "Hey, Chief." He called all administrative assistants "chief." He believed they knew as much if not more that their bosses. The tall, thin lady with graying hair looked up.

"Yes, what can I do for you?" she inquired.

He pulled out a wad of bills and slipped them to her. "I need someone to tell me who this license plate belongs to." He glanced over his shoulder, knowing that what he was asking was probably impossible and illegal but worth a try.

She glared at Nate. "I know who you are, and I know that you know you are asking me to break the law. Take your money and leave. If you ever come back here asking me to break the law, I'll call my boss."

"Fine. It was worth a try." He shot her a quick smile.

*Strike one. I really didn't think I'd be successful. I doubt I'll get much help from the Clerk of Courts Office either. But I've got to try.* He climbed into his car and returned to the courthouse. The assistant clerk he'd talked with earlier glanced up, stood, and walked his direction.

"Well?" Nate queried.

She smashed her lips together and shook her head. "Sorry, the official record didn't give the names of the complainants. Don't know if you'd find out any more information from the clerk that was in the courtroom. Sorry, that's the best I can do."

"Well, thanks for nothing," he growled. Although he didn't get an answer, he slipped her fifty dollars. "I appreciate your effort." He spun around on his heels and left.

Since he had left the department, Nate found that he did his best thinking at church. Community Church allowed Alcoholics Anonymous chapters to meet in their fellowship hall. The club asked Nate to be the liaison with the church. If problems arose, it was Nate's responsibility to talk with the pastor or trustee chairperson. Nate preferred to talk with the pastor, and in that capacity, Nate had become friends with the pastor. During one of their conversations, the pastor informed Nate that the sanctuary was always open for prayer or contemplation. Nate found himself in that place of solitude quite often.

Today would be no exception. Having had his two simplistic solutions shut down, Nate sought out his place of solace. Sitting quietly in the third pew from the front, Nate mulled over the information he'd collected. He reached for a pew Bible and simply prayed, *Give me direction, please. I don't deserve your help, but I need it. KC, Rose, and Charles need this nightmare to end. Please, give me advice.* He'd never been much of a churchgoer, but he knew he really needed divine intervention. He let the Bible fall open and read, "Trust in the Lord and do good; dwell in the land and enjoy safe pasture. Take delight in the Lord, and he will give you the desires of your heart. Commit your way to the Lord; trust in him and he will do this: He will make your righteous reward shine like the dawn, your vindication like the noonday sun. Be still before the Lord and wait patiently for him." He sighed heavily and prayed, *I don't know how to do this, God. I've always done things my way. I don't know how to trust you. How do I know you'll give me the right answer?* He was so intent in his prayer that he didn't hear the door open. He heard a man clear his throat. He quickly returned the Bible to its place and stood. "Oh, hi, Pastor. Didn't hear you come in. How are you?"

"I'm fine. But I sense you have a troubling problem." He let the statement hang between them as he sat down in the pew behind Nate. Silence was broken only by the shuffling of shoes.

"Pastor, I've got a case that really needs resolution. But every break I get seems to be shut down because of the law. It's the law I've pledged to uphold. I don't know how to solve the case without breaking the law." He ran his hand through his hair. "I even offered bribes to people also sworn to uphold the law. Fortunately, their morals were higher than mine." He let a sarcastic laugh slip out. "I'm so desperate, I've decided to try prayer. Humph! Can't even get God to help me."

"Nate, I don't know what your case is, but I can assure you that God does and God will help you." He reached inside his suit jacket, pulled out his smart phone, flipped through a couple pages of apps, and clicked on one. "The Bible often gives us answers to our problems. The psalmist wrote, 'Trust in the Lord and do good; dwell in the land and enjoy safe pasture. Take delight in the Lord, and he will give you the desires of your heart. Commit your way to the Lord; trust in him and he will do this: He will make your righteous reward shine like the dawn, your vindication like the noonday sun. Be still before the Lord and wait patiently for him.'"

"That's the same scripture I just read," he sighed again. "I don't get it. I don't understand it." He turned to face his friend. "What's it mean? Why don't I feel like I'm getting any direction?"

The pastor began to break down the verses. "'Trust in the Lord: Nate, do you trust in God?" He let Nate think about the question. "I don't mean, do you believe in God. Do you trust God?"

Nate shrugged his shoulders. "I don't really know. I do believe in God, but I don't know that I trust God."

"Another verse says, 'Commit your way to the Lord; trust in him and he will do this: He will make your righteous reward shine like the dawn, your vindication like the noonday sun. Be still before the Lord and wait patiently for him.' The problem with us is that we like to think we can handle all of life's challenges. Right?" He waited for Nate to respond.

"Yeah, I guess you're right."

"Well, when we try to do things in our own knowledge and with our own abilities, we often fail. So, I suggest you think about asking for God's help. Okay?"

"I'll think about it, Pastor." Nate stood and shook hands with the pastor. "I'll try to do that, but I might need your help occasionally. If you don't mind, I'll sit here for a while."

"Not at all, Nate. You can stay here as long as you need." He reached into his pocket and pulled out a business card. "If you need anything, any time, give me a call."

The pastor left, and Nate sat quietly. A sense of peace flowed throughout Nate's body, and a smirk spread across his face. "Thanks, God. I think I know how to get the information I need."

CHAPTER 42

J oyce Goen realized that KC was humming. She hadn't heard her humming for weeks. *God, I thank you for bringing KC into our lives. Richard and I love her like a daughter. It's so good to hear her humming. Thank you for protecting her. Please keep your arms of protection around her.* As she finished preparing tea, she heard KC walking toward the break room. "Hi, there! You seem to be rather cheery today." KC smiled in response to Joyce.

"It's been weeks since I've received any notes or indication the stalker has been around. I'm hoping he's gone. I almost feel free again." She snickered. "Free again. That sounds strange. I got out of prison and was freed. But I was suddenly was in prison again, imprisoned by a stalker—a coward who doesn't even have the courage to show his face."

"KC, you haven't any idea how many times Richard and I have prayed, even fasted, for you. We love you, dear." She reached across the table and tapped KC's arm. "Please don't get too comfortable as you're out and about, dear. The police haven't arrested anyone yet, have they?"

As if a cloud passed over KC, her expression fell and the knot in her stomach enlarged. "I know. But it's been nice not to look over my shoulders all the time. Mom has actually gained some weight, and her color has improved." She smiled weakly. "I guess I've known I shouldn't feel so safe." She sipped some tea and added, "I promise, I'll be careful."

"Good," Joyce replied. Standing up, Joyce continued, "Okay, young lady. It's time to get back to work."

"Taskmaster!" She saluted Joyce and headed back to work with a smirk on her face.

Nate Conover had been watching Stewart Alexander for two weeks. He hadn't done anything remotely connected to stalking KC or anyone else. He followed him to the courthouse, restaurants, the Salvation Army, Goodwill, and numerous places of business. Nate glanced at his watch. By agreement, he and Charles were meeting at the diner across from the courthouse. He scrambled into his car and pulled into the parking space next to Charles.

"Cuttin' it close, Conover," Charles smirked.

"Yeah, you too," he countered. The two shook hands and entered the diner. The server showed them to a booth, and they both ordered black coffee.

"Well ... do you have anything, yet?" Charles questioned.

Nate swirled his coffee and then ran his finger around the lip of the cup. "Been following that guy around for days now. He's hasn't done anything illegal. Hasn't been near KC." He sighed heavily. A hush fell between them.

Charles thumped his large hand on the table. His growing frustration was visible. "Nate, I'm paying you to get this stalker. Now get him. I'm giving you one more month. Got it?" He slid out of the booth. "One month, no more." He threw down a five-dollar bill and walked out.

Nate slipped on his grubby clothes at dusk. He jumped in his car and headed toward Stewart's apartment building. He sipped some whiskey and spit it onto his shirt, continuing his ruse as a drunken bum. One difference was that now he wore glasses. He'd ordered a pair of spy glasses. He planned to befriend Stewart Alexander and hopefully find out why he'd been stalking KC, if, indeed, he was the one stalking her.

He put himself in Stewart's path and then casually called out, "Hey, buddy, think you could spare a couple of dollars? I haven't eaten for a couple days."

"Naw, don't have extra. Try the food pantry down the street," Stewart retorted.

"Got nowhere to cook," he countered. "Soup kitchen near?" he quizzed.

"Yeah, couple blocks down Madison Street. Heard they have good chili on Wednesdays." Stewart paused briefly and added, "Wait a minute. This *is* Wednesday, ain't it?" He looked at Nate. "If you didn't smell so bad, I'd ask you to go with me."

Nate didn't let that deter him. "If you got a place where I can stash my coat, maybe I'd pass the smell test," he replied as he removed his coat. He wasn't going to let this opportunity slip away. "Is there a place where I can hide this?"

Stewart tilted his head toward a box near a heating conduit. "Can't promise it will still be there, but it's worth a try."

The two stumbled the two blocks to the soup kitchen run by a local church. Nate was hoping none of the servers recognized him. The voice of one of the servers sounded familiar, but he kept his head down, avoiding eye contact. He and Stewart sat at the same table, but exchanged very little conversation.

Stewart shoved his chair back quickly and announced to Nate, "Gotta go. Got a meeting. Hope your coat's still there." He left rapidly, glancing over his shoulder.

*Stay quiet. Don't leave too soon,* Nate reminded himself. He finally left the warmth of the soup kitchen. Rather than walking toward Stewart's apartment building, Nate jogged around the block and curled up on the heating vent near a store that was closed for the night. However, it was close enough to see and hopefully hear anything that Stewart might have to say in his appointment. He waited ten minutes before a car pulled up. Stewart didn't move, and the car drove off. Another few minutes passed, and another man approached Stewart. He nodded his head toward the box where Nate had left his coat. *Son of a gun, he just gave away my coat.* He shivered. *Guess I'll go to the Salvation Army and get another one. Not like I have to wear it every day.* He huddled over the heating vent for another twenty minutes. As he started to leave, he saw another car approach. Stewart opened the passenger door and climbed in. Nate began videoing the encounter. He saw the driver hand Stewart what looked like an envelope, which Stewart slipped under his shirt. *Give just about anything to know what's in that envelope.* Nate watched as Stewart left the car and gave the driver the thumbs-up. As the car passed by, Nate tried to identify the driver. He slammed his hand on his thigh. *Couldn't really see who it was. Hope these glasses recorded everything. If so, maybe I can get some help improving the images.*

Three weeks had gone by with no threatening phone calls, no notes, and no harassment from the stalker. At the end of each quiet day, KC thanked God for the protection given. As Friday drew to a close, KC decided to ask Richard to discontinue his nightly escort. "Mr. Goen, I'm so thankful for your and Joyce's support. You both have gone out of your way to care for me. I know the two of you have been praying for me since before I was released from prison. I know you continue to pray for me, and I really appreciate it. But it's been over three weeks since the stalker bothered me. I think maybe he or she has given up. So, beginning tonight, I relieve you of your bodyguard responsibilities." She smiled and extended her hand to shake his.

"KC, I know you want life to return to normal, and we want

that for you too. But are you sure you want to do this? I really don't mind walking you to your car."

"I know, Mr. Goen. But you can't be with me twenty-four/ seven. At some point I have to take care of myself. Besides, I've been taking self-defense classes. If I feel I need your help, I'll let you know. Okay?"

"If you're sure, but—"

"I'm sure. Thanks so much. See you Sunday at church and 8:00 sharp Monday morning. Night!" She grabbed her portfolio and keys and was out the door.

Joyce and Richard pulled on their coats, turned off the lights, and locked the door. Walking to the parking lot, they talked about how much KC's confidence had grown as well as her faith. Richard unlocked the car doors, and as Joyce climbed in, she thought she heard something. "Richard, listen," she whispered. "I think I hear someone crying." Quietness filled the air. And then ...

CHAPTER 43

"W haddya mean? Nearly three weeks with no notes, no phone calls, and now she gets a note?" Nate said. "I still think I know who it is, and I'll catch him. I promise, Charles.... I can only imagine how terrified she is.... I know. I'd feel the same way.... Stepping up surveillance immediately." *Wow! That's one angry man, and I don't blame him,* Nate thought, his own anger increasing.

The burnt orange sphere was slipping beyond on the horizon of the lake. The heat from the sun lessened as the sun turned from blood red to pink to pale blue to eggplant purple and then finally disappeared from sight. Nate sat in his beat-up car, gagging because of his putrid homeless clothes. *Tonight I'm going to take some drastic measures, but I need to be careful. That Stewart guy probably is suspicious of new people. Still ...*

Nate turned the key, and the engine roared to life. Although the weather was cold, he drove with the window down. The fresh air helped him think. He also needed it to alleviate the stench in the car. *I really hate undercover surveillance,* he thought. Approaching the flophouse where Stewart lived, Nate decided he would hang out in the stairwell.

Sheltered there, Nate waited for Stewart and prayed that he would show up. Nate shifted from one step to another. Every few minutes, he'd pull out a brown paper bag with a bottle hidden inside. He'd take a nip and let it trickle from the corner of his mouth. *Have to give the impression I'm a drunk. But I'd rather be drinking coffee right now. Oh, wait,* he chuckled to himself. *I am an alcoholic, but I'm a recovering alcoholic.* Nate staggered down the stairway and started toward his car, ready to give up for the night. Just then, he saw Stewart walking toward him. Nate reached into his pocket and switched on the spyglass camera. As Stewart closed the distance between them, Nate deliberately stumbled and fell. Stewart paused but then continued walking. "Hey, buddy! Can ya help me get up?" Nate slurred his speech. Stewart's footsteps slowed, stopped, but continued again. "Aw, come on," Nate said, garbling his speech. "I need help gettin' up. Blew out my knee in the war. Can't you just help me up?" he begged. He heard the footsteps stop and then get louder. Nate was looking at the torn blue jeans Stewart always wore. He reached out for Stewart's outstretched hand. "Thanks, buddy! I owe ya!" He looked into Stewart's eyes and said, "You the guy that went with me to the soup kitchen, ain't ya?" Stewart shrugged his shoulders.

"Weak moment. Don't usually care about people like you," he responded.

"Whaddya mean—people like me?" Nate tried to sound offended.

"Drunks. Stinkin' drunks, that's what I mean." Stewart spoke with contempt.

"Well, ya don't know what it's like livin' with the pain I have." Nate began to sob. "Stupid doctors won't give me any drugs to help the pain. Whiskey's the next best thing." He hobbled over to lean against the building. "Can't get aid from anyone, so I just live on the streets ever since I got to town a couple weeks ago." He shivered. "Gettin' cold too. Any shelters I can go to?"

Stewart glared at him. *Just got paid for leavin' a note on Elliott's car. Got money to get a couple hits of cocaine. Wish he'd go away.* "Listen, pal. I'm no public aid worker. Gonna have to find help the best way ya can. Barely makin' it myself."

"But it's cold. Ya don't wanna find me frozen on the steps in the mornin', do ya?" Nate appealed to what little sense of compassion Stewart might have. Stewart rubbed his hand over his face; his hand paused over his mouth, and he tugged on his nose.

"Well, I guess I could let ya in the building. Ya could sleep in one of the stairwells or laundry room in the basement. Just don't tell anyone how ya got in, hear?" He glanced up and down the street, as he didn't want anyone to see him helping a drunken bum. "Come on, lean on me." Stewart got him in the building and pointed toward the door leading to the stairs. "Laundry room, downstairs."

The morning sun streaked through the dirty windows in the laundry room. It felt warm on Nate's whiskered face. He walked to the laundry sink. It was rusty and moldy, but the water was hot. He splashed cold water on his face and then hot water. It felt good. He needed to get out of the building, but first he needed to figure out how to get back in without Stewart's help. Climbing the stairs, he looked about for another door. He found one opening into the alley. The lock pick set he'd ordered last year would open the lock. He tottered to the street and then to his car.

Nate slept for a couple of hours. With a cup of strong, hot coffee and a cinnamon roll for breakfast, he was ready to review the video from the previous evening and the evening before. He was hoping the spyglasses were good enough to get a decent picture of the driver. He fast-forwarded through much of the video but stopped when he saw Stewart approaching a car. He slowed down the video. Nate's eyes narrowed and his brows furled as he focused on the driver's face. *What? That can't be. Gotta get this to someone who can enlarge this.* Nate sat at his computer desk deciding whom he could call.

With his elbow on the desk, he flicked his thumbnail on his front tooth. *Ah, yes. I'll call my friend at the forensic lab.*

Nate jogged to his work car and punched in Charles Phillips's phone number. He reached his voice mail. "Charles, it's Nate Conover. I'm onto something. Need to talk with you. Meet me at the diner at 11:30." He then tapped the Bluetooth button on his steering wheel and said, "Call 555-339-2357." He waited for the phone to ring.

"Forensic Labs of Monroe County, how may I help you?" the receptionist answered.

"Nate Conover calling to talk with Anthony Haines, please."

"Certainly, Mr. Conover. Please hold."

*She certainly has a pleasant voice. Hope she's as attractive as she is pleasant.*

"Well, Nate Conover. Haven't heard from you for a couple of years. How's your new business?" Anthony inquired. He was one of the few people who had encouraged Nate to begin his own business.

"It's a little slow, and I absolutely hate the cases of spousal cheating. But the one I'm working on right now might be the biggest case I've had since leaving the force. I need your help."

"Wow! I can't imagine what it might be. Haven't seen anything in the papers that would snag my interest. How can I help you? You know my assistance won't be cheap, right?"

"Not a problem, Anthony. Need you to enhance some video I shot the last couple nights. How soon could you do it?"

"We're backed up for several weeks. Realistically, I couldn't get to it for, oh"—Nate could hear his friend flipping through pages—"I don't think I could do for three months. That's the earliest."

"That won't do, Anthony."

"I'd be happy to recommend—" he started.

"Naw, that won't work. You're the only one I trust."

"Why don't we get together for a beer?" He paused. "I'm sorry, Nate. I should have known better. How about a pizza?"

"Now that will fly with me," Nate answered. "How soon could we do that? Tomorrow night?"

"You're really eager to get this done. Must be big. Yes, let's have that pizza tomorrow night. Pizza King, seven o'clock, okay?"

"Yep, that works." He hung up as he was pulling into a parking spot near the diner.

Charles Phillips was already waiting. Sitting in rear of the diner, he raised his finger to get Nate's attention.

"Thanks for meeting me, Charles. I'm really onto something, I promise. However, what needs to be done to prove my theory will cost some money. I'm talkin' two or three thousand dollars unless I can get my friend to do it as a favor." He sipped some coffee and added, "I know I've been tellin' you I'm close to solving this, but I really believe I am. I'm asking you to trust me. Are you prepared to pay—"

"Listen, Nate, I'll pay whatever it takes to find out who's stalking KC and why. It isn't only for KC, but my wife has lost weight, she's not sleeping well, and she's fearful all the time. It's got to stop. So do whatever is necessary. Whatever you do, be sure it's legal because I don't want a technicality to get this case tossed. Understand?"

"I'm with you. I don't want it tossed either. I'll let you know as soon as I know something, okay?" He gulped the remainder of the coffee. "I'll pay this time," he joked. He paid every time because Charles usually left in a huff.

Nate copied the videos to his computer and to a thumb drive. He grabbed his spyglasses and the thumb drive and headed to his car. He slipped into the car seat and patted his breast pocket where he'd placed the thumb drive. It was missing. *How could I have lost it from the desk to the car?* Hurriedly, he ran back to his computer, where he found the drive beside the computer. His stomach felt as if he'd swallowed a ball and it was bouncing around. He opened drawers and slammed them shut as he searched for an extra thumb drive. *Found it! Deep breath! I'll make an extra copy when I get a chance.*

Anthony was waiting for Nate and had already ordered the pizza, as well as iced tea for Nate and a beer for himself. "About time you showed up. Hate to tell you this, but you're on the clock. I've got to make money too."

"You're kiddin,' right? Pizza and a beer, and you're gonna charge me? Give me a break," groaned Nate. He slapped Anthony on the back. "Nice to see you. Appreciate you meeting me. Let's eat and then I'll fill you in on what's goin' on, okay?"

They joked together. Anthony showed Nate photos of his family. Finally, Nate broke the reminiscing. "Anthony, let's talk business. Do you remember that young lady convicted of embezzlement— KC Elliott?" Anthony leaned his head to the left a little.

"Well, I think so. Didn't she get released recently?"

"Yeah, she's doing well. But someone's stalking her. I think I've found the stalker, but I think someone else is involved too." He reached into his shirt, pulled out the thumb drive, and slid it across the table to Anthony. "The other night I was tailing a guy I have reason to suspect, and I got this video. I used these," he said as he pulled out his spyglasses. "I think I know the guy driving the car, and I think he gave my suspect an envelope. Can't prove it, but I'd bet my life it was filled with money."

"It's all interesting, but what do you need from me?"

"I need you to enhance the video. Between you and me, maybe, just maybe, we can ID the driver."

"Then what? What if the driver can be identified? He or she hasn't committed a crime. At least from what you've told me, no crime has been committed. I don't know if I can do this."

Nate blew out a long breath. "It isn't illegal, is it?" He shook his head. "If it isn't illegal, what's holding you back? What's buggin' you?"

"I don't know. It's legal, but I don't know if it's ethical," he said with a sigh.

"Fine," Nate uttered in disgust. "I'll see if I can get someone else." He stood and walked outside. Suddenly, he realized he'd left the thumb drive with Anthony and returned.

"Give me the thumb drive," he demanded.

"Naw, I'm gonna do it. Give me a week. Give me your e-mail address, and I'll send a brief report. For a more detailed report, we'll have to do pizza again." He smirked, and they shook hands.

"Oh, thanks, buddy. I'm sure you won't regret it." Nate picked up the tab and paid for supper.

Nearly a week passed. Nate had tailed Stewart Alexander almost every night. The spyglasses worked, but identifying the driver was still difficult. He got home and as usual checked his e-mail. Bingo! Finally, Anthony's response came through. Nate clicked on the JPEG file. The picture was clear. Questions Nate still needed answered included, Why is he involved with Alexander, and is Alexander really the stalker?

CHAPTER 44

KC's cell phone rang. It was Logan Parsons again. She sighed heavily, her shoulders sagged, and her head dropped to her chest. *God, how much longer will I have to see this guy?* "Hello, Mr. Parsons.... Yes, I know I have an appointment.... Of course, I can reschedule. When?... Six-thirty this evening? Yes that will work for me. Where? ... Okay, I'll see you there." KC punched the end button on her phone. Sitting quietly at her desk, she decided to talk with Joyce. She saved the project she was working on and walked to Joyce's office.

"Got time for tea?" she asked quietly.

"For you? I've always got time for tea with you." She looked intently into KC's eyes. The enthusiasm usually present was gone. Replacing it was anxiety. Joyce said a quick, silent prayer. *Whatever is bothering this young lady, God, please give me the right words to comfort and encourage her.* "What's your flavor of tea today?" she queried.

"Anything will do," she answered flatly.

"Stalker or parole officer?" KC had worked with Joyce long enough to be able to read her emotions.

"I guess I should be relieved that it is my parole officer. He wanted me to meet him at his office after hours. I told Mom I didn't trust him the first time I met with him, and he's done nothing to change my mind. We're meeting at McDonald's on College Avenue at 6:30." She breathed in deeply and exhaled. "I wanted to tell you because you're always so understanding. I can't tell Mom any longer. She's so fragile. She worries about me when I leave the house and while I'm at work. Social life? Zilch. I don't know who I can trust." She stared off into the distance. "I just want all this to end. This is almost worse than being in prison."

Joyce listened quietly. "KC, I can't say I know how you feel because I don't. I understand your Mom's concern. I agree that you should only meet with Mr. Parsons when others are around. In fact, I don't think you should meet with anyone alone." She paused, chewed on her lower lip, and added, "I probably shouldn't tell you this, but Richard and I have been screening your business contacts."

"What? Joyce, why would you do that?"

Joyce couldn't tell if KC was angry or wounded. "Why? Because we care for you. We love you."

"But I don't want to be a charity case. I will not be a charity case." Her voice trembled as she spoke the words through clenched teeth.

"KC, you aren't a charity case. In fact, since you started working for us, our income has increased significantly. We choose clients we know you will amaze with your talent and will be able to close a deal." She leaned forward and lifted KC's head slightly. "And there is the fact that we know you'll be safe."

KC sipped her tea. She looked into Joyce's eyes and responded, "I don't know exactly how I should feel—relieved, angry, or flattered." She snickered. "I don't know; maybe I feel all three." She touched Joyce's arm and added, "I'm sorry, but my emotions are so raw. I never know how I'm going to respond. I do appreciate everything you and Richard have done and are doing. I really do. Please forgive my reaction."

"Nothing to forgive, dear. Please continue to be careful."

They hugged briefly and returned to their workstations.

Logan sat at his desk bouncing a Nerf ball off the wall. Occasionally his sadistic nature became overwhelming, and he'd bounce the ball off the back of the head of a coworker. "Oops! Sorry, didn't mean to hit you," he would exclaim with a snigger. Greeted with a sneer, Logan would snap, "What? You don't believe me? Would I really hit you" And he'd laugh again.

As five o'clock arrived, the other parole officers checked out, but Logan remained. Still bouncing the ball against the wall, Logan's disdain of KC Elliott grew deeper. He began slamming the ball against the wall even harder. *I hate that woman. I hate that woman. I absolutely hate that woman. She's such a Goody Two-shoes. Passed every drug test, showed up for every appointment. Can't find any reason to revoke her parole.* He banged the ball against the wall with such force that it caused a mirror to crash to the floor. *Oops! Too bad! Guess I'll have to get a replacement. Would hate it if these narcissistic idiots couldn't comb their hair.* He glanced at his wristwatch and thought, *I have just enough time to clean up this mess, go to the dollar store, and then meet Elliott at McDonald's.* He stomped to the utility closet and grabbed the broom and dustpan. *Can't believe I'm doing janitorial duty. If the guys in the office hadn't seen me bouncing the ball, I wouldn't have to do this.*

Logan was deliberately late. *Is she going to leave?* He waited in his car where he could see KC. *Ah! There she goes. Now I can write her up.* Sitting in his car, he observed the door. Reaching for his notebook, he jotted down the time, place, and name of the parolee. He was delighted—he finally had something on the Elliott girl. Glancing up, he saw KC sit down at a booth. Slamming his fist against the dashboard, Logan uttered an expletive and shouted aloud, "Ah! Thought I finally had something. Delayed this meeting long enough." Logan unwrapped himself from his car, slammed the door, and headed into McDonald's for a meeting he didn't want to go to.

"Sorry, I'm late, Elliott. Something came up at the office." He pulled his wallet from his pants pocket and announced, "I'll be right back." He approached the counter, where he ordered a large cup of black coffee.

*"Sorry, I'm late." I doubt it. I met your kind in prison. You're waiting for me to goof up so you can send me back to the joint. Well, you're not going to find it. I'm going to do everything I humanly can to stay out of that place.*

"Penny for your thoughts, Ms. Elliott," he said, breaking her contemplations.

"Mr. Parsons, my thoughts aren't worth a penny, nickel, or quarter. You'd be wasting your time and money." *Just like you're wasting mine.*

"As I recall, you've had some problems with a stalker. At least, that's what you've told the—"

"Excuse me." She looked straight into Logan's eyes and pinched her lips together. Through gritted teeth, she added, "It is *exactly* what I've told the police, and every word of it is true. Someone has been stalking me. My mother's health has been affected, and ..." She felt her cheeks heating up. Her heart was racing, but each word was more pronounced. She glimpsed about the restaurant. No one seemed to notice. "My mother was in the hospital because whoever is stalking me left a note on the windshield of my car, which she was driving that day." KC leaned nearer to Logan and through clenched teeth added, "If you want, I can produce the doctor reports." She sipped some coffee. "Yes, I have a stalker. Am I enjoying it? Absolutely not! I daresay I'll have no help from you to stop the stalker either. You are an egotistical male chauvinist who gets his jollies from making parolees squirm. Now, if this meeting has satisfied all your requirements, I'm out of here!" She grabbed her purse and left.

# CHAPTER 45

*Oh, that was a stupid thing to do,* KC thought as she scrambled into her car. Immediately she regretted the outburst. *But it felt good to finally say what I've been thinking.* The car roared to life, and she headed home. While it felt good, KC's stomach was churning. *What have I done! Could that sudden outburst send me back to prison?* She stewed about it all the way home.

Like a fish out of water, KC flip-flopped all night. Sleep was as elusive as the stalker. She tried to read, but just as she began to doze, she'd jerk awake. The deep, restorative rest she needed never came. She wanted a cup of tea but feared waking her mom and Charles. Finally, she pulled out her laptop and worked on a project. Sleep eventually came, but it was restless.

*Bang! Bang!* Rose knocked loudly on KC's door. "KC, you'd better get up. You're going to be late for work." She woke with a start. She glimpsed at her clock and jumped out of bed. "Oh, Mom, why didn't you wake me sooner?" KC grabbed her gown and stomped down the hall. *Today will be a quick shower.* Checking her hair, she decided she would forgo a shampoo. "Mom, will you fix me a couple pieces of toast and a cup of tea? I'm going to eat on the run!" she shouted downstairs. Ten minutes later, KC kissed her mother's cheek, grabbed her laptop and purse, and headed off to work.

She arrived just in time. Dropping into her chair, she sighed. *Can't wait for the end of the day to arrive. I'm so tired.*

"Charles," Nate texted, "we need 2 meet. Onto something. Need to talk with u. Meet @ café for coffee? 11:15? Text me." *I really hate texting, but Charles doesn't want me calling him.* He looked at the photo. He knew who the driver was, but he needed to find out what his connection was to Stewart. *I'm pretty sure there was money in that envelope, but I can't prove it.* Nate drove to the city park and walked the track. The fresh air and exercise gave him time to think.

He and Charles arrived at the café at the same time. "This had better be good, Nate. It's getting expensive, and at the rate I'm going, I'm going to be spending more money on medical expenses. Rose isn't doing well at all—still losing weight, worries about KC all the time." He sipped some coffee and demanded, "So what do you have?"

"Listen, Charles, I need you to promise not to interfere with my investigation. I *think* I'm beginning to piece things together, but I'm going to have to ask KC to help me in a sting." He gulped his coffee, letting Charles think about what he'd just said.

"You want KC to be a guinea pig?" he questioned. "What kind of danger would she be in?" With his index finger, he circled the rim of his coffee mug, pondering the plan.

A wry smile crossed Nate's face before he answered. "I happen to know she's been taking karate lessons, so I think she can handle herself." His eyes narrowed as he continued, "Besides, I won't be far away, and she'd be wired." He paused as he asked the server to refill his coffee mug. "I'll talk with the instructor without her knowledge and ask him to accelerate her lessons so she'll be able to protect herself."

"You going to tell me who the stalker is?" Charles queried.

"Nope, for a couple reasons. One, I don't want *you* to interfere.

And second, I think the stalker is being paid to do his dastardly work." Nate looked intensely at Charles. "I need you to stay out of this. But I want your okay to ask KC to help. Can I count on you?"

Charles licked his lips and chewed on the inside of his cheek as he deliberated his choices. "I don't think I have much choice. If we are to catch the stalker, we have to do something." He paused, stared out the window, and asked, "You really think she'll be safe? If she gets hurt, Rose will never forgive me." He lowered his voice, and through clenched teeth, he threatened Nate. "If KC gets hurts and Rose turns against me, there will be no one to blame but you. And you don't want to know what I can do to you."

"Well, Charles, I'll take that as the threat it was intended to be. I promise she won't be hurt. She might be scared and might have nightmares for a while, but we are going to wrap this up." He sat silently to allow Charles time to consider the situation. "Well, do I have your permission to talk with KC?

Hesitantly, Charles nodded. "Just remember, if she gets hurt ..."

CHAPTER 46

As the door opened at Advanced Web Designs, KC nearly jumped out of her skin and her heart began beating a mile a minute. She and Joyce were reviewing a contract. Joyce walked, as calmly as possible, to the front desk.

"How may I help you?" she asked very professionally, considering she felt like to was going to faint.

"Well, I'd like to talk with KC Elliott," the man answered.

"And why might you be looking for Ms. Elliott?" Joyce asked. "I suggest you come talk with me." She stepped aside and motioned for him to follow her.

He hesitated, so Joyce reiterated, "You will talk with me first."

KC's mouth gaped. *Oh, my! I've never heard Joyce speak so abruptly.* She stood looking down the hallway until the door was closed firmly.

Nate Conover stretched his hand forward and introduced himself. Joyce ignored the gesture. "Sit down, Mr. Conover. Now why do you need to talk with KC?"

"May I ask who you are? Are you KC Elliott?"

"I am Joyce Goen. I am one of the owners of this business and will not tolerate someone disrupting KC's work. Now," she said as she reached for a notepad and pencil, "why do you want to talk with KC?"

*Wow! She is one tough cookie.* He reached into his shirt pocket and pulled out a business card. "Well, Ms. Goen—"

"It is *Mrs.* Goen," she interrupted.

"Very well, Mrs. Goen. I'm Nate Conover, and I'm a private investigator. I—"

"And why are you investigating Ms. Elliott, if I might ask."

He wanted to respond, *You might ask and I might answer,* but he remembered his mother's words: "You catch more flies with honey than with vinegar." So instead, he said, "Mrs. Goen, I can tell you are very protective of KC. I want to thank you for that." He cleared his throat. "I was hired to find out who has been stalking her. I believe I've found the person, but I need to talk with KC. I want her to help me get the guy. I actually think two men are involved, and I really need KC's help."

He paused, letting his words sink in. "I've talked with her stepfather, Charles Phillips, and he's given me the okay."

Joyce asked, "Why didn't you talk with Rose? After all, Rose is her mother."

Her brows furled tightly.

"Good question. Charles hired me, not Rose. And it is my understanding that her emotional health is quite fragile right now because of all of this idiocy. Charles is protecting her."

Joyce nodded her head. She was well aware of the health issues Rose was experiencing. "Well, let me talk with KC. If she agrees to talk with you, I'll leave the two of you alone." She rose from her chair, crossed the room, and walked to KC's desk. Speaking quietly, she explained the situation.

"Of course, I'll talk with him." KC stood and started toward the conference room. She stopped. Looking at Joyce, she added, "I'll stay after work to make up whatever time this takes. The company should not pay me for when I'm not working."

"Nonsense," Joyce retorted. "You're not staying after office hours. Now, go talk with him."

KC continued to the conference room.

"Mr. Conover," she said, entering the room. "What is it I can do for you?"

Nate stood and stretched out his arm to shake hands with KC. She allowed him to take her hand into his. It was large and somewhat calloused, but he held her hand gently. She pulled her hand away. *I must have held her hand too long. But they were so cold and clammy. She certainly is frightened.* He motioned to the chair across the table from him. "Please have a seat."

KC nodded briefly. "What can I do for you?" she repeated.

"Well, it seems we have a problem." Nate noticed that she glanced at him through narrowed eyes.

"*We* have a problem? Is someone stalking you too?"

"Good one," he said with a smirk. "You've a quick wit. So let me rephrase the statement. You've got a problem, and I believe I will be able to help you. How's that sound?"

Her eyes were steely. She pressed her lips tightly together. "Mr. Conover, if you think you have a plan, then I'm willing to try it. I cannot live like this forever." A tear rolled down her cheek, and she quickly wiped it away. "And I'm afraid it's going to kill Mom." A silence fell between them. The second hand on the clock sounded like a dripping faucet. KC sat with her elbows on the table and fingers steepled, thinking. "Better tell me your plan. I think I'm in."

# CHAPTER 47

S melling of urine and whiskey, Nate huddled near the door of Stewart's apartment building. With his hat pulled down over his eyes and wearing the spyglasses, he waited and waited for well over three hours. Shifting from one cheek to the other, he was ready to call it a night when the click of a key in the lock caught his attention. *Don't move,* he reminded himself. *Gotta be sure it's Stewart.* His sense of hearing was intensified, and his heart felt as if it was going to beat out of his chest. *Stay calm.* He attempted to keep his breathing normal as if he were sleeping. He even attempted to snore. Soon he heard someone start up the stairs. He raised his head enough to see that it was Stewart. Nate turned on the spyglasses to record the encounter and pulled out a six-inch dowel rod.

Stewart saw the bum sleeping on the stairway and kicked him. "Outta my way, buddy." He spat out the words.

Nate grunted. Stewart kicked him again and then stepped over him. It was then that Nate grabbed Stewart's leg.

"Hey! What are ya doin?" he demanded. "Let go!"

It was dark in the stairway. Nate stuck the dowel rod into Stewart's back. "Shut up and nothin's gonna happen to ya. Hear me?"

Stewart's heart was pounding like a jackhammer. "I ain't got no money, so let me go!"

Nate spit out, "I said shut up." He attempted to pull him to his feet, but Stewart was so high on drugs that he could barely stand. Nate finally got him upright, and he whispered loudly in Stewart's ear, "Listen! You're gonna walk out of here quietly. Hear me?"

Feeling what he thought was a gun in his back, Stewart nodded.

"Move it," Nate commanded.

Stewart stumbled down the stairs, but he put up no resistance. Once outside, Nate shoved him against the wall in the alley.

"Don't shoot me, man. I got some dust in my back pocket. I'll give it to ya. Just don't shoot me."

"Stewart, you're such a loser," Nate spat out. "Don't want your dust, pot, or anything else. But I need your help, and you are going to help me, hear?"

"Whaddya want?" His voice was slurred. He shivered, "I'm cold."

"Yeah, I bet you are." Sarcasm dripped from Nate's mouth. "We're gonna go to the diner down the street. You aren't gonna make a scene, are ya? Remember what I've got in my hand." Nate pushed the dowel rod harder into Stewart's back.

"No, man. I'll be good."

"Excellent! Let's go, and remember what I've got. Trust me, fella, I'm not afraid to use it!" *Don't know what I could possibly do with a six-inch dowel rod, but I gotta make him think I can hurt him.*

The all-night diner was about three blocks away. Stewart could barely walk a straight line, but Nate managed to keep him upright. They passed several men sleeping on heat grates. Some had blankets pulled tightly around them as they slept and snored. *Drugs and alcohol! So destructive. What a waste!*

Stewart and Nate wandered into the diner. Nate shoved him toward the booth in the very back. As they passed the counter, he looked at the server who was working a Sudoku puzzle. "We'll have a couple of cups for now. Might order something else later. Just keep the cups full, okay?"

She nodded as she turned to get the mugs. She filled the cups and took them to the booth where the two men sat.

"Let me know when you want more. Just hold the mug up, yell, or whatever. Middle of the night and not much is happenin'," she said matter-of-factly. Then she went back to the counter to work on the puzzle.

"Listen, Stewart, I know you're getting money from Logan Parsons," Nate said before he swallowed some coffee. *I really don't know that, but I'm fairly certain.*

Stewart's head lifted suddenly. His eyes were wide, not only from the drugs but from the statement.

"Don't know who that is," he said dully as he, too, drank from his coffee. "Awful coffee."

"Oh, I have proof that you know who he is. Got pictures of you meetin' him and him givin' you an envelope with something in it. I suspect he's givin' you money. Am I right?" Silence hung between them like humidity on a hot summer night. "What's he payin' ya for, Stewart?"

"Need something to eat," he reluctantly replied. "Ain't had nothin' for couple days."

"Fine." Nate reached for the menu stuffed behind the condiments tray. "Decide what ya want. Then we'll order. Don't waste my time either, got it?"

"Yeah, I got it. How about pancakes, sausage, eggs, and hash browns?" He looked at Nate. "You payin? I ain't got no money."

"Yeah, I'm payin' … this time." He raised his mug, and the server walked over.

"More coffee?" she asked flatly.

"That would be fine, but he wants some pancakes, sausage, eggs, and hash browns. I'll have the same thing minus the pancakes."

She jotted down the order and walked to the kitchen. She worked on her puzzle while the cook prepared the food.

"Okay, Stewart, I'm tired of your stalling tactics. I want an answer. What's Parsons giving you—drugs or money?" Nate was persistent in his interrogation.

The food was delivered. Nate pulled Stewart's plate to his side of the table. "If you want this food, you better start talkin'." He glared at Stewart.

Stewart didn't say a word. Nate picked up the plate and put it under Stewart's nose.

"Mmm, doesn't that smell good?" He put it down and added, "It's yours as soon as you spill your guts." He swallowed some coffee. "Now the question was, what's Parsons givin' ya—drugs or money?"

"Come on, man. I'm really hungry." Stewart stared at the food. "Let me eat, and then I'll tell ya."

"Ain't gonna work that way. And by the way, the food's gettin' cold. Nothin' worse than cold eggs."

Stewart swallowed more coffee. "Ugh, it's cold. Can I have a warm up?"

"Nope, not til ya talk." Nate's police tactics were still intact even though he'd been off the force a while.

"Okay, okay!" Stewart slumped in the booth. "Parsons been payin' me to stalk some woman. He gives me a C-note every time we meet."

Nate raised his cup for the server to indicate that they wanted more coffee. She acknowledged his request with a nod. As she approached, he lifted his finger toward Stewart. "Stop just a minute." After their coffee mugs were refilled, Nate pointed his index finger at Stewart. "Continue," he demanded.

"Well, he's been doin' it for several years. I use the money to get dope." He hung his head in humiliation. "Yeah," he said, his speech slurred, "I know I'm a hopeless druggie."

Nate relaxed in the booth a little. "So, who's he's havin' ya stalk right now?" he quizzed.

"Come on, man. Can I have some food before it gets too cold?" he begged.

"Oh yeah, I forgot about that," Nate responded sardonically. He shoved the plate across the table.

Alexander took a bite of the eggs, and Nate pulled the plate back again.

"Need more info, Stewart."

"One of his parolees. Don't know why. Seems like a nice woman."

Nate pushed the plate back. "And?" Nate's eyebrows raised questioningly.

"Just let me eat the eggs 'fore they get much colder, okay?" Stewart pleaded.

"Eggs only."

A stillness lay in the conversation as Stewart wolfed down the eggs and Nate enjoyed his breakfast.

Stewart finished eating the eggs and started on the sausage too.

"Naw, ya don't," Nate said as he pulled the plate away. "Sausage getting' cold too?" He swallowed some coffee. "You can eat sausage cold. It's not the best, but you can do it."

The two looked at each other in total silence, waiting to see who would cave first. "So, what's this woman's name?" Nate asked.

"Name's Elliott. He's tryin' to get her to break parole so he can send her back to prison." He eyed his plate and finally pulled it to himself. "He's done that lots of times. Keeps reminding me that if I don't cooperate, he'll send me back. Don't wanna go back there." He stabbed a huge piece of sausage and stuck it in his mouth.

"Whaddya mean, 'He's done that lots of times'?" Nate pulled the plate back to his side of the table.

"I mean, he pays me to stalk women on parole." He sighed loudly. "Can I have my plate now? Let me eat, and I'll tell you everything I know."

Nate shoved the plate across to Stewart. As he gulped his coffee and breakfast, Nate tried to sort through the information. *Why would Parsons want to send female parolees back to prison?* Suddenly, Nate's head fell backward against the booth. *Now I get it. I bet he was having sex with them.*

"Listen, Stewart, do you remember the names of the women you've stalked for Parsons? It's real important, so think hard."

Stewart swallowed a bite of pancake and drank deeply from his coffee. "Need more coffee." He paused. He reached into his pants pockets and then padded his overcoat. "Oh, here it is." Alexander pulled out a small notebook and tossed it across the table. "Saved all the addresses and names. Don't know why, but I did."

Nate grabbed the notebook before Stewart could retrieve it. *Stewart might be a druggie, but he sure knew how to keep records. Not only did he keep records of whom he was stalking but also how much money he'd received. This is more than I could have hoped for.* "Listen, Stewart, you've been real helpful. Mind if I keep this book?" Nate asked politely. "I'll get you another one."

"Nah, you can have it. Can I have more pancakes?" he answered, wiping his mouth on his sleeve.

"Stewart, you can have anything you want." He called the server over, and Stewart ordered more pancakes, eggs, and sausage.

Nate sat in the booth across from Stewart for another hour and three more plates of pancakes, eggs, and sausage. *Poor guy! Probably hasn't eaten well for weeks.* Nate drank more coffee and mulled over how he could use the information he had gotten. *What do I know? 1) KC Elliott is being stalked. 2) The stalker is Stewart Alexander. 3) Stewart says he's being paid to stalk her by her parole officer, Logan Parsons. 4) Stewart says Parsons has paid him to stalk others. 5) Stewart is a druggie. 6) Who's going to believe a druggie. 7) If it's true, why would Parsons want his parolees stalked?* He had lots of questions and absolutely no solid answers.

"Hey, buddy, do me a favor," Nate began. Stewart looked up from his plate.

"Don't know. What? What's it gonna cost me?" he replied.

"What did you say Parsons is payin' ya?"

"Usually a hundred every time I meet him."

"Tell ya what. Next time he meets with you, I'll double the amount if you call and tell me what he wants you to do. Deal?" He held out his right hand. In it was his phone number. "I'll get ya a throwaway phone. Only call me on that phone, got it?"

"Parsons will send me back to the joint if he finds out I'm goin' against him."

"I'll protect you. Okay?"

"Well, I guess."

"I'll get that phone for ya and meet ya in the hallway of your apartment building. See ya tomorrow night at 10:45."

Nate grabbed the tab for the meal and coffee. He paid at the register and handed the server a generous tip.

CHAPTER 48

Hot water coursing down his body felt good. Nate hated going undercover, especially when he had to play a bum. The urine smell stuck in his nostrils, so he grabbed a jar of Vicks vaporizing rub and wiped an ample amount under his nose. He knew he was clean, but he continued to stand under the water. *I do some of my best thinking here, but I'm really stymied. I need to talk with someone—someone I know who keeps confidences.* Nate reached for his towel and towel-dried his hair and then the rest of his body. With the towel wrapped about his waist, he traipsed down the hallway to his bedroom. He pulled on his undershorts, slipped on a T-shirt, and laid down to rest.

Honk! Honk! Honk! *What in the world! What's that noise?* He finally woke up enough to realize it was his cell phone. His long arm reached for the phone, and he answered, "Yeah, Conover."

"Sleeping, huh? Can't get the job done if you're sleeping." It was Charles Phillips. "I'm not paying you to sleep. Regular diner in forty-five minutes." He didn't wait for an answer. Nate was left holding a phone with no one on the other end.

*Guess I better get movin'! When Sir Charles calls and orders a command performance, one jumps.* He brushed his teeth, combed his hair, and dressed in his khaki slacks and dark blue polo shirt. He slipped his wallet in his back pocket, grabbed his car keys, and headed toward the garage. The engine thundered to life. When the garage door lifted, Nate backed out. *Oh, I could have slept a couple more hours. I'm really tired.* He yawned again and again.

Charles was waiting for Nate and had already ordered a cup of coffee for him. "Sorry I woke you." He sipped some coffee and added, "Well, not really. I want a report. Now!"

"Yep, I know you do. Mind if I order some breakfast?" Nate questioned.

"Breakfast? Don't you know it's two in the afternoon?"

Glancing at his watch, he realized he'd slept most of the day. "Wow! Didn't know it was so late. Got to bed very early this morning." He ordered some pancakes and orange juice to go along with his coffee. While waiting for his food, he smirked at Charles. "You're going to be happy with what I learned in the middle of the morning. But I can't tell you everything—no names, nothing other than that I learned some really interesting information. I've talked with KC about helping with a sting. But I might not have to use her."

"That would be good. I hate to involve her."

"I said, I *might* not need to use her. Truth is, I still might need her help. So, you're going to need to be patient for a few more weeks. I guarantee you we are close to solving the case."

Charles reached his hand across the table, and Nate shook it. "You know what, Nate? I believe you this time. Keep me informed, hear?" Charles picked up the tab, laid down a tip, and left. Nate finished his breakfast/lunch. He ordered another cup of coffee and slowly drank it. He thought of all of his friends still on the police force. He considered all of those he could confide in but settled on one person.

"Thanks for meeting with me Sandy," he said as he motioned to the server. "Would you like something to eat? I'm buying." Nate smiled.

"Sure, that would be great." Her eyes tightened as she added, "But don't consider this a date. I'm already seeing someone."

"No, no, this is strictly business."

The server took Sandy's order and left.

"What kind of business?" she questioned.

"Long story short," he said, trying to smile, "my client is being stalked. The police don't seem to take it seriously because she was an offender and spent time in prison—"

"Wait," she interjected. "I think I know who you're talking about. Can't remember her name, but she lives on a lake. Right?"

Nate nodded. "How did you know?"

Officer Roberts explained their brief encounter. "I remember seeing her parked in front of the station, and she told me she was being stalked. She was surprised I believed her." She looked into Nate's eyes. With her brows raised, she asked, "You mean she's *still* being stalked?" She was incredulous.

With a slight nod of his head, Nate answered, "Yeah, and I know who's stalking her, but he claims he's being paid to do it." He dropped his voice to a whisper. "I need your help, and what I need done needs to be held in confidence."

Sandy cleared her throat, puckered her lips, and remained silent. "Well?"

"I don't know, Nate."

"I'm not asking you to break the law, but I need someone to verify some information. I'll keep your name out of it as long as possible. You must know that it is possible I will have to tell others how I got my information."

She dropped her head, clasped her hands tightly on the table, and twiddled her thumbs. "But why me? Of all your contacts on the force, why me?"

"Two reasons. First, you have a reputation for being honest and fair. Second, I've heard you know when and how to keep confidences. Okay, three reasons—you also know when to stop, when you've reached the line and mustn't cross it." Nate stopped talking.

"Well, okay. But not only do I not cross the line, I try not to get too close to the line. If you're okay with that, I'll see what I can do to help."

"Sandy, that's great. Here's what I know." He and she talked for the next two hours. Nate handed her copies of Stewart's notebook. She had her assignment, and Nate was left to wait for several days.

Nate yawned, concluding that he needed sleep. He'd done all he could until he heard from Officer Sandy Roberts. He rubbed his hand over his five o'clock shadow and pinched the bridge of his nose with his index and thumb. *Gonna grab some grub and eat at home, shower, shave, and call it a night.* He rubbed his neck and rolled his head to the right and then the left. *These nightly surveillances are gonna kill me. Note to self: Call chiropractor after case is solved.* He pulled into a local deli and ordered a sandwich and bowl of soup to go.

"That will be $12.95, sir," the server announced. Nate pulled out a twenty-dollar bill, handed it to the server, turned, and walked out. "Hey, mister, wait! Your change." He simply waved his hand. *I'm so tired, I don't care.* "Keep it!"

His resolve to shower and shave fell apart as soon as he sat back in his recliner to watch the news. Sleep overcame him. It was nearly midnight when he was startled awake by his snoring. His head was pounding. He stumbled into his bedroom, stepped out of his clothes, and fell into bed. Pounding his pillow into his favorite position, he settled his head into the fluff, and sleep rescued him from the cares of the last few weeks. His fatigue was so complete that he barely moved most of the night. His REM sleep provided him the much-needed rest.

It was around eight o'clock in the morning when Nate began stirring. He stretched, yawned, rolled over, and tried to sleep again, but the sunlight streaming into his bedroom window prohibited it. He sat on the side of the bed rubbing his eyes and his face. He massaged his neck. His first thoughts were of KC, the stalker, and Logan Parsons. Why would Stewart Alexander and Logan Parsons be cohorts? One was a drug addict and exconvict, and the other was a parole officer. The story Stewart had told him seemed too farfetched. It didn't make sense.

Nate pulled on a pair of jeans and a shirt and headed to his kitchen. He tore open a package of oatmeal, added the water, and put it in the microwave. Grabbing a coffee pod and popping it into the coffee maker, he let Stewart's account rattle around in his head. *It only makes sense if it's true. But who is going to believe a druggie?* Nate slammed his fist on the counter and shouted, "God, I need your help! I want KC safe, and I want whoever is involved to pay for the suffering they've caused this family. Please, let Sandy Roberts be successful. And let it come quickly." The aroma from his coffee tickled his nose, and the microwave beeped, indicating his oatmeal was ready. As he ate breakfast, he watched the news. He found very little of interest. He turned the television off and ambled into his office. After switching on his computer, he checked his e-mail. He began deleting all the spam he had received, and he almost deleted an e-mail from Officer Roberts. His heart beat quicker, and he clicked open the e-mail.

"Need to see you today! Call me at 555-1715 ASAP."

*Could she have the information already? Could I be so lucky?* He grabbed his cell phone and punched in the number. It rang four times. He almost ended the call when he heard, "Roberts here."

"Sandy? Whaddya have?" He was so anxious to learn what she'd found out.

"Not on the phone. Break is in about forty-five minutes. Meet me at Kelso's Diner."

"I'll be there," he said, and he hung up. It was all he needed to kick into high gear. *Oh, God, please let this be what I need. Please.* He pulled on a sweatshirt, slipped into his loafers, brushed his teeth, and splashed on some aftershave, and he was ready to face the day. *Sure hope this proves promising.*

Nate slipped into his Toyota Corolla and backed out of the garage. He was so pumped that he had to use his cruise control. Excitement or anticipation usually resulted in speeding, and the last thing he wanted today was to be pulled over by the police. He turned on the radio to listen to some country music, but it did nothing to calm him. His fingers tapped the steering wheel as his expectation grew. *Don't get your hopes up, Conover,* he reminded himself over and over. *Kelso's? Why Kelso's? It's just a greasy spoon joint.* He considered that for a bit and then remembered, *That's where Sandy is well known and respected, and she'll have an almost private room.* He thought about that for a bit and concluded, *She's really got something for me. I knew she would come through. Thank you, God.*

Sandy and Nate arrived within seconds of each other. Sandy carried a file folder with her and had a smirk on her face. When Nate saw her grin, he concluded it was good news. Opening the door for her, he remarked, "Well, based on that smirk on your face, I'm assuming you have good news." Sandy didn't answer.

The hostess, if a greasy spoon diner can have a hostess, showed the two to Sandy's table. She brought them each coffee and a menu. "I'll be back in a few minutes."

"Well?" Nate was so hyped he couldn't wait for her report.

"Can't we order something first?" she remarked.

He raised his index finger to get the attention of the waitress. She arrived with a carafe of coffee. "Can I get you something?"

"I'll have a cinnamon roll, and she'll have …" Nate glanced at Sandy.

"Gotta watch my weight. Coffee . Thanks."

"It will be a just a few minutes."

Nate replied, "That's fine. I've got all day, but she doesn't." He smiled.

"Okay, we've got the preliminaries out of the way. Whaddya have?"

"Easy tiger!" She opened the file and began explaining what she'd learned. "I have the names of each of the complainants. Each one accused Stewart Alexander of stalking them, and each one dropped the charge. All the women served time in prison, and each was assigned the same parole officer, Logan Parsons. I have the last known addresses and phone numbers for the women. The rest of this is in your court."

Nate glanced over the information. "Hmm. Looks like I've got some leg work to do. I really want to thank you. I didn't expect this so quickly. Thanks."

"Hey, listen, I saw how frightened KC was that night I drove her home. She doesn't trust the legal system right now, and I know we cops failed to take her seriously in the beginning. This is what you are going to have to resolve. If and when you've built your case and submitted it to the DA, let me know. I want to be the one to arrest these creeps." She glanced at her watch and said, "Gotta go."

Nate pulled out his money clip and announced, "I've got this. Thanks for your help."

"Last of the big spenders, huh?"

"This will have to do until I can pay you better. Supper at Kenyon's Palace sound okay?" He winked as he stood to leave.

She was already out the door, but he knew he owed her big time. This case had already consumed much of his time.

Nate drove to the lakefront to review the records Roberts had given him. Page after page seemed to indict Alexander, but a verification by each of the victims would certainly indict Logan Parsons. *I just don't understand why Parsons would take such a chance. What's in it for him?*

Nate sat in the warmth of the sun for a couple of hours, but as the evening approached, he watched the huge ball of fire change from yellow to orange to blue and to purple, and it finally disappeared into the lake. The temperature in the car cooled as the sun disappeared. Nate always enjoyed watching a sunset, especially when he was near water. *Oh, God, you did a great job painting the sky tonight.* He revved his car to life and turned toward home. As he drove past a cul-de-sac, another car engine started. Nate thought nothing about sharing the road with another car. It was dark, and he was formulating his plan to solve the case. Focusing on the case but carefully driving along the curving road, Nate was stunned to see the driver attempting to pass despite the clearly marked yellow line. *What an idiot!* He slowed to allow the car to pass safely. Yet the car slowed too, and then it swerved toward Nate's car. Nate's police training instantly came to mind, and he, too, swerved to avoid an accident. The car rammed the left front bumper of Nate's car. Nate careened to the right and pulled the steering wheel to the left. He slammed on the brakes, and the offending driver sped away in the darkness.

# Chapter 49

"Officer Roberts, here," he heard on his cell phone. "Sandy, someone tried to run me off the road tonight. I'm okay. My heart rate raced for a while, but it's back to normal."

"Hey, listen, I have a break in an hour. Let's meet at the diner. I'll take a report then."

Nate knew he should have reported it immediately. However, he wanted to talk only with Sandy Roberts. He tried to recall all the details of the attack. With trembling hands, he wrote every detail he could. *So thankful for my police training.* "Oh, God, help me remember everything. I'm sure this has to do with KC. She's trying so hard to get her life together. She and her family need resolution. Please help me," he prayed. Sandy and Nate talked for nearly an hour. He gave her all the details he could remember.

"I know this is going to sound crazy, but I *think* I know what's going on. Let me tell you what I think is happening." He shared his assumptions with Sandy. Occasionally, she nodded her head as if agreeing. Other times, doubt reflected on her face. Her brows furled, her eyes narrowed, and her lips turned in opposite directions as if she was thinking.

"Tomorrow morning, I'm gonna try to contact those women. Any suggestion as to how to approach this?" Nate asked.

"Best I can offer you is to play it by ear with each one. But if your assumptions are correct, you are going to have to verify, verify, verify." Sandy tapped the table each time she said the word. She cautioned Nate that the women, most likely, will be suspicious. "You will have to be sure they are willing to refile a complaint and testify against the guys. I know you understand that, but I needed to say it." She left, and Nate was stuck with the tab again.

It was another restless night. Nate awakened twice in cold sweats after dreaming of the car bumping his car. *Sometime today I'll have to report this to the insurance company and then get an estimate on the repair.* He showered, shaved, dressed, and was out the door by a quarter til nine.

Nate approached the entrance of Advanced Web Designs hesitantly. *I wonder what kind of welcome I'll receive today.* He smiled wryly as he recalled his first visit. *I should have called first, but I have no time to waste.* He opened the door and noticed KC sitting at her desk. He cleared his throat. "KC, will you ask Mrs. Goen if I could talk with you, please?" The color drained from her face. Noticing the strain, Nate added, "Nothing's wrong. I need to bring you up to date."

KC nodded her head and disappeared down the hallway. He paced the small entryway. As he thought about what he wanted to say, he could feel his heart thumping in his chest. *Breathe, Conover. Breathe. Can't show KC how frightened you've been.* He turned when he heard footsteps coming down the hallway.

"Mr. Conover," he heard her say softly. "You may follow me to the conference room." He did as he was directed. "Please be seated. Would you like some coffee?"

"Thank you, but no." He attempted a smile, but KC could tell it was forced.

"Well, then, let's get on with it. What do you have to tell me?" *She certainly is very businesslike ... or scared,* Nate observed.

"You may remember Officer Sandy Roberts." He paused to see her reaction. She nodded. "I trust Sandy. She's a good officer, and she's helped me with other cases. She's one of the most ethical cops I know. She knows how long she can help and when to stop. What I'm saying is, I've enlisted her help. I've learned that Stewart Alexander, your stalker, has stalked other women. Best we can determine, your parole officer, Logan Parsons, has been paying him to terrorize many of the female parolees assigned to him."

KC's expression switched from fear to anger. "For what purpose? That's just insane. I haven't trusted him from the very beginning, but could he really be responsible?"

"Well, Officer Roberts and I hope to find out." He paused, wishing he'd taken her up on the offer of coffee. Swallowing the huge lump in his throat, he added, "If, and that's a big *if,* we verify what we think happened, I'll need you to help catch him." He looked across the room, letting that information sink in. He glanced back. "KC, do you think you could help me? I'm not sure how the scheme will work out. You might feel as if you are in danger, but I promise I'll never be far from you." His head tilted slightly to the right, and he reached across the table to touch her arm. "I'll let you think about that for a while. I'll call you later today for your answer, okay?"

Silence filled the room. He could hear the tick-tick-tick of the clock. He stood, and as he did the chair scraped the floor. Reaching the conference door, he heard KC clear her throat and say with a sigh, "No, no need to call. I'll do it. I simply cannot go on fearing for my life and watching my mother's physical and mental health slide." She stood with her head held high and her jaws clenched tightly in determination. "I'll do whatever is necessary, Nate."

"Thank you, KC, and please extend my appreciation to the Goens," he said as he turned the doorknob. He smiled. "Oh, by the way, if you hear about me being run off the road last night, don't worry about it. I'm fine."

"What?" But Nate was already out the door.

*Run off the road? What is he talking about? And if* he's *in danger, what can happen to me?* KC spent the better part of the day working on a project. Occasionally, her mind drifted back to Nate's comment.

"KC," Joyce said, staring at her. "KC, is everything okay? You seem to be a little distracted at times. Did Nate upset you?" She touched KC's arm and added, "I think it's time for another tea break. Let's go." She led KC to the break room. "Now what did young Mr. Conover want?" Joyce was rather terse.

*She doesn't mince words, does she? I think that's one of the reasons I like her so much. That and the fact the she and Mr. Goen really care about their employees.* KC had recently learned that in all the years they'd been owners of the company, only five times had they had to dismiss employees.

KC let out a huge sigh. She began telling her what Nate had said. Joyce was shocked to learn KC was going to be used as bait. At least, that's how she saw the situation. "Are you sure you want to do this, KC?"

"Honestly?" she looked deeply into Joyce's eyes and then looked away. "No, I'm not sure I want to, but I absolutely need to do this. Mom's lost more weight and rarely leaves the house. I need to do this for Mom. Charles has already given his approval"—she stopped briefly before adding—"and his warning." She grinned as she continued, "And I know Nate Conover doesn't want to experience the wrath of Charles Phillips." She smiled at Joyce and gulped down the last of her Earl Grey tea. "Better get back to work. I work for tough taskmasters, ya know."

Joyce stayed in the break room long after KC had returned to work. Sitting in the quietness of the room, she felt the strongest need to pray for KC's protection. *Oh, God, I've grown to love and respect KC. I've known her mom for a long time and was delighted when she married Charles. I know KC and Rose have clashed like cymbals at times, and I know*

*there is a lot of love being tested right now. KC sees an end to the stalking coming soon, but she's been asked to do something that might place her in more danger. I fear for her life, for her mental health, and for Rose and Charles. Whatever she needs to do to bring resolution to this nightmare, protect her. Build a hedge of safety around her.* Joyce had barely finished her prayer when she heard KC scream.

CHAPTER 50

N ate, dressed in khaki slacks and a dark blue polo shirt, entered Kelso's Diner. He had wanted to go to the diner across from the courthouse, but the first woman he needed to talk with refused to meet him there. So Nate suggested Kelso's, and Alice Bushong agreed to meet him there. She told him she'd be wearing an Indiana University sweatshirt, and he told her how she could identify him. He chose the booth near the back of the diner. Soon, a young woman wearing an IU sweatshirt entered. She had shoulder-length, thick auburn hair and goth makeup. He stood and waved. She walked over with an attitude.

"Okay, I'm here. Whaddya want?"

*Yep, she's got an attitude all right.* "First, can I buy you breakfast or lunch, coffee or soda?" He wanted to break the ice before the two began a serious talk.

"Well, I am hungry. I'll have the breakfast special and a Diet Coke." She *was* hungry. The breakfast special was sausage, pancakes, and hash browns. She'd eaten almost all of the food when she looked up at Nate and asked, "So, what is it you want to know?"

"Are you sure you're ready to talk? Maybe you'd like to finish breakfast, or do you want more? Remember, I'm buying." He smiled weakly.

"Naw, I think I can talk." She peered curiously and added, "Are you sure you're not a cop?"

"I used to be a cop, but now I own my own private investigation service. However, I do need to talk with you about your prison record and, more specifically, how your parole period went, okay?"

"Don't know why," she answered sarcastically. "No one wanted to listen to me when I was complaining a couple years ago."

Nate's left eyebrow raised a little. "I'm willing to listen if you're willing to tell me."

She drew long and slowly on the straw in her Diet Coke. "What's in it for me?"

*This is going to be as hard as I anticipated.* "Alice, how does revenge sound?" That question got her attention. "Now, neither you nor I will be harming the person who hurt you."

"Hurt me? Is that what you think this is about? I wasn't just hurt; I was forced to have sex with the jerk."

Nate's head jerked up in shock. He whispered hoarsely, "You were raped? By whom and why?"

"Yes, I was raped, but the police didn't believe me. No one believed me. I was forced to have sex with that creep every time I met him." She looked down at her hands. She had long acrylic fingernails painted bright red. She softly tapped her nails on the table.

"What was his name, and why did you continue to meet with him if he was raping you?" Nate had a good idea, but he needed Alice to say it.

"By law, I had to meet with my parole officer, Logan Parsons, whenever he called," Alice spoke quietly, yet her voice was tinged with anger, and she clenched her jaw as she spoke. "When I told the police, they refused to believe me because I was a convict. No one believes an ex-con. You know that, right? You were a cop. Would you have believed me?"

Nate's face was flushed and grew hot. He knew she was right. He wouldn't have believed her.

"Well," she waited. "Would you have believed me?"

"I'm ashamed to admit it, but probably not."

"So, Mr. Investigator, why should I help you?" Contempt dripped from each spoken word.

Nate had expected Alice to be uncooperative. The legal system had failed her. She had every right to be angry and skeptical.

"If you decide not to help, I understand. But let me ask you this question: Do you want this guy to continue abusing his female parolees?" His fingers covered his mouth, his thumb rested on his cheek, and he sat quietly. *Give her time to ponder the question.* "If it happened to your daughter, what would you want done?"

Alice sat stoically, shrugged her shoulders, and asked, "How many women did he rape?"

"Truthfully, we don't know. So far, we know that three women filed complaints, and all three withdrew their complaints."

"Are the other two going to refile their complaints?"

"Don't know. You're the first one I've talked with. If you asked the question, you can be sure they are going to ask it too. What do you want me to tell them?"

Tapping her fingernails on the table and chewing on the inside of her cheek, Alice contemplated the situation. If testifying against him could put him behind bars, it would be worth it. But it would mean her name would be in the news again. She had a job. It didn't pay much, but she had a job. *If my boss finds out, I might lose my job and then—*

"Tell you what: if I decide to testify, I could lose my job. So, here's my deal. My boss knows I served time, but I don't want his business to suffer, so if and only if he agrees not to fire me, and if the other women agree to testify, I'll do it." She slapped the table and added menacingly, "What I wouldn't do to see him in shackles."

"I'll take that as a yes." Nate's left eyebrow rose quizzically. "Would it help if I talked with your boss?"

Alice nodded her head. "But do you have to tell him I was raped repeatedly?"

"Probably," he said as he swallowed the last of his coffee. "I'll do my best to avoid telling him about it, but I suspect he's going to want to know why you are worried about your job and why you are testifying about a crime that happened a couple of years ago." He reached for his wallet and continued, "Alice, I've had to have that type of talk at other times. I've learned how to approach it carefully. The most important thing is that we all want justice, right?"

"Absolutely! You don't want to know what I really want to do to him, but I'll settle for this form of justice."

The two rose to leave. Nate had the check in his hand, put a generous tip on the table, and headed to the cashier. "Hey, Alice, if you move or change your phone, please, I beg you, please let me know. I'll need to know how to contact you." He noticed that she looked nervous. "Remember, you're not in trouble, okay?"

She nodded and left the diner.

Nate brooded over the information Alice had shared. *Why in the world would Parsons take advantage of his parolees?* Nate knew that Parsons's mother was on the state's parole review board. Rumors indicated that she rarely granted parole to prisoners she interviewed. He'd heard she smoked like a chimney, but, *Hey, that's her problem. Probably will die of lung cancer.* However, it didn't explain her son's behavior. *It's criminal behavior if it's true and is proven to be true. Whether he raped Alice or not, Parsons abused his authority as her parole officer and at the very least should be terminated.*

Nate reached for his cell phone and called another complainant, Susan Berg. On the third ring, it was answered. "Susan speaking, how many I help you?" *She sounds pleasant enough,* Nate thought. *Hope that bodes well.*

"Ms. Berg, this is Nate Conover. I'm a private investigator." He heard her breathe in deeply. "Let me explain. You aren't in trouble—"

"Well, let me tell you this: I know I'm not in trouble. I don't leave my apartment unless I'm going to the doctor. And I don't know why you are calling me."

"Please don't hang up. I need your help. I need to know the name of your parole officer. Can we meet somewhere?" he asked.

"Didn't you hear me? I don't leave my apartment unless I absolutely have to. I suffer from agoraphobia, the fear—"

"Of being with people or in open spaces. I understand. Do you allow people to visit with you?" He was desperate to talk with her. But suspecting that she, too, had been raped by Parsons, he didn't want to meet with her alone. He couldn't allow himself to be alone with the opposite sex in private for fear of being falsely accused of impropriety.

"Usually, I don't allow men in my house if I'm alone. Can't trust them," she answered with profound sadness.

"I believe I understand the reason why." He hesitated for several seconds. "Tell you what. You invite whomever you wish and trust to be with you, and I'll bring a female friend. But I really need to talk with you. I'm asking you to trust me. I want to help you."

"Leave me your phone number, and I'll see who I can get to come sit with me. I might call my therapist."

"That would be great. I'll ask a female police officer."

"I thought you said I wasn't in trouble." Fear tinged her voice.

"You're not, but this officer is trying to help me. You ask your therapist what time works for her. Let me know, and I'll call the officer to sync our schedules. Okay?" he questioned hopefully.

There was silence on Susan's end. He heard her sniff and instinctively knew she was crying. He didn't continue the conversation; instead, he waited for her to answer. His heart was beating rapidly in anticipation.

"If you're sure I'm not in trouble, I'll do it," Susan replied. "But I'll sue your pants off if you're lying to me."

"Susan, you can trust me. I know you've paid your debt to society. My goal is to see that you and others—"

"You mean there were others?"

"Yes, there were others, and I want you and the others to get justice."

"I'll call you back as soon as I can make the arrangements." Her voice held a note of hope.

"Very well, then, here's my number. Call me anytime." He hit the end key on his phone.

*Great! I believe we will be able to nail that unethical representative who's a rapist.* Nate suspected it would be several hours before Susan returned his call. He glanced at the next woman on the list Officer Roberts had given him. He punched in her phone number, but after five rings, he heard, "I'm sorry. The number you called is no longer in service." *Well, I didn't think I would be successful with all my calls, but I'm not giving up.* Looking again at the file, he noted that complainant number three used to work at the hospital in housekeeping. *Hmmm, who do I know that works at the hospital?* A name didn't come to mind immediately so he decided to take a break. *I think I need a cup of coffee and a quiet place to connect the dots.* A drive to the lake would be relaxing, but he didn't want to take any chance that he might be followed again. *I know I won't be followed again because I'm watching my back always. I won't go to the lake, but I could go to Cascades Park. Should be safe there.* He put his coffee cup in the car's cup holder, turned on the car, and headed to the park just north of town. Every few seconds he glanced into the rearview mirror. He drove around for several minutes and finally decided it was safe to park. However, he didn't pull into a parking lot. Instead, he parked along the roadside, leaving the engine purring. It would give him plenty of time to drive away when another car approached, friendly or not.

Sitting along the roadside, he felt his body relax a tad. He sipped his coffee slowly and enjoyed the warmth of the sun. He felt his cell phone begin vibrating and then heard the ring tone. "Conover." That's how he always answered his calls.

"Well, Conover, this is Officer Roberts. Want more information?"

"Are you kidding me? Of course, I want more information. Anything that will help catch this perp." His heart jumped and thumped excitedly. "Whaddya have?"

"Not right now. Meet you tonight at Kelso's, okay? 6:15."

Before Nate had the opportunity to agree, he heard silence. *Guess I have a date tonight at 6:15. But it's not a date. Would love to ask her out, but don't want to do anything that might scare her off. I need her help right now. After we solve this, maybe then I'll ask her out.*

His thoughts were jarred when he heard a car approaching. Looking in the rearview mirror, he didn't sense danger, so he put his car in drive and off he went.

CHAPTER 51

KC wouldn't talk about the stalking with her mother or Charles. Charles had hired Nate, and she knew Nate was giving him periodic reports. She saw no reason to talk about it at home. Occasionally, she'd find a note under the wiper of her windshield. Nate had asked her to save all the notes she received and put them in plastic bags. She mused, *I'm probably the only person in Bloomfield carrying a box of baggies in my purse.* Yet she knew Nate was right. All notes needed to be kept as eventually they would be used as evidence.

Sitting at a stoplight, KC heard her phone ring. *Oh, no. Not now. I can't answer. Please, please leave a message.* The light changed to green, and she was off. *Where can I pull over to check messages? Gotta see who called me. Wish I had a car with built-in Bluetooth.* Five minutes slipped by, and then she saw the shopping mall. *There! I'll pull in there.*

She circled the parking lot several times. KC wanted to be sure she hadn't been followed. Convinced she was safe, she parked in the "back forty" of the mall lot. Always aware of her own security, KC kept the engine on and doors locked. Her purse was on the floorboard, requiring her to lean over to retrieve her phone. *Excellent! Nate called.* She tapped the voice message icon and listened.

"KC, it's Nate Conover, but you already knew that. So far, I've talked with two women who had problems with Logan Parsons.

One jumped at the opportunity to talk about him. The other suffers from agoraphobia. I'm waiting for her to call me back with a time when she and I can talk at her home. Long story so I'll tell you in person. In the meantime, do not—I repeat—do not meet with Logan Parsons privately. Always schedule your appointments in a public facility. Still working on a plan. Hopefully within a couple of weeks we'll be able to wrap this up and you can get on with your life. I'll call you. Tomorrow I'm having lunch with Charles. You don't need to talk with him. This is just an FYI. Talk later." KC listened to the message again. She took a couple of deeps breaths and exhaled slowly. *Nate Conover, I hope you're right. Mom is definitely ready for this to be over. And I'm more than ready to begin living again.*

It was nearly six o'clock in the evening, and Nate pointed his car in the direction of Kelso's Diner. He opened the door and seated himself in the booth at the back of the restaurant. "What's your special for tonight?" He tried to guess by the aroma. "Beef stew, perhaps?"

"Oh, no, sir," the server replied. "But you're close. Roast beef, mashed potatoes, green beans, side salad, and a drink. Does that sound interesting?"

Nate felt his stomach growl and answered, "I'll take the special. Ranch dressing, cup of coffee. Any pie left?"

"Sure, couple slices of apple pie."

"Then I'll have apple pie with a scoop of ice cream on top," He winked at her and added, "I've heard, 'Life is short; eat dessert first,' so I think I'll have the pie while I wait for my companion."

"Yes, sir. I'll get your pie—"

"And ice cream," he interrupted her and smiled.

"And ice cream. And coffee?" Mischievousness showed in her smile. Nate started to answer, but she'd already walked back to the kitchen. She brought his pie, ice cream, and coffee at about the same time Officer Roberts arrived.

"Hi there! I waited for you like one hog waits for the others."

Sandy slid into the booth, and he continued, "I haven't eaten since breakfast. Decided I deserved the dessert."

"I don't know that you *deserved* it," she remarked, "but I'm sure it looks better on you than me. So I guess I'll have to decline it." She smiled briefly as she looked over the menu. "I wonder if they have a half-size serving of their special. It sounds good, but I don't need a full serving."

"You know I'll pay for it, so why not ask for a take-home box," he suggested. "You can take it to work with you tomorrow."

"Maybe I'll do that. Thanks for the suggestion." Sandy leaned on the table with her right hand over the left. "I don't know if this is good news or not. That third name on the list ..." She looked at Nate.

"I wasn't able to contact her. The file you gave me said she used to work at—"

"The hospital," they said together. They laughed.

"Well," she began, "ignore that. She violated her parole and was sent back to the women's facility in Dwight."

"Thank you, Officer Roberts." He stopped briefly as their meals were delivered. "At least now I know where to find her. Phone number was out of service. I knew the personnel department at the hospital wouldn't give me information." He shoveled into his mouth a bite of roast beef and gravy. "Mmm! That's good!" He swallowed some coffee and inquired, "Any chance I could get on her visitor's list?"

"I pulled some strings, and you're already on it," Sandy said with a smile.

"Keep it up, Roberts, and you might be promoted to detective soon." During the rest of the meal, Nate brought her up to date on what he'd learned. When he shared what he'd learned about Susan, he questioned Sandy as to her availability to meet with Susan and her counselor.

"Well, it depends on the day and time. I honestly don't know if it's appropriate. You're getting me close to a line I won't step over now. I think I need to talk with my supervisor."

Nate frowned disappointedly. "I was hoping we wouldn't have to involve the higher-ups." He sipped on his coffee. Reluctantly, he answered, "If you think you must, then you must. Is there someone you really trust?"

She wiped her mouth with the paper napkin and replied, "I think so, but let me think about it overnight. The information I gave you on complainant number three is a matter of public record, so that shouldn't be a problem. I'll call you tomorrow, okay?"

He nodded his head, wiped his mouth, tossed a twenty-dollar bill on the table, and escorted Sandy Roberts to her car. Nate watched her pull out of the parking lot, making sure she wasn't being followed.

CHAPTER 52

The only good thing about the drive to Dwight was the interstate highway. The weather was rainy and cold, and Nate wasn't excited about making the drive on this dreary day. However, he was eager to talk with Trish McMann, complainant number three. She had a name, and he'd read her criminal records. Trish was a drug addict and a dealer. This supposedly was her fourth incarceration on drug charges. *I'm really eager to hear her story. I know most convicts claim innocence, but she might actually be innocent. If her story checks out with the others, she can help us solve this case.* He took the next exit to fuel his car. While he was waiting for his tank to fill, he plugged in his tablet and selected an album of Christian rock. With the tank full and another cup of strong coffee, Nate was on his way again.

Tapping his fingers on the steering wheel to the beat of the songs kept him awake. He glimpsed toward his GPS and learned that his estimated time of arrival was twenty-three minutes. He dropped the volume of his tablet and began reviewing the questions to which he and Officer Roberts needed answers. If Trish was willing to talk and if her answers matched those of Alice's and, hopefully, Susan's, he would agree to talk with the district attorney to have her sentence commuted or reduced.

Arriving at the prison in Dwight, he checked in at the desk.

True to her word, Officer Roberts had worked miracles and gotten his name on the visitors' list. "Sit over there," the prison clerk said matter-of-factly. "Will take some time to find her." Nate sat in the crowded waiting room. The other visitors ranged in age from infants to grandparents. Most of the adults sat stoically, while the children poked one another. Some of the children talked to other children, and some tried to converse with the adults. One by one, names were called, and the families, whatever they consisted of, rose and headed to the large visiting room. It was close to an hour that Nate sat silently brooding about what direction this visit would go. *Trish could refuse to talk with me. That would send me—I should say, us—back to square one.* Finally, Nate heard his name called. He walked to the desk, where he received directions. "Here's your locker key." The clerk rattled off a list of all things prohibited in the visitation room that should be placed in the locker. "Go to the gate and wait for the guard." The clerk pointed in the direction of the gate. Nothing more was said. *I think they need a course on courtesy,* he thought, but then he reminded himself that this was nothing more than a job to most of the employees. It had become humdrum. *I would bet the front desk clerks have seen many of these visitors many, many times.* This guard pushed another coded keyboard and electronically opened the gate. Nate stepped in and immediately was frisked for contraband. "You've got an hour." He opened the door to the visitation room. It was loud, as if everyone was shouting to be heard.

Nate explained to the guard that he didn't know what Trish looked like and asked if he might point her out to him. Surprisingly, he did. Nate walked over to where Trish was sitting. "Trish, I'm Nate Conover, a private investigator." He reached out to shake hands, but the guard announced, "No touching." He pulled his hand back.

"Yeah, so whaddya want?" She slumped down in the chair with her arms crossed and a sour look on her face.

"I need your help," he replied.

"Sure. You and who else? And why should I help you?" Her disdain for authority was evident.

"Well, it's been brought to my attention that you were assigned Logan Parsons as your parole officer. Is that right?" he asked assertively.

She spat his name. "Logan Parsons can go to—"

"I can see there's no love lost between the two of you." He waited for a retort.

"He's the reason I'm in this freakin' place."

Nate's antennae went up. His eyes widened, and he paused to see if she would offer anything else.

"Okay, I admit I was usin' again. But what he did to me should never have happened." Fear and hatred were clearly evident in her answers.

"Tell me about it, please," Nate requested.

"Why? You guys never believe cons. You always believe people in authority." She clammed up and twirled her hair nervously. Nate sat silently. He surmised she would continue sooner or later.

"I was doing pretty good—stayin' clean, had a job, and never tested positive for any drugs. I hated Parsons from the moment I met him. I didn't like the way he looked at me. Well, to be honest with you, I didn't like the way he leered at me. It was as if he was undressing me." Nate listened. "One night after I peed in the cup, he called me back to the office. Told me I'd failed the drug test. I said, 'Naw, no way. I haven't taken any drugs and haven't been around anyone taking drugs. I knew the provisions of my parole.'" She stopped and waited for Nate to ask questions. He didn't, so she persisted in explaining her encounters with Parsons. "He walked around to my side of the desk. Said, 'Ya know, I could overlook this transgression if you'd...' Then he walked behind me and began giving me a shoulder rub. I shrugged his hands off and told him where he could go. He grabbed my arms and said, 'I'll make you pay for that.' He demanded I take off my clothes. I refused. He pushed me against the file cabinet and raped me. When he was done, he said he was going to have my parole revoked. I slapped him. Yeah, I know I shouldn't have, but I did. Said since I didn't give it up to him willingly, he was going to teach me a lesson. So, now you know why I'm here. Whaddya gonna do about it?" It was clear she expected an answer.

Nate glanced at his watch and noticed that their time was running out. "Trish, thank you for sharing this information with me. I've recently learned about several similar complaints against him. If I can arrange for a court reporter to meet with us another day, would you be willing to recount this event?"

"You bet I will. I want that egotistical idiot to pay for what he did to me."

Nate thanked her and added, "I hope to see you in a couple of days." He turned and walked toward the door, which the guard opened. Before Nate stepped through, he looked back at Trish, knowing she probably was going to be strip searched. Why? He didn't know. They hadn't been allowed to touch each other.

"Come on, fella. Move it," the gruff guard announced.

Nate couldn't move quickly enough. The code for the electronic box had to be punched in, and then the gate opened. He opened his locker, grabbed all his belongings, and signed out. Stepping outside, he took a deep breath of air. *Part of me is glad I only had an hour. I'm thankful I can breathe fresh air. It smelled like no one ever takes a shower in there.* Inside, the odor of wet and soiled diapers, not to mention sweaty bodies, was prevalent. *Remember, you will probably get to do this again in a couple of days.*

Climbing into his car, he thanked God that his mother and father had reared him in the church and that he had never strayed from the straight and narrow ... except for his alcoholism. He buckled his seat belt, brought the engine to life, and left the parking lot. Reaching the interstate, he sighed heavily. *I hope and pray we can wind up the case very soon. I'm spending too much time with Sandy Roberts and enjoying it very much.* He smiled at the thought of Sandy. *Remember, you've promised to take her for dinner.* He laughed aloud.

His gut told him he was being followed. Every few seconds, he'd glance in the rearview mirror and see that a black Equinox SUV was behind him. *I'm certain I'm being followed.* He'd speed up and then slow down. Whatever he did, the driver of the SUV did the same. Nate began weaving in and out of the traffic. The SUV driver mimicked what Nate did. Arriving in Bloomfield, Nate drove straight to the police station, but the SUV drove on past. *At least he didn't try to run me off the road. This is a loaner car. Don't think the insurance company would appreciate it if I called and reported that I'd been run off the road again. Gonna see if Sandy's on duty. Maybe she can give me a ride home.* He shivered as he thought about the possibility that her life could be in danger too. *Gonna change that plan. Maybe I'll call for a cab.*

# CHAPTER 53

F inally arriving home, Nate noticed that he had a voice message from Officer Roberts. "Nate, got a meeting scheduled with Susan and her therapist on Friday at 9:00 at her apartment. I've stuck my head out on this case for you. You better be there, got it?"

Nate snickered and deliberated whether he should return her call. Yawning and rubbing his whiskers, he decided he'd wait till morning. *I'm tired, and she didn't seem to be in a very good mood. Friday is a couple of days away, which gives me the opportunity to organize the information we have already gathered.*

Morning sunlight streamed through his bedroom window as Nate stretched and yawned. Punching the pillow, he rolled over, hoping sleep would overcome him. Fifteen minutes passed and, after flopping like a fish, he forced himself to get up. After a brief stop in the bathroom, he stumbled to the kitchen to get a cup of coffee. *So glad I invested in that one-cup machine. Coffee in less than a minute.* While he waited for his coffee, he put a bowl of cereal in the breakfast nook. *Beep, beep, beep.* The coffee was ready, and so was his breakfast.

Following breakfast, Nate showered, shaved, and dressed in faded blue jeans and a sweatshirt. *No need to overdress. All I'm doing today is trying to make sense of the information we've gathered.* Walking into his living room, he noticed a piece of paper on the floor near the door. A bit of a neat freak, Nate grabbed it and began to toss it in the trash, but something in the pit of his stomach told him to read it. "Listen, big shot, back off or else!"

His first instinct was to crumple the paper into a wad. Yet his investigative training overcame his initial instinct. Walking into his office, he carefully slipped the paper into an evidence bag. *Whoever left this dropped it in the mail slot. I knew last night I was being followed. Thought I'd given him the slip by going to the police station and calling a cab. I'm sure Logan Parsons is involved. I've got to talk with Sandy. Maybe she can get fingerprints off the paper.*

Later that day, Nate's cell phone vibrated. Glancing at the caller ID, he quickly answered, "Sandy, do you have anything for me?"

"Slow down, Nate. The paper had two sets of prints: yours, and an ex-con's named Johnny "Cokehead" Bailey. He has a record going back fifteen years. He's on parole right now. Wanna guess who his parole officer is?"

"Logan Parsons."

"That's right. All we have to do is find Johnny and have a talk with him. Logan Parsons doesn't realize it, but he will soon be facing his victims, and more than likely he's going to go to prison for several years. Abuse of power is also a crime."

"Are you going to keep the note in your custody? I think it would be best if you could."

"Well, I think we are at a point where a complaint needs to be filed. I think it is the only way I can keep the evidence."

Nate ran his hands through his hair. He considered her comment and came up with another idea. "What if I put it in my safety deposit box at the bank until we get signed affidavits from the other women? I really don't want Logan to know how close we are to requesting an arrest order. We'll need to talk with the DA and lay out our information to get an indictment."

Silence greeted Nate for a few seconds. Sandy finally spoke, "I really think we should do that sooner rather than later. I'll call the DA's office to set up an appointment. Call you back soon." There was no good-bye, but Nate knew the conversation was over for the time being.

Evidence upon evidence was piling up. The most difficult to establish was a motive. *What motive would Parsons have to terrorize the women? Rape is about more than sex; it is about power. He'd been placed in a position of power, and he'd been abusing it.* Nate was reviewing the information gathered to prove it. The more Nate reviewed the data, the more angry he became. He almost wore a path from his desk to the kitchen as he paced. He smacked his fist in the palm of his other hand. "Why, dear God? Why? I don't understand why he would do it. I'm absolutely sure he did what those ladies said. Even though it is hard to believe a druggie like Stewart Alexander, I even believe him." Nate repeated it so often that it was almost a mantra.

His cell phone alerted him to a call. "Sandy?"

"You must have had that phone in your hand. I didn't even hear it ring once."

"Come on, Sandy. When's the meeting?" His eagerness was so apparent. Sandy could picture him pacing anxiously.

"How's today at 1:30 sound? Got everything you need?"

"All but signed and notarized affidavits from the victims. I know KC's ready. I think Susan is iffy, and if I can get permission to get a court reporter into the prison, I have no doubt that Trish will sign. Stewart Alexander, I think, will cooperate. He told me he wanted to get clean but doesn't have the money to go to rehab. Don't know anything about Johnny "Cokehead" Bailey. I'm almost afraid to approach him until we have Parsons in lockup.

---

"You folks have really done your research," District Attorney Solomon Prescott said. "Get the affidavits signed by the women and Alexander; find Johnny Bailey and get his side of the story; and I'll issue a warrant for Logan Parsons. You *do* know that Parsons has connections in high places, don't you?" He didn't wait for an answer. "His mother, Geraldine Grossman, is the chair of the state's parole board. She's gonna fight this tooth and nail." He paused. "But I believe you have a powerful case against her son. Now, go get the rest of the documents you need to wrap this up."

Sandy and Nate left Prescott's office. Sandy was filled with relief that she hadn't gotten reprimanded for working behind the scenes, and Nate was thrilled to see the light at the end of the tunnel. "We should have asked the DA to issue a permit to the court reporter to visit with Trish," Sandy said. "But I think it would be good for her to have an attorney present, don't you?"

"Absolutely! I think I need to go back to Dwight to explain all this to Trish and verify that she's going to press charges. I'll take care of finding out who her attorney is. You talk with the DA again. It's too late to go today and we've got the meeting with Susan tomorrow, so the earliest I could go is Monday." He mashed his lips together. "No. That's not soon enough. Ask Prescott if he could arrange a telephone call. I'll contact the attorney. Sound okay?"

Sandy couldn't decide if she had been given more work to do or not. "Nate, most of this investigation you've done, but I've worked behind the scenes. I think I need to ask my supervisor to allow me to focus on this. He's likely to tell me I'll have to use personal time. I won't make any money while I'm doing that."

Nate smiled slyly. "Not a problem, Sandy. I'll pay you for the time you miss at work. It's really important that we close this case. Justice has to be done." He turned to walk away but stopped and said, "Let me know what Prescott says—and your supervisor, okay?" He was out the door before Sandy answered.

CHAPTER 54

N ate and Sandy arrived at Susan's apartment at the agreed-upon time. Her counselor was with her. "Thank you for meeting us, Susan," Sandy began. "We want to assure you that you are not in any trouble. We need your statement so we can bring Logan Parsons to justice. I assure you—you are not his only victim."

Susan sat opposite Sandy and Nate, and her counselor, Dr. Walters, sat beside her. Susan twisted a napkin in her hands.

"Are you ready?" Nate inquired.

She dabbed at her eyes and twisted the napkin tighter. "Yes, let's get this over with."

Sandy and Nate asked questions and sought details for nearly an hour. "Did you report the rape to the police?"

She shook her head no and covered her face. "I didn't think they would believe me, so I didn't say anything." Silence filled the room. Sandy and Nate sat quietly. It seemed as if they sat saying nothing for an hour. Finally, Susan spoke quietly. "If you're looking for DNA, I can provide that." Tears flooded down her cheeks. "The last time he raped me, I got pregnant. I didn't want a reminder of that monster, so I gave the baby up for adoption. I also went to the rape crisis center because I wanted records of the rape. They have the photos and everything you need."

285

Sandy cleared her voice and broke the silence. Speaking softly and with kindness, she asked, "Why didn't you pursue charges? I know you didn't think the police would believe you, but I don't understand why you'd go to the rape crisis center and then not allow them to follow up."

"I knew I wasn't the only woman he raped—"

"You knew he'd raped other women?" Roberts asked incredulously. "How did you know?"

"He told me. I knew that at some time in the future, he'd be found out. Then I would come forward. I received anonymous letters and phone calls, and at least once someone was in my apartment. Every so often, I felt I was being followed."

"Did you ever see the person following you?" queried Nate.

Her eyes were closed tightly, her brows creased, and her teeth clenched. "Yes," she said, nodding. "Well, not so much saw him, but always gave me a salute." She lifted her hand and raised one finger to her eyebrows. "It's what he always did." She opened her eyes and shuddered.

Sandy glanced at Nate. "Any more questions?" she asked.

"Yes. Susan, we're asking everyone who accuses Parsons of rape if they'd sign an affidavit. Will you? And can we get the photos from the rape crisis center? Was the adoption an open adoption?"

"Yes, yes, and yes," she softly answered. "I really don't want to testify against him, but I will if I must. But only if necessary. I know the adoptive parents," she added, smiling. "They've been kind enough to send me photos once or twice a year. He's a handsome little boy."

"Dr. Walters," Nate said, turning toward the doctor, "do you think you can help Susan prepare for court if it is needed?"

"If Susan wants me to help her, I'll do my best." She looked at Susan, who nodded her agreement.

"Okay, then," Nate announced. "We need to arrange for an affidavit. What time works for you? And Doctor, do you want to be here?"

"Whatever time works for Susan, and I'll be here if Susan wants me to be here."

"How does Monday at 9:30 sound?" he asked.

"Well, with agoraphobia, it's not like I have a calendar filled with appointments. Yes, Monday at 9:30 will be fine." She turned to her counselor and added, "Dr. Walters, I think I need to face the monster who destroyed my life! However, if I have to go to court, I would like your support, okay?"

"I think that's a good step forward."

Nate called Charles to arrange a meeting to report the progress of the case. They sat at their usual booth in the diner. "Conover, I'm glad to hear this," Charles said, pausing briefly. "Do you think you'll have to use KC as bait?" Worry was evident in his voice.

"I'm hoping not. However, if any of the other women back out, I will. I suspect that once the media learns of Parsons's arrest, other women will come forward. I'm hoping he'll be smart enough to cop a plea. I deplore how he's abused his power, but I hate putting the women through a trial," Nate said with resignation. "The truth? I'd love to nail that guy. I want him to go to prison for the rest of his life. I'm not sure we can get it, but that's my hope."

"You'd better hope he gets put away for a long time. If he beats this rap ... well, I don't know what I'll do. Rose has lost so much weight and has lost interest in life. I'm afraid for her, but I'm also concerned for KC."

"Don't borrow trouble, Charles. We don't know how things are going to turn out. Either way, I think you have a lawsuit against Parsons and probably the State Board of Parole." Nate let that information soak in. He sensed that Charles had stopped short of threatening harm to Parsons. *I certainly understand his desire to retaliate against Parsons. I don't know what I would do if it had been my mom or sister or girlfriend.* "Remember, Charles, no threats or assaults. Understand?"

"Yeah, I understand," he acquiesced. Charles rose to leave, and Nate watched a crushed man walk out the door. His shoulders stooped, the twinkle in his eyes was gone, and the furrow between his eyes deeper than before.

Officer Roberts was busy on her end of the case. She hurried back to the DA's office and rapped on the large, solid mahogany door bearing a brushed nickel nameplate that read, "Solomon Prescott, District Attorney." Roberts waited for an answer. Not hearing one, she carefully opened the door and announced her presence. "Mr. Prescott? Are you here?"

*Oh, for Pete's sake. Can't I even have a break to eat lunch?* "Whaddya want?" he yelled, his frustration apparent in his curt answer. Roberts almost backed out of the office.

*No! Don't back out. This is too important to allow him to frighten me.* "Mr. Prescott, I need to ask a favor," she answered.

"Well," he replied, "you've already disturbed me. Come in."

"I believe we all are anxious to resolve this issue. Would you order the warden to allow me, Nate Conover, Trish's attorney, and a court reporter to interview Trish on Sunday afternoon?" She heard him sigh loudly. "It's either that, or would you order the warden to allow Trish to talk via a conference call with us, her attorney, and our court reporter? Or perhaps you can have her come to your office and conduct the necessary discussion."

Prescott cleared his throat. "Officer Roberts, surely you're aware that I can't make the warden do anything. That request will have to come from the Department of Corrections." He swallowed from a cup of tea and continued. "I'm willing to call the director *after* I finish my lunch. Is that soon enough for you?"

"Mr. Prescott, I will await your answer this afternoon." She knew she was pressing her luck by giving him a timeline, but she felt certain he wanted to clear up the issue. *I suspect he's eager for this to hit the papers. He's running for state's attorney. He's a politician. I can imagine his campaign slogan: The Department of Corrections needs correction.*

Prescott leaned back in his leather desk chair. He propped his feet on his mahogany desk and rested his head on folded hands. *This is my chance to surge ahead in the polls. But I can't go to the current director.* He pulled out the directory of state departments. Thumbing through the book, he located the Department of Corrections and ran his finger down the page to Dwight Prison. *I can't believe it! Could it be that simple?* The warden of the prison was an army buddy.

His lunch period was over, but he asked his administrative assistant not to disturb him. Rather than use the office phone, he grabbed his cell phone and punched in the phone number listed in the directory. He paced in his office. After being transferred from one department to another, he finally reached the warden's office. "I'm sorry, Warden Shafer is out of the office right now," the receptionist informed him. "I think he'll be back in about thirty minutes. Can I have him call you back?" Prescott gave her his phone number and emphasized the importance of a return call. "I'll tell him Solomon Prescott called," she assured him

Solomon sat quietly for several minutes. Still trying to process all he'd learned, he did something he hadn't done for years: he prayed. *God, I believe everything Roberts and Conover told me. I don't know that I can trust the current attorney general or the director of the corrections department. I hate to bypass the chain of command, but I feel I must. Kevin Shafer is the only one I can trust. Please make him agreeable to what I'm going to ask. Please, all the evidence indicates that Logan Parsons has been abusing his power and sexually assaulting the women assigned to him.* Again, he sat silently. *I can't sit here any longer. Gotta take a walk.*

He yanked open his door and stepped out onto the plush carpet. "I'll be back in about an hour," he told the receptionist. "I've got to work through some stuff in my brain. Walking always clears my mind. I've got my phone," he said, holding up his cell phone. "If something comes up, call me." He left without another word.

The weather was getting cooler, but it didn't bother Prescott. He walked around the block several times. He spotted an empty bench near a tree losing its leaves. He walked over and sat. *Please call, Kevin. I need an answer, and I need to get back to—* His phone rang. *Please let it be him.* Looking at caller ID, he knew it wasn't his office. On the second ring, Prescott answered, "Kevin?"

"Hey, buddy. Who else would it be. My secretary said it was important. So, what's up?"

Prescott shared the theory presented to him by Officer Roberts and Nate Conover. He then said to Kevin, "I need to ask a favor. I'd like to come visit with Trish. And I want Roberts, Conover, and my secretary to talk with her. I need to take an affidavit. Or is it possible for her to come to my office?"

"Why don't you enlist the help of the director of the Department of Corrections?"

"Honestly? I don't believe he would help since I'm running against him. And the evidence convinces me that Logan Parsons is guilty. But you know his mother is the chairperson of the state board of parole, right? Who's gonna believe her son would capriciously rape female parolees? Certainly not his mother, and she always has the ear of the director. I hate to break the chain of command, but I'm begging you—please let us come talk with her."

Silence! Prescott could feel his heart pounding in his chest as he waited for Kevin's answer.

"I'll *allow* it. But it will need to be done here. I'm not letting her out until she has to appear in court. "And I will be present too."

"Oh, that's great. Thanks, Kevin. We can be there Sunday at about one thirty, okay?"

"That's fine. You'll have one hour. That's all."

CHAPTER 55

Officer Roberts's cell phone vibrated. She quickly answered it when she saw who was calling. "Roberts, here. How can I help you, Mr. Prescott?"

"You can help me by being available Sunday to travel to Dwight. Turns out the warden is an old army buddy." There was a hint of satisfaction in his voice. "And we will only have one hour to interview her."

"Oh, that's great." She suddenly heard exactly what he had said. "We? As in me and Conover?"

"No, as in you, Conover, me, and my secretary." This time, Roberts could sense a smile in his voice. "And, I believe Warden Shafer will allow her to type and print the affidavit while we're there. Then Ms. Barker can notarize the statement. We will be well on our way to obtaining an arrest warrant," he announced confidently.

"Thank you, sir. It is great news, and your special efforts are appreciated. I'll let Conover know." She pressed end, and the call was over.

As soon as the call was over, she called Nate. Unfortunately, he did not answer, so she left a text message for him to meet her at Kelso's Diner ASAP. She pointed her car in the direction of the diner. *I'd rather sit in the car and wait for him, but I think Parsons is crazy enough to have me followed and I don't want to be a sitting duck for him.* She threw open the squad car's door, made sure she had her radio with her, closed the door, and locked it.

Once again, she chose the booth in the back of the diner. The server asked what she wanted, and the answer was simple: "I think I'll have hot tea. It's getting a little nippy outside. I have a gentleman meeting me." The server nodded and returned within five minutes with a cup of steaming hot water and a tea bag of Earl Grey tea.

Sandy sat alone for about ten minutes and wondered if Nate would show up. *I'll wait another ten minutes,* she thought. Just then, the door chimes rang, and she looked up to see Nate enter. He walked to the booth and sat down.

"Well, you must have heard something," he said. "You didn't text me, so I figured we needed to talk face to face."

"Now I know why you're a private investigator. You're so observant and smart," she remarked.

"Flattery, flattery, flattery will get you everywhere," he joked with her. "But I could read between the lines. You've got something, right?"

The server approached and asked what Nate would like to drink. "Just coffee, please," was his reply.

"Well," Nate said, drawing out the word. "What do you have?"

"We have a date with Solomon Prescott and his secretary, Ms. Barker, this Sunday at 1:30. Ms. Barker is going to record the conference. Prescott is fairly certain that the warden, who is an old army buddy of his, will allow her to use the computer, print off the document, witness, sign, and notarize the affidavit. And—I'm making an assumption—I think he will allow her to e-mail it to keep it handy." She took a deep breath. "How does that sound?"

"Like Christmas came early!" A broad smile was plastered across his face. "Only one question—well, more than one, but for right now one question." He swallowed a mouthful of coffee. "Are we all riding together, or what are the arrangements?"

Laughing, Sandy responded, "We didn't even talk about that. I'll call him to ask him."

Darkness clouded Nate's face. Sandy stopped laughing. She skewed her head, and her left eyebrow elevated just a tad. "What's wrong, Nate?"

"Wrong? No, nothing really. I was just thinking. We need to come up with questions to ask her."

"I was so excited about setting up the meeting, I forgot." Sandy sighed heavily. "Want me to ask Prescott if we can have a powwow to clarify our questions?

"Might be a good idea. When you call to check on the transportation, ask about that?"

"Sure, but I don't think this is the best place to make the call. I think I'll stop by the office." She rose to leave. "I'll call you with the information." She left.

The server brought the check for the coffee and tea. Nate laughed. *Can't believe it! I got stuck paying for her again.*

As previously arranged, Nate, Officer Roberts, Solomon Prescott, and Ms. Barker arrived at the prison at about one fifteen. Warden Kevin Shafer greeted Solomon with a firm handshake. Solomon introduced the remaining members of the group, and they were led to his office, where they exchanged pleasantries for a few minutes. A knock at the door interrupted their conversation.

"Enter," was the only word Shafer uttered. After the sound of keys in the locked door, the door opened. "Prisoner Trish McMann?" Shafer asked.

She wore handcuffs and shackles. She nodded and replied hesitantly, "Yes, sir." Her voice was soft and quivering. It was clear to Sandy that Trish was nervous.

"Ms. McMann, you know why you are here, don't you?" Shafer asked.

"Yes, Warden Shafer, I do," she replied, but her eyes didn't make contact with his.

"Then let me introduce these people." Pointing first at his army buddy, he announced, "This is District Attorney Solomon Prescott." Moving down the line, he added, "This is Ms. Barker. She's Prescott's administrative secretary, meaning she runs the office and Prescott does what she says." Ms. Barker was embarrassed by the compliment but thought, *You have no idea how true that is.* She smiled at Trish. He continued, "This is Officer Sandy Roberts, and I believe you've met Nate Conover."

"Yes, sir. I have."

"I will be staying in the office while you answer questions. I realize it isn't what you want, but it's necessary." She nodded her understanding. "Then let's sit down and get this going." He looked again at Trish and then the others in the room and continued, "You remember, you have only one hour, right?"

Ms. Barker pulled out her steno machine, and the others waited while she set it up. She bobbed her head slightly to Prescott to indicate that she was ready, and the questions began. Shafer listened raptly. The more Trish opened up, the more he was convinced that she had been railroaded. Rather than stopping the questioning after an hour, he allowed an additional hour of questions. By the time Prescott, Sandy, and Nate were done questioning Trish, Shafer was biting back his anger. He rang for a guard to escort Trish to her cell. After she left the office, he exploded.

"What kind of monster is Parsons? I know his mother. The inmates call her a battle-ax, among other names. I know she's a"—he checked his words—"I know she's a tough cookie. I can't imagine how she could raise such a depraved and corrupt person." He asked Ms. Barker if she would like to use the computer to transcribe the session.

"Mr. Prescott, what's your pleasure?" she questioned.

"Yes, absolutely." He glanced around the room and back to

Shafer. "Would it be possible to have something to drink and maybe something sweet to eat?"

"Yes, I'll see that it's here within fifteen minutes," Shafer replied. He turned to Barker and said, "Please take your time. If what she said is true, I want this criminal behind bars as quickly as possible." He walked to his phone to call the kitchen guard and asked for coffee, sodas, and cookies to be brought to his office ASAP.

Ms. Barker was escorted to the secretary's desk, where she began transcribing. The interview session had lasted an hour and a half; It took Barker about forty-five minutes to complete the job.

"Mr., or should I say, Warden Shafer, I have my notary equipment. If you can bring Trish McMann back, I can notarize her signature."

"It might take thirty minutes or more to bring her back. But yes, I can arrange that."

While they waited for Trish to return, Barker sent the document to the printer. She checked that all papers were in order.

While the group waited for Trish, they reviewed what they'd heard.

Sandy said, "Trish indicated that there were other victims of Parsons. We need to find them and question them."

"Even if we do, they may not testify against him," Prescott countered. "I know we can find several of them. Our police department has some very good detectives." He cleared his throat and added, "But at this point, I'd rather have Nate continue doing the investigation."

The eyes of everyone in the room looked quizzically at Prescott. He smiled sadly. "You're probably wondering why I don't want to use the police department." They all indicated that his assumption was accurate. "This is what I'm thinking: If Parsons is corrupt, has the dishonesty infiltrated the entire department? Present company excluded," he declared.

Sandy's mouth hung open in stunned disbelief. "You really think the department could be that corrupt?"

"Not the whole department, but some. Yes, I do," Prescott retorted.

Nate jumped into the discussion. "I believe some corruption exists. I agree with Solomon. I think I should continue the investigation. I also believe more victims will come out of the woodwork as soon as this hits the media. If I'm correct, I think an arrest warrant will be issued in less than two weeks."

"Ms. Barker, I need to ask you a question. Please come to my office right away."

"Right away, sir," she replied through the phone intercom. She grabbed her notebook and rapped on Prescott's door until he answered. Invited in, she sat across the desk from her boss. "Now, what can I do for you?"

Prescott leaned forward, placed his elbows on the desk, and replied, "I need your help." He breathed deeply, adding, "Is there anyone in the judicial clerk's office you trust, someone you would trust with your deepest, darkest secret?"

Barker didn't take thirty seconds to answer. She smiled broadly and announced, "Sure. My sister Vivian works there. She knows that if she ever breached confidences, I'd kill her."

"Oh, please remember who you work for—the district attorney. I don't want to issue an arrest warrant for you!"

They both laughed. Prescott leaned back in his chair. "Here's what I need you to do, rather what I need your sister to do. See if she can access a list of Logan Parsons's parolees for the last five years. I need copies, including current addresses and phone numbers." Barker was writing quickly. "And I need them as soon as Wednesday afternoon. Think you can do that?"

"Oh, without a doubt I can do it, but I don't know if Vivian can do it. But I'll ask her at noon. We'd planned to have lunch, so it's no big deal."

"Thank you."

"Well, now I have a question for you."

"Okay, shoot!"

"Will you quit calling me Ms. Barker? My name is Ruby. I really don't like to be called Ms. Barker. It makes me sound old." She laughed, adding, "Well, let's face it. I am old."

"Oh, I'm smart enough not to say anything to that." A shadow fell across Prescott's face. "Remember, this needs to be done not just quietly but with utmost confidentiality."

CHAPTER 56

It was a beautiful autumn morning. The sky was bright blue with absolutely no clouds. The cold air was nippy, and the pungent fragrance of burning leaves drifted in the breeze. The sounds of leaf blowers could be heard periodically. Sidewalks were decorated with large lawn bags filled with fallen leaves. Nate always questioned the need to rake up leaves when the trees were still wearing some.

Nate called Joyce for permission to keep KC longer than her regular lunch hour. He knew Charles was often away from home at noon, so Rose wouldn't be suspicious with Charles being gone for lunch. Nate picked up KC at work and drove to Kenyon's Palace, where he asked to be seated in the rear of the restaurant. He sat facing the door, and Charles and KC sat opposite him.

"Lunch is on me today," he announced as he smiled.

"You mean, I'll pay for it later," Charles answered.

"Whatever. I want to let you know where we are on the case." The server approached, and he stopped talking.

He and Charles ordered coffee. KC asked for hot tea, Earl Grey if it was available. The server distributed menus. "Let's decide what we'll eat first, and then I'll get you caught up." There was no questioning him; it was a statement. Silence surrounded them for a few minutes. Nate closed his menu and decided he'd begin his report.

"I want you to know a lot has happened in the last forty-eight to seventy-two hours. We have signed and notarized statements from at least three women who have accused Logan Parsons of rape and sexual abuse." He looked directly at KC.

Her mouth was agape, and all color drained from her face. She kept her hands in her lap. Shaking her head, she declared, "I knew there was something about him I didn't trust. But Mom thought he was 'such a nice guy.'" The last statement was said with sarcasm.

"Now, KC, you can't blame your mom. We both know she always looks for the good in everyone," Charles replied.

"When is he going to be arrested? He is going to be arrested, isn't he?" KC quizzed Nate.

"Honestly, I believe it will happen very soon, perhaps within the next forty-eight hours. But," he said, dropping his voice, "I'm afraid we're going to have to use you as a decoy, KC."

"What?" she said louder than she meant to. Some of the other diners turned to look at their group. She realized she'd spoken too forcefully. "I thought you told me I wouldn't need to do that. Why now? If you've got statements, why do you need me?"

Nate swallowed some coffee before answering her.

"First, I want you to know that the district attorney, Solomon Prescott, says we have a fairly good case. But a more recent assault would really seal Parsons's fate."

The server came to get their orders, refilled their drinks, and left.

"Oh, by the way, did you know Geraldine Grossman—"

"Ugh! She's an evil woman," KC interrupted.

"Well, it appears the apple doesn't fall far from the tree," Nate replied.

"Don't think I know what you mean," KC said. Her left eyebrow raised and the furrow between her eyes deepened.

"I mean, Logan Parsons is Geraldine Grossman's son!" He paused long enough to let that soak in. He could see the server coming with their food, so the conversation stopped for a couple minutes. After the server left, Nate began again. "Geraldine Grossman has a reputation for trying to keep convicts in prison for the entirety of their sentence. She rarely agrees to parole. Why she's been chairperson of the state's board of parole for so long is beyond my imagination. And Logan apparently has an intense hatred for women." He forked a bite of grilled salmon and began chewing. He noticed KC hadn't even picked up a fork and had barely touched her tea. Nodding toward her, he encouraged, "Go ahead and eat."

She shook her head. "I'm so stunned, I don't think I can."

Charles nudged her with his elbow. "Eat, KC. I'm paying for this lunch." He tried to lighten the mood but suspected that KC was in shock. "Come on, honey. You need to eat."

She lifted her spoon, and both men noticed that her hand was shaking. She put a little soup into her mouth and let it slide down. KC grabbed her napkin and held it over her mouth. She scooted her chair back quickly and nearly ran to the restroom. Charles was right behind her. He stood beside the restroom door and heard her vomiting into the toilet. *Oh, God, what I can do?*

Another female diner who saw KC race to the bathroom approached Charles. "Excuse me, sir. Your daughter seemed to be in distress. I'll go check on her."

"Thank you for your kindness," he replied. He stepped away from the door, and the woman entered. In about five minutes, the two women exited.

"I think she needs to go home," the unknown woman remarked.

KC and Charles returned to their table. "Nate, I need to take KC home. Perhaps we can complete this conversation later."

Nate responded, "I know this is very upsetting, but we need to continue this conversation as soon as possible. Could we talk this evening?"

"I don't know. Rose rarely leaves the house, and I don't want her to hear what you're planning." He stopped and then added, "Maybe I can get her good friend to take her out for dessert." Charles took

KC by the elbow. "I'll call you later. Plan on being at our house by 6:15, okay?"

The server approached to see if everything was okay. She noticed that KC's food had barely been touched and asked, "Would you like a take-home bag?"

KC shook her head. "No. Thank you, but no." She and Charles left.

Before they left the restaurant parking lot, Charles called Rose's friend Shirley. "Hey, it's Charles, and I need a big favor." He paused to listen to her answer. "I need you to take Rose out for dessert or shopping, anything. I need her out of the house by 6:00. You can bring her back about 8:30. Think you can do it?... Don't take no for an answer.... I'll let you know why later. And Shirley? Thanks."

Charles sighed due to the heaviness of the situation. "KC, I have one more call I need to make, and then I'll take you home." KC sat soundlessly, her eyes devoid of a sparkle, her face ashen. She watched Charles punch in a phone number. Staring down at her hands, KC showed no interest in the phone call.

Charles finally spoke into his cell phone. "Nate, everything is set for tonight. You'd better have a good plan. Gotta go. Taking KC home." He stretched his hand to KC, who placed her hand in his. *He has such a firm, loving touch. I feel safe with Charles.*

She jarred loose and spoke up. "What about my car?"

"Already thought about that. I'm gonna tell your mom that you were feeling ill, and that's not a lie. You called me and asked for a ride home. So you'd better ask me for a ride so I'm not lying to your mom." He squeezed her hand gently and smiled.

"Charles, I'm not feeling well. Will you give me a ride home?" she replied, and a bit of a smile crossed her face. "I am exhausted, and I will need a nap." She took her hand from Charles and stood absolutely still. "I told Joyce I'd be back this afternoon. I need—"

"Nope, you don't need to do anything except go home and rest." He placed her hand in the crook of his elbow. "Once I get you home and let your mom hover over you, I'll run the remainder of my errands and will stop and talk with the Goens. They understand what's going on." He patted KC's hand. "I'm so glad you work for such godly people, KC. You know you are a very fortunate lady, don't you?" She nodded in agreement.

CHAPTER $57$

Nate, Sandy, Charles, and KC gathered outside the office of District Attorney Solomon Prescott. "Are we ready? I do believe what we've planned is legal," Nate announced. "However, I want to cover all the bases. That's why I've asked for this meeting." Everyone nodded in agreement, though KC's response was less than enthusiastic. "Okay, let's get this done." They stepped into the outer offices of the district attorney's office, and Nate spoke to Prescott's administrative assistant, Ruby. Ruby rapped on Prescott's door to announce the presence of the group.

"Well, show them in, Ruby."

She opened Prescott's door wide and led them in. She glanced around the room to be sure there was a chair for each person.

Nate, taking the lead, introduced the DA to KC and Charles. "We are here because of one Mr. Logan Parsons. Officer Sandy Roberts has assisted me in gathering evidence proving Logan Parsons is abusing his authority as a parole officer. We have signed affidavits from three women who claim that Parsons has forced them to have sex in order to stay out of prison. Sandy and I are fairly certain that more accusations will be made upon the arrest of Logan Parsons." He stopped briefly. "What we want to do is to wire KC, install hidden cameras in his office to verify his actions—"

"Mr. Conover," Prescott cut in, "are you suggesting we entrap him?"

"No, I don't want to entrap him. I'm only suggesting we install the cameras to protect KC."

"Mr. Prescott," KC hesitantly began, "I've refused to meet with Mr. Parsons privately. I've never trusted him from our very first meeting. I was always uncomfortable around him. We've met at McDonald's and other public places. I believe the evidence Mr. Conover has gathered is proof that Parsons has had me stalked. I want him to pay for the terror he has inflicted on me and my family. I want him to pay for raping the other women. So I am willing to put myself in harm's way. Trust me—I'm not going to seduce him. I can't stand to look at him, let alone have sex with him."

Prescott leaned forward in his leather chair. Contemplating their request, Prescott steepled his fingers and focused his eyes downward but shifted in his chair. Silence filled the room. No one wanted to interrupt his thought process, but the quietness was overwhelming. Prescott finally broke the silence. "Tell you what. I believe you have a good case, but we're going to have to have a court order to install the camera and wire KC. I was trying to determine which judge would be most favorable toward us." He turned and looked out the window overlooking the courtyard where leaves still hung precariously on tree limbs. "I hate to admit it, but some judges believe whatever a parole officer says about a parolee." Turning back to the crowd in his office, he announced, "I believe Judge Karsell is the most honest, fair-minded judge on the bench. I'll call him to see if I can talk with him." He stood, adding, "I'll call you, Mr. Conover, as soon as I know. Thank you for coming." He looked directly at KC and said, "Young lady, I want to apologize on behalf of the judicial system for what you've endured." With that said, he strode to the door and showed the group out.

Judge Karsell was reviewing the evidence presented to him, uttering "Hmm" every so often. Closing the file, he looked at Solomon Prescott and replied, "Sol, I'm going to authorize the cameras and the wire on KC. I'm also authorizing Officer Sandy Roberts to supervise the installation. I assume she has friends on the force she trusts?"

"Yes, your honor." He watched as Karsell signed the necessary paperwork. Closing the file, he shoved it across his desk. Prescott stood and stretched out his hand to shake hands with the judge. "Thank you, sir."

"Don't do anything that will void these orders. If these allegations are true, as I believe they are, I want that man off the street and in prison. Having said that, you do know, don't you, that I will have to recuse myself from this case?" His eyebrows rose as he asked the question.

"Yes, sir, I do. Thanks for your help." He turned and left the office.

Sandy talked with other officers and oversaw the installation of the cameras. All the work was done after hours and using night vision equipment. Everything was in place to nail Logan Parsons and send him to prison. KC was given instructions to call them when Parsons set up their next meeting. It was then that she would be wired and given last-minute instructions. Immediately prior to her appointment, she would give Sandy a urine sample because other complainants had had their parole revoked due to allegations of drug violations.

Days passed without any threats from the stalker. KC was beginning to relax, but at the same time she was apprehensive. She jumped when the phone rang or when the door opened. Joyce and

Richard Goen prayed with and for KC daily. Joyce, who was more than an employer, often had break time with KC. Joyce could get her to share her real concerns.

On this bright, sunny, autumn day, Joyce invited KC to join her for tea. "Okay, young lady, what's going on?"

"What? What do you mean?" KC asked. She felt defensive. "Am I not doing my job?"

"Whoa! No, that's not it at all. Richard and I haven't any problem with your work or your work ethics. Heavens, dear, we couldn't have asked for a more diligent employee." She reached across the table and patted KC's trembling hands. "We're aware you are waiting for another appointment with Mr. Parsons. We know you are putting yourself in harm's way. However, we can only imagine the apprehension you are experiencing. If there's anything we can do to ease it, please let us know." Genuine compassion radiated from Joyce's eyes.

Tears filled KC's eyes. She looked down, not willing to allow Joyce to see her raw emotions. "Joyce, you're the only one I can talk with right now. Mom's health, both physical and emotional, is so fragile that I've learned to be a pretty good actress. She sees a side of me that says everything is okay, but I know deep down she knows everything isn't okay. We skirt around the issues." KC looked again at Joyce, adding, "She doesn't even know about—" Her cell phone rang and, glancing at the caller ID, she mouthed to Joyce, "It's Parsons."

"Hello, this is KC Elliott."

"Well, good morning, Elliott. It's a pleasure to talk with you today. You do know it is time for a drug check, don't you?"

"Yes, I do, Mr. Parsons. Work is over at 5:00 p.m. Can I come then?" she asked. "Okay, I'll be there by 5:30. Thank you for accommodating my work schedule. The Goens—" She waited as he interrupted. "Yes, I know your opinion of the Goens." She winked at Joyce. "I'll be there, not a minute late." She hit the end button on the phone. KC took in a very long, deep breath and exhaled slowly.

"Well, I guess this is it. I need a few minutes to get everything in motion, okay?"

"Oh, absolutely. Someone is coming here to, what, wire you?"

"That's right." She reviewed the procedures with Joyce. "Once I make this call, someone will come here to get me wired up and to take a urine sample, another person is following me to his office, the cameras will be switched on—"

"You'll have backup there, right?" Concern filled Joyce.

"Oh, yes. That's all covered." It was KC's turn to reassure Joyce. "I am scared, but I'm confident that the officers and Nate have my back. They will allow Parsons to go far enough to hang himself but not far enough to harm me." She patted Joyce's arm. "But," she said, smiling the smile that didn't match the look in her eyes, "if you and Mr. Goen would like to pray for me, I'm not going to say no."

"Let me get Richard. We'll pray right now." She didn't allow grass to grow under her feet. She was down the hall and ordering Richard to join her in the break room in seconds.

"Now, dear, KC is going to meet with Mr. Parsons early this evening. We need to pray with her. Will you do that?"

"Without a doubt, dear. KC, you know we love you as if you were our own daughter, don't you?" Richard said. "We are concerned for you and want this horrible time to be over. I haven't shown sympathy or understanding, but I hope you haven't taken that as a sign that I don't care. It's been just the opposite. Now, let's pray." They joined hands and bowed their heads. "Almighty God, you sent the Archangel Michael to battle for support for Daniel. Today, we beg you to send Michael in support of this young lady who has lived in fear for months. KC has been a brave young lady who seeks justice not only for herself but for the other victims of Mr. Parsons. Give her confidence in the face of this terror. All the people who have been put in charge of her protection, keep them alert and safe. We know your scripture tells us over and over again not to be afraid because you're with us. Yet, honestly, it's hard to do when faced with evil. God of love, God of power, we pray the words of the song, 'Grant us wisdom, grant us courage for the facing of this hour.' We offer this prayer in the name of Jesus, your son, our King and Savior. Amen." They had a group hug, and Richard turned to leave. He paused, turning back to face the two women, and said, "Go get 'em, tiger." He winked and then left.

Sandy, dressed in civvies, arrived at Advanced Web Designs to collect the urine sample and to immediately take it to an independent laboratory. Sandy introduced KC to another female officer, Linda Galloway. "Linda is going to follow you to Parsons's office. She's not going inside but will be observing from an undercover van. There are other officers staked out inside the courthouse. As soon as we have the goods on Parsons, the officers will come storming in." She watched KC's eyes. They were as wide as saucers, but KC focused on the assignment. The longer Sandy talked with her, the more comfortable KC became.

"Sandy, I know I should be really nervous, but I'm so anxious to get this over—" She stopped midsentence, shook her head, and corrected herself. "That's not true. I am nervous, but before you arrived I asked Mr. and Mrs. Goen to pray with me. I'm not going in there tonight on my own strength. God is going with me, and God is going to protect me."

Sandy shrugged her shoulders and retorted, "Whatever gets you through this." Sandy wasn't one to go to church as she felt it was a cop out. She had been properly trained at the academy and didn't need any help from some supposed higher being. "Regardless, Officer Galloway has a black belt in martial arts."

"I thought she was going to be in the van?"

"She is, until I get there. Then she's going to join the rest of the crew. She's also going to wire you up now. Ready?"

"Let's get it on. I'm ready."

# CHAPTER 58

"Well, Elliott, how do you think you're doing adjusting to life outside of prison?" Logan inquired professionally.

"I'm doing very well. I have a job I love—"

"Yeah, I know. The Goens think they can rehabilitate all convicts."

"No, seriously, I love my job," KC countered. "Yes, the Goens have been very supportive. I've paid off almost half of the required restitution."

"I suppose that's because you live at home and have no living expenses."

"It is true I live at home, but I am contributing to the expenses and that was my decision. Mom and Charles didn't want to accept the money, but I insisted."

"And what about the supposed stalker?" Logan asked.

Indignation filled KC. Her face reddened, and her stomach knotted. Speaking as calmly and confidently as she could, she retorted, "We've had this conversation before, Mr. Parsons. It is not a *supposed* stalker. Someone is stalking me."

"But the police haven't located a stalker. They're telling me they don't believe there is one."

*Stay calm, KC. He's only trying to rattle you.*

"Whatever. It is what it is."

"I understand you reported for your required drug test," he said as he opened her file. Pulling out a report from the lab, he added, "This report indicates you've been smoking marijuana."

"I beg your pardon! I have not been using any drugs," she responded indignantly.

"Elliott, I'm only going by the laboratory report. According to the terms of your parole, you have violated parole. This appears to be the second time your labs indicated drug use. I'm going to recommend your parole be revoked."

"What? You can't do that!" Color drained from her face, and her heart was beating like a snare drum. "I have never taken drugs!"

"I'm only going by what the lab report indicates."

"Mr. Parsons, I can't go back to prison," she sobbed, deep gut-wrenching sobs. "I can't. I didn't take drugs." She grabbed a tissue from her purse and covered her mouth. Tears coursed down her cheeks. She pushed her chair back and rushed to the trash can. Bile worked its way up, and KC began heaving vomit into the trash can.

The group in the van sat in disbelief. They put the crew in the courthouse in motion. "Prepare to breach, but do not breach."

"Why did you do that?" Logan reacted angrily and pushed her aside. "Are you pregnant too?" His abuse was beginning.

"Mr. Parsons, I can't go back to prison. It will kill my mom. Please," KC begged.

Parsons laughed sardonically and mimicked her, "I can't go back to prison. It will kill my mom. You know, Elliott, I don't care about your mom, my mom, or anyone else's mom." He helped her back to her chair. Sitting on top of his desk, one foot on the floor and the other dangling, he casually said, "Tell you what. If you'll have sex with me, I'll forget all about this."

KC stood up and announced through clenched teeth, "I will not have sex with you."

He stood up and walked closer toward her, "Oh, Miss Elliott, I believe you will." He had already invaded her personal space. "As we speak, an order for revocation of parole is sitting on the judge's desk." He smirked and roughly grabbed her hands. He pushed her against the wall and kissed her forcefully. She freed a hand and slapped him.

"Oh, you like it rough, huh?" He began pulling up her skirt.

KC's adrenaline was coursing through her body. She screamed, "No! No, stop!"

The door of Parsons's office flew open violently. "Police! Don't move!"

Logan backed off and raised his hands. "She came on to me."

Seconds ticked off the clock, and the office filled with people. Nate Conover, Officers Roberts and Galloway, and District Attorney Solomon Prescott made their way into the room.

Prescott moved toward Logan. "You bag of scum, you are an embarrassment to the judicial system." He turned to Officer Galloway and ordered, "Arrest that man. Be sure to read him his rights and do it here in front of witnesses. I don't want any misunderstandings." He turned to Logan again and said, "If I have my way, you will go to prison for the rest of your life. Imagine— former parolees learning you're in prison. Umph! Too bad I can't send you to a women's prison. I'm sure they'd enjoy revenge. But I assure you, word will reach the men, and your life won't be worth a plug nickel." He turned and ordered again, "Read him his rights." He walked out the door.

"You'll never make this stick," Logan countered. "Elliott came on to me. She offered to have sex with me—"

"Anything you say can and will be used against you in a court of law," Galloway continued.

Logan's first and only phone call was to his mother. "You

what? For what? I'll get the best attorney. We'll beat this charge," Geraldine replied.

For a man who despised women in general and his mother in particular, Logan didn't hesitate to call on his mother's connections. He was a manipulative man. He used everyone he could and had used his influence to abuse women under his supervision. Logan Parsons was a classic sociopath.

The next morning, Logan Parsons was arraigned for the sexual assault of KC Elliott and three other women: Alice Bushong, Susan Berg, and Trish McMann. He also faced charges of official misconduct.

The judge asked, "How does the defendant plea?" the judge asked.

Although Geraldine Grossman had very little to do with her son, she hired the most expensive defensive attorney in the state, Graham Webster.

District Attorney Solomon Prescott said, "Your honor, the state requests the defendant be remanded with no bail, as other charges may be pending."

"Explain yourself, Mr. Prescott," the judge ordered.

"It is the state's belief that other women will come forward with similar allegations once this case is public knowledge," he answered.

"Your honor, I'm Graham Webster, attorney for the accused. He pleads not guilty. Bail is requested, and I recommend he be released into the custody of his mother, Geraldine Grossman. As you know, she is the chair—"

"Yes, I know Mr. Webster. She's the chair of the State Board of Parole. However, I'm denying your request for bail. The defendant, Logan Parsons, is remanded." The judge banged his gavel. Logan was led away, his hands cuffed behind his back.

Geraldine glared at KC. "Should have denied your request for parole when I had the chance, you—"

"Keep moving, KC," Prescott stated as he led her out of the courtroom. "Don't talk to anyone about this. The media is going to be hounding you. Don't talk with them. Actually, I suggest you, your mother, and Charles refuse to answer the phone unless you recognize the phone number, understand?" KC nodded, and Prescott continued, "I know you are close to the Goens, but I'm asking you not to talk with them about it. Go to work and go home. For a while it will feel as if you're under house arrest, but the defense is going to watch your every move trying to discredit the charges."

"But I have to work. Restitution has to be made."

"Yes, yes, I know. Didn't you do much of your work for the Goens when you were incarcerated?" KC nodded. "Then I'll work something out for you to work from home. Sound okay?"

Prescott's prediction about additional charges was correct. The most difficult task was confirming the allegations. *How does one prove sexual abuse or rape years after it happened?* he thought. He sat alone in his office late into the night considering his next moves. He leaned back in his leather chair with his elbows on the chair arms and his hands pressed together. Weary and heavy hearted, Prescott closed his eyes for a few minutes. The few minutes stretched into an overnight nap.

Ruby came in early the next morning and saw Prescott's office lights on. She tapped lightly on the wooden door and let herself in. "Mr. Prescott, are you okay?" she cried.

Prescott lifted his head from the desk and groggily answered, "Uh, yeah, I'm okay. Guess I fell asleep."

"I guess you did. Have you been here all night?" she asked.

"I was thinking about this case and closed my eyes for a couple of minutes." He smiled and added, "Minutes turned into hours. I better go home and clean up. I'll be back in a couple of hours."

"And don't forget breakfast, Mr. Prescott," Ruby instructed. He waved on his way out.

Prescott received calls from nearly twenty women, each one accusing Logan of sexual assault. The judge issued a search warrant authorizing detectives to search through Logan's records, particularly records of females. The detectives certainly had their work cut out for them. Most of the records were kept in "the tombs," or the basement. They pulled and reviewed the twenty records and found that, of the twenty, seven women had reported the assault to police. Verifying the accounts of the other women would be more difficult as the rape crisis centers held confidentiality as strongly as doctors and attorneys. The detectives gathered the files they needed and returned to their office.

Although Officer Roberts was not a detective, she was assigned to this case due to her connection with both Nate Conover and KC Elliott. The district attorney's office expected her to work in conjunction with another detective, Timothy Justice. It was Prescott's belief that the women accusing Logan of assault would be more at ease if another woman was present. The team's mission was to locate the seven women and interview them, but it was no easy task. The first case, number 12517, had a phone number that was no longer in service. The next three phone calls yielded the same results. "Let's change our approach," Justice said. Sandy looked at him quizzically.

She asked, "Whaddya have in mind?"

"Well, we know they all served time, so let's check the database for prison inmates."

"Makes sense to me." She plopped herself down in front of a computer monitor and demanded, "First name."

Roberts entered seven names. Of the seven women, three were in the prison database. The prison record indicated that their parole had been revoked. Justice and Roberts looked at each other, and Justice said, "Gotta make a trip to Dwight ASAP. Clear your schedule for tomorrow. I'll talk with Prescott to alert the warden. Be prepared to leave at 0700."

"Okay, but shall we check out the last known addresses of the other four?"

"Yep. Grab your jacket. I'll call Prescott while you drive."

As the two drove to the first address, Justice talked with Prescott. "Yeah, thanks for your help." He pushed the end button on his phone. "It's a go for tomorrow." Other than the noise from the police radio, there was silence between the two. Pulling up in front of a house badly needing another paint job, the two noticed a broken window and could hear screaming. They carefully walked to the door. The steps were rotting, and they had to watch where they walked. Justice rapped loudly on the door.

A woman yelled at a crying baby, "Shut up, will ya! Someone's at the door." Justice and Sandy stared at each other. *I'd bet my last paycheck that baby is being abused,* Sandy thought. The door was opened, and a woman stepped out.

"Yeah?" she pulled out the word with contempt. "Whaddya want?"

"Ms. Washburn?" Sandy questioned. Washburn had a cigarette hanging out of her mouth. Her hair was stringy, and she sported a black eye and swollen lip. "Ms. Washburn, I'm Officer Roberts, and this is Detective Justice." She cleared her throat and continued. "We're here to ask you some questions, but first, are you okay?"

"Well, of course I'm okay. I always beat myself up," she answered bitterly. She took a drag from her cigarette and blew it out toward the officers. "Whaddya want?"

"We'd like to talk with you about your complaint against your parole officer, Logan Parsons."

She yelled at the kid in the house and then responded, "Worthless, if you ask me."

Sandy took the lead in the conversation. "Is there a reason you believe that?"

"Is there a reason?" she replied with contempt and hatred. "Yeah, there's a reason. Told me if I didn't have sex with him, he'd send me back to prison." She pulled on the cigarette again. the same results,

"You reported to the authorities that he sexually assaulted you. Do you have any proof?"

"You mean other than that kid that's screaming in the house?"

"The baby is Parsons's?"

"Yeah, the baby is Parsons's. I should have had an abortion, but I didn't have the money."

"Ms. Washburn, did you happen to report this to a rape crisis center?"

"Yeah, but I didn't want to file charges because no one would believe an ex-con, especially one who was using drugs."

"Would you be willing to talk with a rape counselor.? Authorize her to talk with us?"

"Maybe. What's up?"

"I can't give you the details, but let's just say there is an investigation and you might be able to help us."

"Yeah, I'll talk with her. Anything to get that son of—"

"Thanks, Ms. Washburn." Sandy and Justice turned to leave, but Sandy couldn't ignore the signs of abuse. "You know, there's a shelter we could take you to for your protection. And yes, you can take the child with you. Do you want to go?"

Washburn took another drag from the cigarette. "Don't think so, not tonight. He said he was sorry and wouldn't do it again." She was silent for a few seconds. "Guess that's about the fifth time he's said that. I keep hoping he means it, but …" Her voice trailed off.

"If you change your mind, call me anytime." Sandy handed a business card to Washburn. "You don't have to live like this. We can get you to a safe place and arrest him for assault."

"Like you did Parsons? Thanks, but no thanks."

CHAPTER 59

S andy and Detective Justice met with the three inmates at Dwight Prison. In a sterile room with no windows, devoid of pictures and posters, the two interviewed each inmate separately. As each inmate was ushered into the room, the two stood behind a table about six feet long with a Formica top. Cigarette burns on the top were evidence of the age of the table. Both the table and chairs showed wear and tear.

Sandy, again, initiated the conversation. "First, we want you to know that you are not in any trouble. We do, however, need to ask you some questions. We may need a notarized affidavit. Do you understand?" she queried.

"I s'pose," the first inmate answered in a noncommittal tone.

"Do you know Logan Parsons?"

"Know him? He's the reason I'm here—again," she responded.

"Tell us about it, please," Sandy continued.

After the interview, both Sandy and Justice agreed this case was viable. A date would be made to have a court reporter present for the affidavit. The next two inmates reported much the same, and all three agreed to filing a complaint.

"You know our biggest obstacle is proving their allegations," Justice announced as they returned to the car for the drive home.

"You don't think this is enough?" Sandy asked incredulously. "Each woman told us the same story."

"True, but all three are inmates, and all three had their parole revoked under the guise of drug violations."

Sandy slapped her forehead with her right hand as she exclaimed, "Duh! Why didn't I connect the dots?"

Justice slammed on the brakes. "Explain."

"Remember? KC had a urinalysis done just prior to her last meeting with Parsons. Well, I took the specimen to an independent lab. The test was normal. If you look at the video, Parsons told her she'd failed the last two tests. If that's true, then—"

"The lab is dirty too!" Justice exclaimed.

"Exactly," she replied. "More work."

Once again, Justice and Sandy met with Prescott.

"Are you sure?" Prescott inquired.

"There's only one explanation—and only one way to prove it. We've got to set up a sting. And that's going to be difficult with Parsons in jail." Justice hesitated and added, "You know the media is all over this. The lab is going to be dotting its I's and crossing its T's.

"How do you know your lab is clean?" Prescott quizzed.

"Good question. I've checked out the lab. It has been certified by the National Laboratory Certification Program. It has passed every performance test and inspection since 2008." Justice swallowed a gulp of his soda. "I've also already checked with the Drug-free Laboratory, and the lab hasn't been certified since 2010. Drug-Free also has several complaints against it. " He shook his head. "How does that happen?"

Prescott sat reflectively in his chair and sighed heavily. "I don't know, Tim, but we're going to find out," he answered. He slapped his hands on his desk and added adamantly, "And we're going find out quickly."

A quick, yet legal, investigation yielded the information needed to prove a conspiracy between a chemist, Barbara Sutton, at the laboratory and Logan Parsons. Prescott, Sandy, and Justice met with and interrogated her.

"Listen, Ms. Sutton, we've been investigating Logan Parsons, a parole officer. Have you tested any urine specimens for Parsons's clients?" Prescott inquired.

"I've tested lots of urine specimens. I don't always know which parole officer has ordered the test," Barbara said, clearly evading the question.

"Let's look at it this way," Justice said. "Do you sign off on the tests you conduct?"

"Well, of course. It's required." She was adamant.

"Take a look at this paper. Is that your signature?"

She looked at the paper. It was a report she had prepared for KC Elliott.

"Yes, it is my signature."

"Is there another name on this paper?" Justice asked.

She glanced at the document again. "Uh, yes, sir."

All three authorities knew they had the evidence. Sandy sat next to Barbara and inquired, "Whose name, other than yours, is on this report?"

Barbara hung her head and replied, "Logan Parsons."

Prescott demanded, "Why did you tell me you didn't know which parole officer ordered the test?"

"Fear? Confusion? I, I, I don't know," she announced as a tear dripped from her eyes and onto the table.

The interrogators sat quietly for several minutes. Prescott nodded toward the door, and Justice and Sandy followed him.

"Ya know, I think there's more to this. We might be able to make a deal with her if she works with us, and I know that's a big if. Parsons has something on her and has been forcing her to lie about urine specimens. We've got to get her to talk. Actually, Sandy, I think you need to go in and talk with her. See if you can get her to crack, okay?"

"Sure, I'll use my gentle charm," she said with a smirk. "You are going to tape this, right?"

"You bet your life I am," Prescott rejoined.

CHAPTER 60

"KC, this is Nate Conover. Can we meet for lunch?"
"You told me to stay home and avoid the media. Are you sure it's okay?" she queried.

"Trust me, it's safe. I want you to hear this from me before you hear it on the news. Let's meet at Kelso's Diner in thirty minutes, okay?"

"I'll be there." KC saved the project she'd been working on and shut down her computer. She slipped on a yellow sweater. *Wonder what I should tell Mom. She knows I've been told not to leave the house. She'll worry about me.* She bit her lip. *Just have to be honest with her.* "I'm having lunch with Nate Conover," she announced, and without waiting for a response, she was out the door.

Nate was sitting at the table near the rear of the diner. He'd already ordered his coffee and her Earl Grey tea. He stood as she approached and greeted her with a handshake. "Please, please be seated."

The server brought her hot water for her tea. KC glanced up and thanked her. Then she looked at Nate. He was grinning like the Cheshire cat. "What's up?"

"Good news! No, not good news—great news." He could barely contain himself. "We have interviewed seven women. Each confirmed she'd been sexually assaulted by Parsons. The other women admitted to having sex with him to avoid going back to prison. One woman had the best evidence possible: a son. His DNA was tested, and it's a positive match. Some of the women reported the alleged assault to rape crisis centers and, with their approval, the counselors confirmed the women had been raped. Police reports were not made because Parsons had threatened them."

"We suspected that. What's the great news?" she asked apprehensively. She sipped some tea.

"Getting there," Nate proclaimed. "When presented with all the evidence, Logan and his attorney worked out a plea agreement with Solomon Prescott."

"You mean to tell me ..." Indignation filled her voice. Nate motioned for her to keep her voice down. Gripping her cup with a death grip, she glared at Nate. "I'm to keep my voice down?" she questioned through gritted teeth. "Kinda hard to do when the man who assaulted me isn't going to pay for it!"

"KC, calm down. I didn't say he wasn't going to prison. He is. It's just that the coward opted for a plea agreement. To avoid a lengthy trial and further embarrassment to his mother, he agreed to plead guilty in exchange for a thirty-year sentence rather than life."

"But I want more. How can I be sure he can never retaliate? Can I sue for emotional distress? Emotionally, he has harmed my mother, and I want him to pay for that too." She had all types of questions. Revenge is what she wanted. "And what about that Alexander guy, the stalker? What's happening to him? And the lab that falsified my drug tests, what happens to them?"

"The lab has been shut down and is being investigated. I'm not an attorney, but I believe you have a legal case against not only the laboratory but also the technician. I think you could file suit against the state, but it's a long shot. Even if you win, chances are slim to none you'll ever get paid." Nate was trying to be as honest as possible with a young lady who was stressed beyond measure. He allowed KC to mull that over for a few seconds. "KC, look at me." He paused as she lifted her head. "I know you want revenge. You want him and everyone involved to suffer as you and your family have, right?" She nodded. Nate continued, "I understand. I really do. How much money is enough? A million? Two million?"

"No amount of money can give me back my life, my peace of mind, and my mom's health. No amount of money." Her voice was both sad and bitter. "He ruined my life."

Silence hung heavily between them. Nate put his rough, calloused hand over KC's hand and asked gently, "Did he really, KC?"

A tear trickled down her cheek, and she sniffled. "Well, I guess not. I messed up my life when I embezzled the money." She sat quietly. "But after my release, I was determined to turn my life around, and he ruined it!" Anger still burned in her soul.

"In the end, who won? Did Logan Parsons win? Did he send you back to prison? Did you lose your job because of Logan Parsons?"

"No," she sulked. "But what about Mom? She really suffered, she lost weight, and she became a recluse in her own home."

"I know, KC," he added sympathetically. "I understand you and your family have been violated. I do. I suggest you talk with your mother and Charles. Ask them their opinion regarding a lawsuit."

Her tea was cold, but she still sipped it. Nate motioned the server over for more hot water and coffee. The server returned with hot water and a new tea bag and refilled Nate's coffee. "I know what they're going to say, Nate. And I'm not there yet."

He cleared his throat and asked, "What are they going to say?"

She looked deeply into his eyes. "They're going to say I should forgive him and get on with my life. But I'm not there yet. I'm not." She rubbed her finger over her lips. "I know I should, but I'm just not there yet." She sighed heavily. "Guess I need to pray about it, right?"

"That's a good start. After a time of prayer, maybe a long time of prayer, you may still want to sue the lab, the technician, and others. But give yourself time to pray, to really seek God's will. Okay?"

She pursed her lips together and replied, "I guess I should do that. God did get me—no, us—through an awful time." She allowed a hint of a smile to cross her face. "Maybe it is a first step toward restoring a broken relationship with God."

Nate smiled. "I think you've made several steps toward restoring the relationship. I've seen you grow spiritually over these last few months." He sipped some coffee and added, "I've seen you grow by leaps and bounds in your relationship not only with God but also with your mother."

"Really?" she asked incredulously. She chewed on her lower lip as she pondered his comment. "Okay, I don't want to brag or anything, but in ways I do feel stronger. I'm emotionally spent, but I'm learning to stand up for myself. Since I confronted Parsons, I know he doesn't control me. And I can't tell you how many times I prayed to a God I'd quit believing in. I guess God never quit believing in and loving me."

Nate sat quietly, listening and nodding his head in affirmation. "Oh, KC, I believe your family, church family, and community will look at you as a brave, strong young lady—a lady who sinned but has been redeemed."

A tear slipped down her soft cheek, and KC tried to take in the compliment Nate had offered her. That tear was followed by many more.

"God has forgiven me. Mom has too." A smile broke over her tear-stained face as she realized that she had accepted God's redemption.

CPSIA information can be obtained
at www.ICGtesting.com
Printed in the USA
FFOW02n0351150317
33479FF